TRAPP'S SECRET WAR

TRAPP'S SECRET WAR

Brian Callison

This first world edition published in Great Britain 2008 by
SEVERN HOUSE PUBLISHERS LTD of
9–15 High Street, Sutton, Surrey SM1 1DF.
This first world edition published in the USA 2008 by
SEVERN HOUSE PUBLISHERS INC of
595 Madison Avenue, New York, N.Y. 10022.

British Library Cataloguing in Publication Data

Callison, Brian
  Trapp's secret war
  1. Trapp, Edward (Fictitious character) - Fiction 2. World
  War, 1939-1945 - Naval operations - Fiction 3. War stories
  I. Title
  823.9'14[F]

ISBN-13: 978-0-7278-6540-3   (cased)
ISBN-13: 978-1-84751-050-1   (trade paper)

All Severn House titles are printed on acid-free paper.

Typeset by Palimpsest Book Production Ltd.,
Grangemouth, Stirlingshire, Scotland.
Printed and bound in Great Britain by
MPG Books Ltd., Bodmin, Cornwall.

Prologue

Have you ever drifted, alone and vulnerable, at the edge of the Arctic ice barrier nor'east by something-or-other of Bear Island, part way between Franz Josef Land and sudden death?

Have you ever done an unsettling thing like that with your ship's engine stopped and the Judas-benevolent wavelets slap, slap, slapping against her already dangerously submerged war loading marks, and no one daring to drop a spanner, clatter a plate: make the slightest noise that might act as a magnet for the searching hydrophones of the wolf pack you just know is out there?

Even more disturbingly: have you ever done it at the worst possible time? In the middle of a seasonally-brief autumn night, for instance: when, each minute by nerve-corroding minute a star-laden sky is making you clearly visible through a Zeiss attack lens from miles away? Has reduced your floating refuge to being a black cut-out target marker silhouetted against the never-quite-dark ice blink of the Polar horizon.

Have you ever done all that, and done it with your throat so dry with apprehension that not even the freezing crystals inhaled with each laboured breath can alleviate the discomfort, while simply waiting for the first torpedo to strike?

Hopefully not. Almost certainly not if now, so many years on, you've managed to sleep throughout last night without revisiting that long-ago event. But some men have. A few even survived the experience – the more fortunate of those otherwise quite ordinary seamen who sailed the PQ serial-numbered Arctic convoys across the roof of the world from Iceland to the Kola Inlet and Murmansk during the darkest days of World War II.

They called you a straggler from that dreaded moment when your engine stopped and your heart nearly did. A drop-out.

In that split second you'd become the sea war equivalent of Dead Man Walking. God knows it had been fraught enough and terrifying enough even while your lumbering, over laden cargo vessel had managed to keep up with the convoy. At least, then, you'd been able to cling to the hope that, as one among thirty or forty other merchantmen, your particular ship might assume some magical, one-tree-in-a-whole-forest anonymity for as long as you remained within the protective umbrella of the escorts. The merest glimpse of a plunging corvette off the starboard beam, or a lean grey destroyer or a heavy cruiser or – should you be so lucky – a fleet carrier, had even afforded a momentary sense of security. But the delusion hadn't lasted long. You'd always been conscious, deep down, that such protection was both limited and fallible. Even at your most optimistic you'd never quite been able to dismiss the reality that you still had a high chance of dying horribly by fire or explosion: of being parboiled alive in super-heated steam or suffocated under a blanket of fuel oil; by drowning, exposure or starvation before your particular forest could make landfall.

It meant, even before you'd become a straggler, that you were exhausted both mentally and physically, with the out-bound leg of the voyage only part-complete and the return QP-serialled gauntlet yet to be run assuming, Dear Lord, that You further spare me.

For a start, they'd known precisely where you were during each minute of every hour: the black-crossed torpedo planes and the screeching dive bombers and the homing U-boats. For several days the convoy's position, course and speed had been monitored and reported back by the Luftwaffe. That nose-heavy, vampire-like long-range Blohm Voss 138 reconnaissance aircraft had been shadowing you with amiable menace since its first compatriot first scented your blood thirty miles north of Jan Mayen Island – one from a whole belfry of sister bats constantly circling the horizon below the overcast from the moment you and your geometrically arranged consorts crawled beyond the operating limit of Allied air cover based in Iceland.

The chances were that even before you'd reached the south-ernmost edge of the ice barrier you would have come under increasingly regular attack. Had you signed on as one of the deck crowd – as a mate or an able seaman or a bosun or a galley lad – your eyes would have provided the primary instruments to fine-hone your fear. You would have been forced to stand fast at your emergency station and physically watch your fellow seafarers die as ship three in column four abreast of you blew up with a flash and a bang and a climbing pyre of smoke and nothing of her left floating, and you realized she'd been loaded with munitions. While there'd been that beautiful American benzine tanker last night, less than a month old, paint barely dry and still shaking down on her maiden voyage out of Frisco: the one that took two torpedoes and only four minutes to begin burning from end to end with matchstick men ablaze from head to toe flinging themselves shrieking from her taffrail.

Had you, on the other hand, been a member of the black gang, an engineer officer say, or a donkeyman or a greaser, then that most exquisitely cruel inventor of cruelties – your imagination – would have proved the Achilles' heel of your well-being. Mercifully you wouldn't see the ships and men and a host of families' lives back home erupt, but you could sense when they did because your own hull became a kettle drum and the cold sea its diaphragm. The shock waves of the escorts' retaliatory depth charges kicked you in the belly: the muffled, pom-pom-frantic clamour of the ack-ack punctuated even the main engine's roar; the crump of a Stuka's near miss started rivets, rattled the pipe joints around you and flayed your nervous system further.

Some would claim they had the worst of it: the men who worked below the waterline. All but the most phlegmatic of engine room crews in a Russian convoy died at least twice a day: each time they forced themselves to descend those shiny, near-vertical ladders into their cacophonic potential coffin to relieve the previous watch.

You'd still done it, though. Done your duty. And the more frightened you were, the braver a man it proved you to be. Because somehow you'd carried on as if it wasn't happening. You kept your fear a private thing, and your prayers a silent appeal. You still made jokes and laughed at the even worse ones made by your shipmates. You still looked forward to a meal, and gazed in awe upon the majesty of an iceberg and marvelled at the antics of a dolphin. During your precious watch below you'd continued to rig that model of a tea clipper, the one you'd been painstakingly fashioning for the past three voyages, or you knitted oiled wool socks you might never survive to wear, or you unearthed the chipped tin box of Woolworths' watercolours, stuck your tongue out've the corner of your mouth, tried to forget where you were, and began to paint yet another sunset . . .

OK, so maybe you did walk the deck with your knees flexed, more like a self-conscious crab than a man, so's the pile-driving smash of a torpedo wouldn't drive your thigh bones up into your spleen. And maybe you *did* keep all your clothes on, including your seaboots, when you turned in and pretended to sleep and, while doing so, prudently left your cabin door hooked back despite its having had an emergency kick-out panel fitted in case the whole thing jammed solid in a blast-distorted frame anyway, and dragged you down to the bottom of the Barents Sea, pyjama-resplendent or not, should the nightmare become reality.

You'd done all that, and more.

Right up to the moment when the propeller shaft stopped turning.

That's when you *really* began to feel scared.

I ask again, with sympathy. Have you ever found yourself aboard a straggler drifting, helpless and vulnerable around 78 degrees north: just a spit off the southern edge of the Arctic ice barrier, part way between Franz Josef Land and a very quick, or an agonizingly slow, death?

Have you?

Because I have.

Even worse – have you ever done a nerve-jangling thing like that during one of those short autumn nights when the ice-blink still makes you clearly visible from miles away even at two in the morning? And even *worse* than worse – done it in the knowledge that a U-boat commander might just be aligning the cross-hairs of his Zeiss attack lens on your sitting-duck hull in that very second, from point-blank distance and *precisely* below the bridge deck where you stand?

I have.

But there will still be a difference between you and me, even if you can lay claim to having experienced such a traumatic event. Because the captain of *your* ship would only have placed you and the rest of his crew in that position once he'd been left with no alternative. Because the God you'd all been relying on had dropped the ball momentarily, and your propulsion system had failed.

Whereas *my* captain had sat us there *deliberately*! Just rang down 'Stop engine' on the telegraph like he was preparing for a boat drill at sea in peacetime, and waited cheerfully while our late convoy left us behind. And more to the point . . . our escorts.

No, *don't* look all smug and sceptical like that. He damn well DID, I'm telling you! But I'm getting ahead of myself. Chronic hysteria occasioned by having had your ship blown from under you too often tends to do that to a chap. It's why I've decided, on pain of prosecution, to disregard a blanket decree that all involved should remain silent to prevent the British government's continuing embarrassment, and to place on record this chronicle of an avaricious man's manipulation of war to suit his personal ends. To try and lay the ghosts of lunatics past.

Long past now, yet, still, spectres persistent enough to impose upon my every sleeping hour; hover on my waking horizon as constant reminders of the perfidy of man.

Always circling. Never going away. Just like those Blohm Voss reconnaissance planes had done. That time north of the Arctic Circle.

One

'You will be joining a PQ-designated convoy on arrival Iceland, gentlemen,' the Senior Naval Control Service Officer said matter-of-factly. But then, being matter of fact about risking other people's lives was his job. 'The commodore's ship, flying flag X-ray, will commence weighing at 0530 tomorrow morning, ready to depart the anchorage followed by the rest of you.'

The mood in that sparsely furnished hall was sombre. They all knew what they were about to embark upon, those weather-beaten ship masters attending the convoy pre-sailing conference. They'd known since they'd arrived in dribs and drabs at the assembly anchorage over the past forty-eight hours and seen the gathering of other merchantmen, an odd one here and there camouflaged in black and white Arctic dazzle which, throughout the coming weeks, would sail in strictly regimented company with their own.

'Russia', the word had been, even before the NCSO confirmed the worst. To some it engendered a sense of déjà vu. To those it was a case of, 'Russia again'.

But at least they *knew* why they were there, along with their chief radio officers who were attending the convoy communications briefing. They were about to sail to hell and back. Or some of them would: more than half of them would, with a bit of luck. Survive to complete the round voyage to the Kola Inlet, that was. But feeling lucky or not, each master mariner in that grim-jawed throng was acutely aware that, once he stepped aboard the naval launch waiting to return him to his command, the risk was high that he might never, ever, set foot on land again.

But like I said: at least those captains knew *why* they were there in that desolate Scottish sea loch. At least they *had* a ship to sail, and a destination to aim for, and proper orders instructing them on how to get there should they, as one of the more phlegmatic of them wryly commented, be so fortunate as to pick a time to travel to the Arctic Circle that coincided with the Kriegsmarine and Luftwaffe's 1943 annual autumn vacation.

I, on the other hand, didn't even know *that* much. I didn't have the faintest clue as to why I'd been rushed to sit with those distinguished ocean veterans immediately on my arrival: me being merely a lowly reserve lieutenant, and one with a somewhat invidious service record to boot. *Report to NOIC forthwith*, the naval telegram had said. The one that arrived just as I was being discharged from military hospital after my last ship had been sunk.

Sole survivor of that episode, I'd been. Commanded by a lunatic, it had been – my last ship, that is: not the military hospital. Happily he, her captain, had gone down with her, as had the rest of his appalling crew of psychopathic social misfits, so my war to date hadn't been all bad and I couldn't really complain.

Even this, my being inexplicably summoned to sit in on a convoy conference prior to its departure for Murmansk, had to be an improvement on past form, and should it transpire that I was to be sailing with them as a small cog in the commodore's naval staff, then so be it. I was perfectly prepared to continue doing my bit for the war as long as I was ordered to do so in the company of reasonable men. And come to that: aside from having been bombed and sunk in my first warship; torpedoed an' sunk in my second; mined, shelled, machine-gunned and shouted at a lot on account of Hitler's fantasies of world domination, the Führer had never actually proved himself to be my worst enemy by a long chalk. No more than had, albeit by a considerably shorter hair, my former admiral – that bastard— the one who'd appointed me as first lieutenant of the most eccentric, the most bizarre warship ever to be deployed in desperation by the Royal Navy.

No, it was the commanding officer of *that* latter benighted vessel who'd earned himself top spot in my personal annals of resentment against wannabe world dominators. Not that it mattered, I keep telling myself. I can even afford to be generous towards his memory now. No need to continue to simmer over injustices past: to perpetuate the bitterness and animosity I nurtured over what he'd done to me.

Being fortuitously dead, I'd never have to cope with *his*
like again.

Bloody Captain Edward *bloody* TRAPP . . . !

I'm Miller, by the way. Lieutenant Miller, Royal Naval Reserve.
I don't wish to be pedantic or overly formal: it's merely that I
tend not to respond to my first name because, ever since I
joined my first ship when barely fifteen years old, people have
either called me *Miller* or *Sir* or – within earshot anyway –
Mister when wearing my previous hat: my merchant navy one.

But I was Navy at this event: definitely Royal Navy and, as
such, set slightly apart from those four-ringed shipmasters who
might well have been MN colleagues under different circumstances. It made me feel slightly uncomfortable: a bit of a
poacher turned gamekeeper, and placed me in a permanent
quandary considering the differing mindsets of the two ser-
vices. It's been said that the only description more obscene
than a Royal Navyman's view of a merchant seaman, is a
merchant seaman's opinion of a Royal Navy man, and that left
me stranded squarely in the middle – a kind of maritime hybrid
that was neither fish nor fowl: a lost soul regarded with mutual
suspicion by both ends of the sea-going spectrum.

But it had been my own stupid fault. Back in the time of
peace I'd volunteered for the Reserve to earn a little extra bounty
and, true to the Navy's promise, on the day war broke out I'd
been transferred from the tramp steamer I was sailing in as
second mate, in which ragged jerseys and seaboots were *de
rigueur* and slab-sided jam sandwiches considered a special treat
for tea, to an alien world of grey ships and brassbound uniforms
and pink gins and knives and forks held proper, and saluting
an' stuff. Even my allegiance had been compelled to suffer a
sea change overnight. Instead of being required by unfeeling
shipowners to make profit my sole consideration, I became
required by an unfeeling Admiralty to make King's Regulations
my Bible, and the two cultures were totally incompatib—?

But hang *on* a minute, Miller! Perhaps I tell a lie. Are they
really so incompatible: making war and making profit? Do
guns and commercial avarice: bloodshed and balance sheets
necessarily make for inharmonious shipmates? What about
the pirates and the privateers? The buccaneers? The
Blackbeards and the Bartholomew Roberts and the Thomas

Tews an' the Trapps . . . the Edward *Trapps*. The Captain bloody Edward bloody TRAPPs!

But I digress again: lift my eyes from these writings and focus hollowly once more on those spectres from the past. The briefest allusion to Trapp can do that to me. So I must lower my head and force myself to continue this journal or those patiently waiting shipmasters will never sail for Russia. They'll never even get past that pre-departure briefing that began it all.

It would start as a twelve-ship feeder convoy, the NCSO announced. Make the northerly passage to Iceland; there to rendezvous with other Murmansk or Archangel-bound elements comprising a further thirty-odd freighters already en-route from ports in the US and Canada . . . well, link up with those that had run the North Atlantic gauntlet and remained afloat and undamaged, at least. Almost certainly those vessels would have been blooded by the time they even sighted Spitsbergen: their crews already battle-weary.

At that meeting point, the birthplace of the PQ-serialled convoys, the then-forty-something ships would merge into one large formation spread over many nautical square miles, the disposition therein of each individual merchantman carefully calculated according to size, manoeuvrability and priority of cargo. That trade formation, surrounded by its protective screen of fighting escorts, would henceforth become a new entity; an organic thing, orchestrated to behave as one; steaming in columns on a broad front at the same speed – just half a knot less than that of the slowest vessel: the whole zigzagging to hopefully disconcert the U-boats lying in wait ahead and wheeling to alter course together on the coded order of flag or coloured light hoists displayed from the commodore's ship. And if that ship be sunk, then command would revert to the vice-commodore's ship . . . and if she became disabled, then the designated rear-commodore's vessel would take her place. And if she was sunk . . . if *she* was destroyed, then . . .

At worst they might be forced to scatter. At that stage of the war, despite Churchill's clampdown on publishing Allied shipping losses, rumours persisted that an earlier convoy, Convoy PQ-17, had been ordered to disperse in the face of potential attack from the German capital ships *Hipper* and *Tirpitz*, and make their way to Russia independently. It had meant that everyone had, at the drop of a flag, become a straggler, with a straggler's prospects of survival. 24 of that convoy's 34 merchant ships had been sunk within two terrible days following the withdrawal of her escort screen, so rumour had it. While almost as unsettlingly, the subsequent convoy, PQ-18, had lost 13 of its 39-ship formation. And *they'd* been escorted every sea mile of the way.

True or, mercifully, false, we listened *very* intently to what the Naval Control people on the platform said, and took copious notes. Especially me. And I was the one who didn't even know whether he was going or not.

Following that bleak introduction by the Naval Control Service Officer, we were given briefings by the Duty Boarding Officer and the Meteorological Officer and the Convoy Signals Officer and the Convoy Equipment Officer and the Charts and Confidential Books Officer and the Convoy Assembly Anchorage Officer and the Extended Defence Officer and, for a change, appearing somewhat incongruous in a trilby hat and a brown civilian suit amid that impressively uniformed throng, the Man from the Ministry of War Transport. It occurred to me then that, with all those shore-based Naval people who so obviously knew everything there was to be known about convoys, why didn't they just sail the bloody ships to Russia themselves an' let us all go home?

But that was spiteful thinking on my part: right out of order and totally unwarranted. There was one leg short and two arms missing from the platform party – happily not all from the same bloke, and especially not from the Duty Boarding Officer who's job it was to clamber up and down vertical rope ladders for most of his day . . . while I could tell from the looks in the eyes of those men, and from the greying hair and the ribbons on their breasts, that they *had*, most of them, earned their place in harbour: albeit some in a previous conflict.

Except for the Man from the Ministry of War Transport, that was. But he didn't really count. Well, you can't command a ship wearing a brown suit and felt hat, can you? And anyway, I couldn't afford to display too much cynicism. With a bit of luck, and despite my still having all my bits, I might be one of *them* at the rostrum tomorrow. Just as soon as somebody found time to tell me why I was there.

'I'll be there to see you off, help sort out any last-minute hitches, gentlemen,' the Duty Boarding Officer said adding, without a trace of wistfulness. 'Wish I was going with you.'

'You can 'ave my place, *Meneer*,' one of the Dutch ship-masters offered generously. Someone even laughed.

'Typical Arctic autumn forecast for the period,' the Meteorological Officer predicted. Meaning it would be margin-ally more clement than a typical Arctic winter. 'You might,' he supplemented encouragingly, 'be lucky and meet dense fog or blinding snow for part of the voyage.'

Bloody marvellous, I gloomed. Zero visibility: one of the seaman's greatest hazards; an absolute nightmare when steaming only a few cables distant from other ships – and they all considered that the good news.

I hardly understood a word of what the Convoy Signals Officer said; communicating with other vessels being a black art to most merchant service officers other than laboriously by flashing lamp, but the Chief Sparks from the various ships scribbled a lot and nodded sagely so I assumed somebody knew what they were doing. A lot of their job would be confined to listening in, decrypting incoming transmissions and revisiting tattered paperbacks. Radio silence was to be maintained throughout the voyage unless they found themselves becoming stragglers, and then only in an emergency . . . an *emergency*? Like when the first torpedo track crossed your bow offering the racing certainty that a second, maybe even a third were on their way? You were permitted to transmit your position then. Preceded by a frantic SSSS – *Am being attacked by submar-ine*. Or AAAA when the Stukas began to peel off right above you into their screaming, near-vertical dives . . . or when that mast those on the bridge had nervously sighted breaking the horizon grew into the upperworks and, eventually, into a black-printed silhouette that you were already familiar with because you'd seen it before in the well-thumbed recognition book you carried. In the section entitled *Warships of the German Fleet*.

RRRR your Chief Sparks would key then, while hopelessly shrugging into his lifejacket before the first half-ton shell arrived. *Am being attacked by Raider*.

There came a momentary interruption to the proceedings at that point.

I saw the NCS officers on the platform stiffen and make to get to their feet – or foot, I suppose, in the case of the Convoy Equipment Officer – as the door at the rear of the hall opened and a late arrival entered. Presumably sporting serious gold braid, I thought cynically on noticing that even the senior NCSO, a commander himself, had braced respectfully before being signalled to carry on. Without fuss the incomer sat in the last row directly behind me, ensuring that, despite my burning with curiosity about who might be important enough to tell a full commander to continue, it made it impossible for me to swivel and stare without being disrespectful.

I promptly forgot about whoever it was: still more preoccupied with glooming about why *I* was bloody there. And it wasn't unusual for VIPs to drop in on briefings informally: keep a finger on the pulse without disrupting the task.

Odd, though. Him sitting directly behind *me* like that. In an otherwise vacant row of chairs . . . ?

The Convoy Equipment Officer proved to be a pedantic, humourless man: a square-jawed lieutenant-commander bent only on emphasizing and re-emphasizing the importance of each vessel maintaining its War Office-specified quota of life-jackets, Carley floats, blackout screens, signalling lamps and spare bulbs, distress rockets and flares, fog buoys, navigation and special convoy lights, one complete set of international code flags and an officially stamped ship's cat . . . no, I joke about the cat. Surplus to requirements, a cat would prove. Any rat with a modicum of sense would've left those ships soon as they heard the destination Murmansk mentioned.

Happily I refrained from jesting in such light-hearted vein with the Convoy Equipment Officer himself, which was just as well. I later discovered he'd lost both his leg and his zest for the comedic regarding survival matters by the time he was rescued, frozen solid to the bottomboards of a lifeboat full of dead shipmates, after having been torpedoed three days beforehand during one of the first Russian convoys.

The Charts and Confidential Books Officer waxed as enthusiastic about destroying things as preserving them. Chart folios and confidential Admiralty publications and code books and secret recognition signals and ominously weighted canvas bags – *Emergency Disposal: Classified*

Documents For The Use Of – seemingly represented his sole focus, his stock in trade and his passion.

'If your ship is in danger of sinking or capture, it is of vital importance that you do not abandon before collecting all sensitive documents from the master's safe and – having first ensured all listed items are accounted for – placing them in the approved weighted container provided before jettisoning it over the side,' he advised earnestly before running out of breath.

'*That'll* be bloody right,' I thought sourly, having been there twice already. 'Ten thousand tons of bloody boat about to fall over on top of you an' the Navy expects you to tick off a checklist.'

But he hadn't finished. 'If, however, your ship is sinking *inside* the 100 fathom line, gentlemen, there arises the possibility that the publications may be recovered by the enemy. In such event, burning the classified documents prior to throwing their ashes overboard is desirable.'

He was very young, that Charts and Confidential Books sub-lieutenant. He had all his limbs and no medal ribbons. It may have been that over-confidence factor that imbued his closing remark with such foolhardy earnestness.

'I would stress, gentlemen, that a detailed report on the disposal of your classified material *must* be made to an Allied naval authority at the earliest opportunity following rescue. Your report should indicate which documents have or have not been destroyed, and whether or not destruction was in accordance with the instructions given in the Admiralty publication you have been provided with: *The Allied Guide to Masters.*'

He was also very brave to have pushed his luck like that. Or suicidally insensitive. In that stunned moment, the greatest threat to his prospect for surviving the war came from his own side.

It was at that stage of the conference that I'd felt a twinge of apprehension. Or not so much apprehension even, as a first stirring of unease. Quite why, I couldn't fathom, other than that it had little to do with having that still-anonymous visitor sitting behind me: albeit the illogical sense of discomfiture that his arrival had caused me didn't exactly help.

So far the stateboards at the back of the rostrum had remained covered by security blankets. When the Assembly Anchorage Officer, a jolly-looking fellow compared to the

Convoy Equipment Officer, whipped them off with his one remaining hand, he still contrived to do so with the abracadabra air of a born showman. The first blackboard revealed a list showing the timing and order in which each ship would sail from the loch. The second board presented a crude diagram illustrating her subsequent placing in this UK to Iceland section of the convoy, and the third, her eventual station in the main PQ formation assuming all went well en route north.

I found my eyes drawn immediately to the middle board. On it, the position each merchantman would take up once it reached the open sea was simulated by a chalked rectangular box. Each rectangle had been allocated a unique convoy identifying number: a routine shorthand intended to facilitate both security and brevity when signalling within the group. At risk of seeming as pedantic as the Convoy Equipment Officer, the boxes represented four columns of three ships steaming in line ahead, or, in lay terms, one ship following another down four parallel lines, like ducks on a pond. The vertical columns were numbered from 01 consecutively, left to right. Each lateral row was also numbered top to bottom: 01, 02 and 03. As with a crossword, marry any line down and along, and you had that particular vessel's identifier. In, say, column 02, the leading freighter would thus adopt Convoy Formation Number 21. In column 04, the second ship would henceforth be known as Number 42, and so on.

All but one of the rectangles had already been filled in to reveal, in addition to the position indicator, its allocated vessel's name and secret war call sign. Number 21 – the Commodore's flagship, *Pacific Surveyor*. 22 – *Sea Tide*. 23 – *Fort Sedan*, and so on . . . Some of them – *Pride of Tenby*, *Sally*, *Bacchus* – I'd even hailed as ships in the night during happier times. A couple of boxes, those relating to joiners that hadn't yet entered the anchorage, had been further noted with their estimated times of arrival. All straightforward so far . . . except that in this case, one block of information was missing, and it was that particular omission which, for whatever reason, unsettled me.

Because the one ship, or rather the one *box* that commanded my instant attention, contained virtually no information at all. It was the tail-end box of column one. It merely stated NYR: *Not Yet Reported*.

Nothing overly concerning in itself. The tracking system wasn't perfect. Shore telephone exchanges might have been

damaged, their lines disrupted. Merchantmen ordered to sail
deep sea in convoy could be delayed at their ports of loading,
or by having to await bunkers or by weather, although that
latter cause was unlikely as the past few days had been fine
and clear. She could still arrive off the entrance at the last
minute and prove all was well.

No, what niggled at me was a combination of factors. Firstly,
that business of her simply being listed NYR, which, in Naval
Control Service-speak, meant that not only did they not have
an estimated time of arrival for her, but that they were almost
certainly ignorant of her current whereabouts. That suggested,
in turn, that she'd somehow contrived to disappear from the UK
general operations plot: unusual at a time in which the status of
every precious Allied vessel was being closely monitored.

Secondly: she apparently didn't even have a name or radio
call sign. Odd, that; a ship without a name. Furthermore, a
ship seemingly unable, or loath, to supply the one detail
necessary to make contact with her by radio . . . ? In a
nutshell, a so-far non-existent ship supposedly making her
way here at an indeterminate speed from a place unknown
to anybody?

And thirdly – though fanciful in the extreme but nevertheless
the factor most closely related to my cause for unease – was that
ship's allocated formation identifier. Because according to the
formula, the mystery ship was scheduled to sail as Number One
Three.

Number Thirteen.

Now I'm no more superstitious than the next seafarer. Most
of our fraternity are to some degree. Some of our superstitions
are centuries-old illogical. Whistling thoughtlessly on deck is
a definite no-no, guaranteed to incur both a gale and a shipmate's wrath. The mere presence aboard of a minister of religion
is still considered an omen of bad luck by some: a blue-painted
boot topping above the waterline a sign of mourning yet to
come; while the seventh wave of a seventh wave will always
be the one destined to kill you although, by definition, how
they figured that one I've never quite worked out.

The number thirteen has never particularly bothered me.
Come to that, any anxiety engendered on encountering it is
hardly confined to the mariners' world anyway, though I have
come across sailors who'd refused to sail on the thirteenth

day of a month if it also happened to be a Friday and would be prepared even to jump ship rather than do so.

Yet that otherwise empty box struck me as being significant, somehow. But *why* . . . ? Why should I, among all those other veterans of the sea war, feel such unease over a chalk rectangle which, because it was unlabelled, had no purpose in practical terms? No seeming reason to be there until it was validated by entering a name.

No more reason to be there, in that room, than I myself. I still didn't know why *I* was there either, and wouldn't until my box – *my* orders – had been filled in. But that was somewhat tortuous thinking. And far too tenuous a connection.

It continued to worry me though, that vacant box. Increasingly so as the conference began to draw to a close. I hardly registered what the Convoy Assembly Anchorage Officer and the Extended Defence Officer said, I'd become so preoccupied with a nonsense.

A twelve-ship convoy. Eleven of them out there and preparing to set sail on a hellish voyage with the twelfth still merely a non-ship: an anomaly on a diagram graced only by a theoretical number which didn't correspond to the actuality.

Number one three. Number Thirteen.

Get a bloody *grip*, Miller! That means nothing. It's outright shamanism – a silly invention based on ignorance. The position indicator is a mere facilitator: an administrative artifice.

But still – ship *Thirteen* . . . ? in a *twelve*-ship group?

A *ghost* ship? Already beginning to impose further tortured imaginings on me. Could it be that it really was on its way despite having not yet reported? That it would arrive at the last minute to haunt me . . . or would it seek more?

Would it demand something *from* me?

Because a ghost ship would require a ghost crew . . . and I already *had* one. Always there; always peeping above the horizon of my mind. Spectres every last man of 'em, from cap'n to cabin boy. All blown up or drowned weeks ago – no, *months* ago now.

I'd been in that bloody hospital longer than I thought.

'Any last minute hitches anticipated, gentlemen?' the brown-suited Man from the Ministry of War Transport enquired while glancing furtively at his watch. With a bit of luck he might catch the last train back to Glasgow and be home for supper.

I shook myself from my reverie. Or should I say 'daymare'?

'Bunkers need topping up? Got all your stores and water . . . are your crews complete?'

They c'n have some of mine, I reflected morosely; still not quite over my attack of the glooms.

. . . It was *then* that a voice, instantly recognizable despite the therapeutic passage of time, growled from the row of seats behind me.

'I trust you've been listening closely, Miller,' it said. 'Very closely indeed.'

I didn't need to turn round. I wouldn't have been able to anyway. Not right away: not frozen to my chair just as firmly as that grumpy Convoy Equipment Officer had been frozen to the bottom of his lifeboat.

Yeah, OK. I see you smile knowingly again: look all smug an' self-satisfi—?

Now hang *on* a minute! You're *wrong*, you know. Completely wrong. It only goes to prove you shouldn't jump to unfounded conclusions: make a snap assumption based merely on my already deeply regretted and embarrassing admission that, only a short time before, I'd briefly succumbed to my clinical obsession with ghosts and necromancy and the paranormal.

I mean, I may still have been suffering the tail-end of a breakdown caused by being callously exposed to shit, shot an' shell in the company of a fully-fledged lunatic, but I'm not *that* crazy. I'm not so mentally confused as to imagine that was a *dead* man talking from the row of seats behind me.

It *wasn't* Trapp's voice, see? Not Captain Edward late-unlamented Trapp's.

No.

It belonged to the bast— to that damned *Admiral* who'd forced me to *sail* with Trapp in the first place!

Two

L ook, before we go any further we'd better get this over
with once and for all – this Trapp business. I'd hate to
leave any impression, however inadvertently, that I still carry
a grudge against the egotistical, grasping, impossibly over-
beari— against him. For a start, I'd never dream of speaking
ill of the dead and, anyway, I'd be a pretty small-minded sort
of chap to wish to perpetuate a feud with a corpse.

Whereas the Admiral behind me . . . now *he* was different.
He was still alive: still very much alive and domineering,
therefore he doesn't qualify for my charitable reflection.

So, the mood I'm in right now, maybe I should alter course
a moment and get *him* out of the way first.

I'd previously collided with him in Malta. Rather as a rowing
boat might, with a battleship. Our somewhat lop-sided brief
encounter had taken place during that beleaguered island's
fight to remain a key strategic British outpost at the most critical phase of the Mediterranean war. Just under a year ago,
that would have been: during early August '42 following my
having been landed there as a survivor from my first sinking.
The island had proved a particularly unpleasant place to be
right then. Only days before, it had stood-to for its two thousand eight hundredth air raid alert. And Maltese mothers and
children were still dying.

I remember the concrete walls of the underground command
bunker shaking; light bulbs dancing from the crump of bombs
falling on the north side of Valletta and the vicious, almost
continuous percussion from the anti-aircraft batteries.
Occasional trickles of powdered sandstone filtered through
cracks in the overhead on to the surface of the operations table,
to be fastidiously swept away by determinedly calm Wren plot-
ters. It had been hot and airless down there: oppressively so,

and not eased by the press of bodies belonging to so many senior Navy, Army and Air Force officers attending the PEDESTAL conference.

And my own, of course. I'd been called there too, to that conferen—? Now *that's* an odd coincidence, come to think of it. As with this current Scottish briefing, I, an apparently unemployable administrative oversight kept hanging around on a besieged sliver of rock bombed by most of Hitler's magnificent men in their flying machines, had been the only one *then* who hadn't been told why I'd been ordered to attend. No bloody wonder I'd felt uneasy even before the Admiral snapped in my ear . . . Déjà vu, you say? Yeah, right – and in spades!

Hardly surprising the merest whiff of the number thirteen had rung alarm bells. Me finding myself elected Flying Dutchman of the Royal Navy's War Appointments Board on that previous occasion in Malta, had ultimately led to my being press-ganged into the most appalling, the most horrif—

But, no.

No, dammit: I *won't* be diverted! Right now I'm telling my story the way *I* want to: not the way HE would've demanded me to—

Easy, Miller. Steady as she goes.

Remember what they kept telling you in the hospital.

It had represented the final throw of the Allied dice, had *Operation Pedestal*. If the convoy bearing its name failed to get through, then Malta was lost. Two previous convoys, code named VIGOROUS and HARPOON, had been decimated by the Luftwaffe and Dönitz's U-boats before they'd reached halfway. Bomb Alley, they called it: a course line drawn from the Gibraltar Straits to Valletta's Grand Harbour along which scores of gallant men had already died. Only two of the seventeen merchant ships despatched had got through with their desperately needed cargoes, and the garrison had been brought to crisis point. The island had run out of food days before. A rat had become a coveted source of protein in some inland areas. There was virtually no ammo left for the ack-ack batteries; no diesel fuel for the boats of the 10th Submarine Flotilla operating from the island; no avgas for its few remaining Spitfires . . .

This time fourteen merchantmen had been committed. Only one was a tanker. Her name was *Ohio*. They were escorted by a massive force of fighting ships: the battleships *Nelson* and *Rodney*, three carriers, six cruisers, thirty-two destroyers . . . thirty-*two*, f'r Heaven's sake – yet even with that awareness, not one of those high-ranking officers around me appeared confident that any of them would get through.

When the telephone rang even the air raid seemed to still momentarily, such was the tension in that concrete pit. The Admiral had answered it himself, listened for a very long moment, then replaced the receiver while turning to face us expressionlessly.

It presaged yet another kick in the guts.

'I'm sorry, gentlemen. *Eagle* has been confirmed as lost. She went down in seven minutes.'

It was all very British. But then, at that time we were getting used to defeat. Only one Wren, a pretty third officer, allowed a stifled sob to escape. The stiff upper ranks with the stiff upper lips just nodded calmly and continued to pack their briefcases in preparation for leaving. One, I think it was Captain (S), murmured, quietly stoic: 'Then thank God they've still got *Victorious* and *Indomitable* to maintain their air cover.'

I'd particularly prayed they would be able to maintain it over the *Ohio*. Of all primary targets to fuel a Luftwaffe bombardier's dreams of winning an Iron Cross First Class, that solitary tanker was the one who's destruction would be most sought after. Sink her, and they sank a whole island. As the heavy metal departed in thoughtful groups to continue to orchestrate their own parts of battle while awaiting further news, I walked over to stand gazing up at the neatly chinagraphed ships' names entered on the *Operation Pedestal* stateboard.

You could tell I was merchant navy at heart: the trade ships in convoy immediately became the subject of my focus. *Deucalion; Clan Ferguson; Melbourne Star; Almeria Lykes; Empire Hope; Santa Elisa; Glenorchy* . . .

The third officer Wren came up beside me and silently erased *Eagle* from the escort group tally. Several names had been deleted already, from both lists.

'Not the most pleasant of tasks,' I said awkwardly.

'My fiancée's in her, sir. One of her pilots.'

'Then he might not even have been aboard. He could well have been flying when . . .'

I ground to an embarrassed halt, realizing what stupid, empty reassurance that was: the skies above *Pedestal* almost certainly dominated, as we spoke, by black-crossed wings.

She hesitated briefly as if to say more, then gave me a brave, desperately sad smile and went back to the plot.

It was then that I heard the voice from behind. That voice I'd heard again today. But I hadn't had cause to be affected so greatly by it then. I still hadn't met the Admiral.

'Probably the most powerful escorting force ever assembled during this war, Miller. Over forty warships,' it said flatly. 'And with only one purpose – to smash a way through for the convoy. Forty ships, to protect fourteen . . . yet even now I'll count myself damn lucky if three, even two of those merchantmen ever reach us.'

I turned. He was looking up at the stateboard with . . . was it a touch of perplexity?

'Yessir,' I'd said, coming to attention. Lieutenants, particularly Reserve lieutenants, didn't feed fuel to conversations with admirals. And anyway, I suspected there had to be a punchline.

When it came, it was straight to the solar plexus.

'So tell me, Lieutenant, how in God's name,' he'd shaken his head, unambiguously incredulous that time, 'can an eight-knot coal burner with no intelligence reports, no routing or mining information, no radar and not even a damned radio – how could she *possibly* have maintained a contraband run between this boxed-in fortress and the North African coast with the regularity of . . . of a Birkenhead *ferry*, dammit?'

I'd wondered briefly if he was joking, but one of his aircraft carriers had just been sunk and I saw the look in his eyes.

'Well it can't be done, can it?' I muttered lamely, even forgetting to add the *Sir*.

The very suggestion was ludicrous, conjuring, as it did, a vision of some phantom vessel – some impossibly antiquated Steamboat Annie loaded to the gunnels with smuggled cigarettes; whisky; Dutchman's gin; fine ales . . . even tinned salmon – chugging invisibly through shot and shell between the Allied and Axis Navies.

'Oh, but it *has* been done, Miller,' the Admiral assured me grimly. 'Consistently. Over the last fourteen months.'

'Good God!' I'd whispered weakly.

'She was arrested last night. They're bringing her into Grand Harbour now, under the guns of two fleet destroyers. She took a bit of catching.'

I remember frowning then. Had I detected a hint of grudging respect in the Admiral's tone? Personally I felt only resentment at the disclosure that he'd deployed two fighting ships desperately needed for more vital war tasks, merely to prevent some low-life smuggler owing, seemingly, no scrap of allegiance to any Flag, from swanning about out there intent on making a fast buck out of chaos while the rest of the world was fighting and suffering – like ME being sunk, f'r a bloody start. And in a *frigate* at that, when I'd much preferred to have been sunk in a decent tramp steamer.

. . . Mind you, he must be a damn good seaman, I privately conceded; that contraband runner's captain. With a capacity for skulduggery to rival Machiavelli's.

Nevertheless: 'Destroyers are precious resources, sir. I'm surprised you didn't order her to be sunk on sight. Ideally, with all hands.'

'Geneva Convention apart, that is why I am an admiral and you are still a lieutenant, Lieutenant,' he'd retorted levelly, not at all put out by the implied criticism. 'I look at the bigger picture.'

'With respect, sir, I'm not required to. I'm Hostilities Only. I was a merchant service officer before the Navy decided, in its wisdom, to offer me a temporary career break.'

'Perhaps we were wrong,' he retorted unexpectedly. 'Perhaps you would be better suited to ships that aren't painted grey and fly the White Ensign. Not openly, at least.'

'Sir?' I muttered uncertainly.

He'd swung away abruptly. It appeared I'd been dismissed. An' I *still* didn't know why I'd been called there?

But then he'd turned back, almost as if struck by an afterthought. 'Got your seabag handy, Miller?' he'd queried slyly.

'In my billet, sir.'

. . . Assuming one *could* call a hole in the ground with a corrugated tin sheet laid across it, a billet, that was. A very *deep* hole, mind you. Custom burrowed. I'd had a lot of spare time on my hands, and shrapnel is a great motivator.

'Get it. Given your evident nostalgia for the merchant service way of life, we may be able to offer you an option. I suspect the ideal berth for you might just be entering harbour.'

He must have read the look in *my* eye then, as realization dawned.

Because for the very first time, the Admiral smiled.

Two hours later I'd met Trapp.

Di'n't I *say* that admiral was a bastard?

I'd captured my first sight of the impounded vessel just as the island's sirens wailed to signal the start of yet another hit and run attack on Valletta's Grand Harbour.

It had scared the absolute *shit* out of me. I don't mean the umpteenth bombing raid – I meant my first sight of Trapp's ship. My ship too, as things were to turn out, though I hadn't been aware of it at the time because that devious bast— because the *Admiral*, being an admiral, didn't deal in 'options' for junior Reserve officers. It seemed he'd endorsed my appointment as first lieutenant to her the moment I'd naively left his bunker. Without so much as a 'Well, what did you think of her, Miller . . . ?'

I hadn't even been certain of which vessel I'd been looking for. They'd told me at the gate I'd find two small tramp steamers – moored discreetly out of sight to prevent the garrison's morale from plummeting any lower, they'd warned me – up a foetid backwater of the dockyard proper. One had been there a long time: a burnt-out hulk which had been a very old ship even before the Stukas had got to her, and from which the Navy had since stripped everything salvageable . . . and the other was Trapp's blockade runner.

Yet the only way I'd been able to tell the two wrecks apart lay in the clue offered by two steel-helmeted Naval armed guards resignedly taking cover yet again along the scarred upperworks of the outboard vessel.

She'd been a caricature of a ship even when seaworthy: a demented cartoonist's parody of every sailor's nightmare. Shelter decked from counter to roughly half her two-fifty-foot length forward, she boasted a tiny foc'slehead surmounting a battered stem as straight up and down as a plumber's plumb line. There was a hole precisely the diameter of a four-inch naval shell, clear through it. Where her buckled decks weren't rusty, they were filthy: where they weren't filthy, they'd been eaten away altogether. Her mushroom ventilators had mushrooms growing under them. There was a gaping shake in her ancient wooden mainmast you could've stuffed a cabin boy's head into. Most of her wheelhouse had collapsed, while what little canvas was left of her bridge dodger was as grimy and tattered as a coffin ship stoker's underpants. The wires making up her standing rigging had so many parted strands sticking out, they looked more like terrified cats' tails. The only neatly finished thing about her was a second shell hole through her corroding, spindly funnel – presumably the final straw that had persuaded the buccaneering Trapp to give up thoughts of escape and follow the White Ensigned path of true British righteousness into close arrest.

Well . . . that hole, plus the bizarre presence of a plate bearing her name which confronted me at the head of her rickety gangway. Absolutely beautiful, it was: a magnificent example of some proper sailor's art. Highly polished fretworked brass letters mounted on a gloss-varnished mahogany board embellished by ropework so white and expertly crafted it could've been worked by God's Bosun himself.

Which it evidently hadn't been, considering the name her captain had chosen to call his vessel. I was, it loftily informed me, about to venture aboard the not-so-good-ship *Charon*.

How appropriate, I thought sardonically: Charon being that grim spectre of myth who's eternal task is to ferry the Souls of the Damned across the River Styx.

To Hades.

Thanks, but no thanks, I decided grimly while promptly about-turning and making to head back to my suddenly immensely attractive hole, and to face an Admiral's wrath. 'The answer's negative. So shoot me f'r mutiny if you want. It'll be over quicker.'

. . . Just before the first shout from the sandbagged ack-ack emplacement on the wharf. *Take POST . . . ! Hostile – forty plus . . . low level, bearing wun niner fife!*

Gun layers swinging expertly into their seats, reaching for

elevating and traversing wheels. And a man – big, stocky, weather-beaten as a clipper's figurehead – suddenly materializing at the head of the gangway and yelling abuse at me.

'You got no authority to hold this ship, Mister. She flies no Flag, belongs to no country. She's a free-trader: a neutral, an' so am I . . .'

Single Messerschmitt Wun Wun Oh . . . The barrel of the 3.7 swinging downwards and vectoring towards the harbour entrance. *On target!*

'No you're not. You're a parasite, Trapp. An exploiter.' I'm getting furious myself now. And scared because he's blocking my way to the nearest point of refuge. 'You've made a business out of war: a . . . a *profit*! Only now your luck's run out. The war's finally caught up with you an' this bloody atrocious junk heap you call a ship.'

Fuze six.

'Not *my* war – YOUR bloody war, Lieutenant.'

Fuze six . . . SET!

A roar rising to a thundering howl. One stark glimpse of a twin-engined bomber blasting towards us from the harbour entrance so low I can see the prop-wash ripping feathery scuds of spray astern of it.

Me bolting back up that gangway like an Olympic sprinter, barging past Trapp, heading for the illusory shelter of the *Charon*'s corroded, paper-thin bulwarks to join the two already-prostrate RN armed guards. 'Take COVERRRR . . . !' I'm bawling. But I've been here before. Seen it: done that. They'd taken exactly three minutes to sink my last ship.

The blood-curdling shriek of Daimler-Benz closing at three hundred an' fifty miles an hour.

FIIIIRE!

Crash!

A second plane banking low and hard across our stumpy bow, smoke streaming from its starboard engine . . . the swelling screech of Stukas peeling off above the centre of Valletta while every gun on Malta looses off with an ear-shattering concussion. Aircraft . . . *dozens* of bloody aircraft high in the sky above us all intermingled with puff-ball bursts of flak. An enormous explosion from somewhere inland, while my nails dig into the filth and rusted scale of the *Charon*'s scuppers.

'Gerroff my *ship*, Mister. I'm non-aligned – a neutral vessel.

If you wasn't a reservist I'd heave you back over the side myself, tiddley Navy rig an' all!'

He's still *standing*! And again, from the 3.7 emplacement. *Crash!*

'If I wasn't a *reservist*, Trapp . . .' I'm clamping my steel helmet hard down over my ears now, while screaming into the rust that's dancing and spiralling under the ack-ack muzzle blast, 'I'd be aboard a PROPER bloody ship. Not playing errand boy to a contraband-running copy of a Port Said fuckin' CLAP barge!'

I feel the prop-wash battering down on me as that first Messerschmitt slams in above the bulwarks, red-painted decal gaping wide as a shark's maw an' the twin underslung cannons in her nose winking little spurts of yellow flame. Parallel lines of holes race past me across the scabrous deck, more rounds spanging and ricochetting from the *Charon*'s accommodation . . . an' he's gone! Thank Christ he had *some* discernment when it came to target selection, that Luftwaffe bomb aimer. He hadn't bothered to dump his load on a wreck so obviously bound for the breaker's yard, shiny nameplate or not.

Trapp shaking his fists apoplectically at the sky, still erect and yelling epithets at the German Air Force while loftily ignoring the neat lines of cannon shell holes, one on either side of him.

'*Neutral*, I am. Non-ALIGNE—!'

CRASH . . . ! Reloaaad!

On TARGET . . . Fuze four . . . Set!

FIIIIRE . . . !

'Not any longer, you're not, Trapp. It's *your* bloody war too, now.'

I roll on my back and start laughing up at him: my snarl of derision overcoming even the rictus caused by terror.

'That's what I've been sent to tell you – you've been *drafted*, Trapp. Called up. You and your ship an' whatever crowd of misfits you have the gall to call a crew. Called up to fight for King and Country. Without even a little profit in sight!'

He still wasn't going to go to war, Trapp wasn't. Even refused point blank to accompany me back to the Admiral's bunker to discuss any part of his participation in the conflict. Not unless I was prepared to guarantee a charter rate for use of his ship and sailors – I venture the term loosely – that would've bankrupted the British War Treasury. Bloody usury, it was: the figure he demanded. The Germans would've rented us the *Scharnhorst* for less, with *Tirpitz* thrown in as a sweetener. Complete with crews and ten thousand rounds of assorted Krupps ordnance.

But Trapp simply wouldn't listen. Kept harping on and on about being a civilian an' neutral and non-aligned, and jus' an international business man, and how he wus goin' to sue the British Admiralty f'r damage inflicted on the *Charon* an' . . . *and* f'r loss of profits while detained under wrongful arrest an' . . . an' . . . he didn't pause for breath all the time he was being frog-marched from the dockyard to the bunker by my commandeered Naval guard.

Didn't even run out of steam on finding himself face to face with an admiral. Just kept getting more and more red in the face and quoting his Right of Internashnul Passage and how he'd been entitled to a warning shot *across* the bows, Mister – not bloody THROUGH 'em!

Until the Admiral said, ever so sympathetically, 'I hear what you say, Lieutenant Commander.'

. . . Whereupon Edward Trapp, probably for the very first time in his life, ground to a speechless halt.

Look, I do realize I'm equally guilty of going on at excessive length, for that matter. Certainly more than I should about a man who'd become history by the time I reached Scotland, when I'm supposed to be writing about a Russian convoy that was about to make it. But having disclosed that the Admiral achieved the seemingly-impossible by getting Trapp to shut up, I should really explain why the conjunction of those two words, *Lieutenant* and *Commander*, had succeeded in so doing.

And explain, perhaps, just why an unrepentant contraband runner arrested off Malta had become an international pariah in the first place. How he'd come to harbour such deep contempt for the concept of patriotism, and for what he came to see as the pursuit of futile ideals.

It seemed that, when Trapp was a mere child-sailor, he'd developed a conviction that not only was he always right and that the rest of the world was out of step, but also that he would continue to be a survivor in this dog eat dog world only if he became hard enough and selfish enough. He'd come to that opinion when, as a starry-eyed first-trip midshipman during the First Great War, he'd found himself alone in mid-Atlantic: the only remnant of a four-hundred-man ship's company who'd fought and died for King and Country when their very gallant but inadequately armed merchant cruiser had been sunk.

He'd endured nineteen days of utter loneliness and suffering, sharing his life raft only with the head and upper torso of a rating whom – which? – he hadn't been able to bear the thought of cutting loose because, for a little boy cast adrift many hundreds of miles from land, to be able to enjoy the company of a part-friend was better than having no friend at all.

But, sadly, even his part-companion had got smaller and smaller thanks to the depredations of various sea creatures, until he had vanished altogether to become only a disappeared friend. And that doubly-exquisite bereavement marked the moment when the child Trapp grew to resent what his King and his Country had done to him, and to generate a bitter hatred of all in authority and, particularly, for those who prescribed the laws of a society that he, according to his own experience, believed to be set firm on a course for self-destruction anyway.

It had been on the twelfth day of his ordeal, just as Midshipman Trapp had made up his mind to die, that a little red fish flipped clean out of the water and landed in the raft. It was his second moment of truth. The boy had frowned at it for a long moment, and decided that the personal feelings of others did not necessarily equate with the will to survive. So he'd said 'Sorry, Fish', picked it up and, while still gasping and staring up at him with bulbous, reproachful eyes, had swallowed it whole, whereupon he finally confirmed that putting one's need first can prove a much more fulfilling emotion than self-sacrifice. Especially when it can keep you alive for another seven days.

Ironically, the act of being rescued had only served to further reinforce Trapp's conviction that nothing was fair in love and war, and that he could never, ever rely on his own side to do the right thing by him. Because even his salvation, such as it was, had been provided by the enemy. A German raider had picked him up, patched him up and, ultimately, trans-shipped him to a prisoner-of-war camp where he'd starved once more before concluding, yet again, that animal cunning and self-ishness and looking after Number One, were to serve him far better than being a jolly decent chap.

And so it was that Edward Trapp became every bit as much a casualty of man's inhumanity to man as any blinded airman or soldier amputee. And why, when finally repatriated after that war to end all wars, he hadn't hesitated to turn his back on the country of his birth and, instead, seek his fortune as a global entrepreneur owing loyalty to no creed other than that of self-sufficiency and the principle of doing unto others before they do unto you – only more violently, just to make sure. He was to become a mercilessly unforgiving man, as many who later underestimated him were to discover to their ultim-ate cost, and indeed, a most terrible man to take liberties with – especially when it came to money.

But he still hadn't learned the most elementary survival rule of all. Not until he met the Admiral. And that was: *Act in haste: repent at leisure . . .*

'Talk all you want, you ain't getting me, my Queen o' the Seas an' my top-drawer internashnul crew for sweetie money, an' that's flat, Mister,' Trapp had declared truculently, playing his ace card of indifference. 'And if you don't like it, then jail me 'til the war's over. I reely don't mind.'

'Unfortunately I can't do that,' the Admiral demurred regret-fully. 'Being bound by the terms of the Naval Punishment Act of 1859, I am compelled to have you shot by firing squad at dawn tomorrow, Lieutenant Commander. For mutiny and disobeying a lawful command in time of war.'

'You keep *callin'* me that. Calling me Lieutenant Commander,' Trapp had yelled, somewhat missing the main thrust of the Admiral's statement. 'Whaddyou mean – *Lieutenant* Commander?'

'But . . . ah . . . surely you couldn't have forgotten, my dear chap?' the Admiral had responded silkily.

'Forgotten *what*?'

'That you, in common with, er . . . Miller here and myself, are a Naval Officer. And have been for the past twenty-odd years.'

. . . Which statement marked the moment when, for the second time in his life, Edward Trapp ran out of words. And so did I, albeit as a very junior fly on the wall who'd never been invited to comment anyway. Well, I mean – Trapp? A Naval *officer* . . . ? A man wearing filthy, gap-toed plimsolls laced with codline, and a reefer jacket so decrepit it'd developed a mould-green patina, surmounted by a merchant service cap so battered that the white top had virtually separated from its headband around 1929 to bob wildly like the half-opened lid of a Popeye tin o' spinach every time Trapp moved his head . . . ?

And I'd thought *I* was the maritime odd man out? Neither Merchant nor Royal, fish nor fowl, with my two Wavy-Navy rings?

'Do you remember,' the Admiral had persisted with much the same considerate quality of a cat playing with a mouse, 'the events which took place after you were repatriated. During November 1918?'

'I took a ship the next day,' the Mouse retorted huffily. 'Outward f'r the Far East. So what about it?'

'Which didn't leave much time to settle your affairs in Britain, did it?'

'Time? Time for what, Mister?'

'To attend your demobilization centre, for instance?'

Trapp grinned derisively. 'Demob . . . ? Christ but I'd had enough, Mister. Enough o' your Navy, an' little men with supercilious . . .'

At which point, for the *third* time in his misbegotten life, Trapp lost the power of speech as realization began to dawn.

'Exactly. And because you never offered your resignation, your name was never removed from the Royal Navy's List of Reserve Officers. Your promotion over the years has been entirely automatic – Lieutenant Commander Trapp!'

'Christ, Mister!' Trapp had echoed. Dead shattered.

'Which brings me to a further point,' the Admiral concluded with a sudden hint of steel. '*Mister* is so very merchant service. From now on, Commander, when in my presence I shall expect you to modify your form of address. You will call me *Sir*.'

I couldn't help it. I started to laugh. But such unseemly mirth had been short-lived: serving only to demonstrate that Edward Trapp would never, ever, lose his irrepressible capacity for rising above adversity. He'd turned to fix me with a malignant eye, as if it had all been *my* bloody fault.

'You heard what Sir said, Mister. I'm a lieutenant-commander, Royal Navy.'

'It appears so, Trapp,' I'd grinned enjoyably.

'While you're only a two-ring, weekend bloody wonder, reserve lieutenant.'

I hesitated uncertainly. 'Yes, Trapp.'

He gathered himself with anticipation. It would be this way for ever, until one or the other of us ended up in Davy Jones's Locker. That Trapp would *always* have the last word.

'Then from now on, Mister, when in my presence I shall expect you to modify your form of address. You will call me *Sir*.'

But *wait* . . .

Although having thoroughly warmed to the theme of my first – and, I must bitterly interject – *only* triumph over Trapp, I simply have to hold back now and force myself to be sparing at this juncture. About relating what happened subsequently. About how the SS *Charon* – or what then became HMS *Charon*, God Save His Majesty from such cruel embarrassment – had been hastily converted to a Q-ship packed to the gunnels with concealed weaponry, then despatched to the North African coast intending – or so the Admiral had imagined, not having blackmailed Trapp quite as successfully as he'd thought he had – to entice any unwary U-boat within point-blank range while, to fill in our war diary during the quiet spells, sinking every enemy supply ship we came across.

A sound strategy, it could have proved. First World War in concept admittedly, but nevertheless worth a try. For a start, no U-boat man worth his salt could have resisted the impulse to take a closer look at her, even if only to help figure how the crumbling *Charon* could possibly float, never mind fight. Except the Admiral's plan of battle hadn't allowed for the T-factor – the Trapp Factor. Meaning he hadn't taken into account the Captain's unmitigated avarice, further compounded by his obsessive aversion to authority. It completely over-looked Trapp's personal mission statement, resurrected Naval officer or not, which stated very clearly that, if you gotta go to war, then such irritating inconvenience should not be permitted to divert from life's primary objective: the pursuit of commercial gain.

But *no* . . . No, I'm *not* going to fall for going on an' on about HIM again. I *won't* give him the satisfaction, albeit posthumously what with him being in his watery grave and everything . . . no way.

Because I've already chronicled the shambles of that voyage, and I mustn't bore you with repetition. Apart from which I've no intention of going against medical advice by recalling any more of it than I have to. I've done the therapy to rid me of that memory . . . my *first* course of therapy, I mean – the one I underwent after the Admiral's grand strategy to tip the scales of war had left me sole survivor of his misconceived plan.

Though I suppose, looking on the bright side of my life as a fighting sailor, in addition to the consolation of knowing that the rest of the *Charon*'s villainous crowd had been consigned to the roll call of ex-pirates along with their boss, that spell of post-Trapp catharsis had at least afforded me a change from the previous routine imposed on me by the Navy.

Instead of leaving me hanging around for weeks in a hole in the ground in Malta as an unemployed target for the Luftwaffe, it left me hanging around for several more weeks in Libya. As an unemployed target for the bloody *Afrika Korps!*

A desert hospital, it had been. Meaning a tent with a few bomb-eviscerated sandbags across the entrance that couldn't have withstood a good strong breeze, never mind the blast of an 88-mil round from a Panzerkampfwagen VI Tiger.

'Write it all down, Lieutenant,' the military psychiatri— well – the *doctor* had urged at that point. 'Everything you can remember about your war deployment with Trapp: right up to the moment when you were found drifting alone on that hatch cover off the Libyan coast after your – his – ship had been torpedoed. Write it down while you're being treated here in exotic Araby, and the act of so-doing will rid your mind of the spectres it continues to raise. Trust me. I'm a head doctor.'

Yeah, right. Like I trusted that soddin' Admiral.

Anyway, I did. Pages an' pages of it. It helped take my mind off the shell fire. Bloody soldiers. Noisy people. Always digging holes in the sand and shouting technical army stuff to each other, like *Incoming* and *Take cover* an' *Medic – where's the fucking MEDIC . . . ?*

Yet even when I'd finished, I still hadn't entirely convinced the doctor that I was well enough to be let out. For a start, he argued the title I'd devised suggested I hadn't distanced myself sufficiently from all association with the outcome.

Miller's War, I'd proposed to call it. I'd felt quite proud of having incorporated that proprietary touch. My journal would stand forever in public libraries as a personal valediction: my legacy to the peace that was bound to follow, even if I never actually saw it.

But: 'Not really accurate, is it, old boy?' he'd said dubiously. 'I mean, it wasn't as if *you'd* taken any decisions during the mission, was it?'

'He wouldn't let me,' I'd protested grumpily. 'No one took decisions when Trapp was in command. Not even *Trapp* took decisions. Things just, well . . . happened.'

'Exactly,' he'd mused. 'So it couldn't be construed that *you'd* had any influence over the course of that voyage, could it? None of that business about improperly utilizing one of His Majesty's Ships as a privateer? Pretending to be Italians . . . stealing all that gold before losing it again . . . siding with the German Navy then persuading them to fight the German Army . . . ? None of those unfortunate by-products had been *your* fault, had they?'

'I suppose not,' I'd agreed uncertainly. 'Putting it that way, I suppose I had been more of a . . . a what-you-might-call horrified observer, than Trapp's executive officer *per se*.'

'Well, there you have it,' he'd spread his hands in professional vindication. 'One minor editorial concession and you can absolve yourself from all guilt; all responsibility for the mission's outcome, dear chap. I can't cure you – the great Professor Freud himself couldn't have *cured* you – but I *can* help you embrace the therapeutic last resort of self-denial: lay the Captain's ghost as of now. Because it wasn't really *Miller's* war at all, was it . . . ?'

I've always felt a tad bitter since, mind you. After all I'd gone through. My being shot at, and verbally abused an' torpedoed and everything.

At his insistence – in fact his direct order eventually; him being a full Medical Corps colonel and me only a lieutenant, and him having lost his temper by then an' screaming terrible

threats involving funny farms an' throwing bloody *keys* away
– that I should change the heading on my magnum opus.

That I should entitle *my* personal Odyssey – *TRAPP'S War*.

Right! Got the chronology sorted now, have you? And the story
so far? Malta – the Admiral – Trapp – *Bang!* – sole survivor
– Libya – hospital . . . ? Followed by my eventually being flown,
without a word of explanation, up to Scotland and that Russian
convoy conference – the one I intend to start writing about
NOW, without *any* further diversion.

Which will make what follows my second journal. My
second course of bloody therapy!

And this one, I AM going to call *MILLER's War*!

Three

W hat was it my still-disembodied Admiral had growled over my shoulder?

'I trust you've been listening closely, Miller,' hadn't he said? 'Very closely indeed.'

Well, that was pretty clear, wasn't it? It implied that any optimism I may artlessly have cherished, about having been posted to this remote backwater to join the NCS staff, had been thoroughly misplaced. I just knew, from the lack of empathy implicit in his tone, that the Admiral had taken time out from his war to complete *my* box personally.

Not that I could blame him. Having been given every reason to be displeased with my recent performance as non-executive executive officer of the Royal Navy's only commercial arm, it would never have been his intention that Lieutenant Miller, Royal Naval Reserve, should sit out the rest of the war in some nice, safe location while polishing his shoes and brushing down his number one uniform each evening for dinner in some UK wardroom. Meaning that, as of 0530 on the morrow, he was destined to set sail for Russia. Quite in what capacity I didn't yet know, but the upshot would be much the same. Cold, wet, apprehensive; up to the Arctic Circle, dodge the bombs, torpedoes, mines and icebergs, an' turn right.

But in the company of nice people, though. I *had* to cling to that thought. Sane, well-adjusted people united in common patriotic endeavour.

I determined not to turn and acknowledge my persecutor, not even after I found myself released from the paralysis of anxiety that gripped me. Tempting providence had long disappeared from my list of things to do, though I wasn't naive enough to imagine that the Admiral's presence was anything other than peripheral to an operational visit to the base. But the mere fact of his being there *did* encourage me to listen even harder to what the next officer had to say: in part because his wisdom might help to keep me alive but, of more immediate concern to my well-being, in case the Admiral asked me questions after.

He was last to speak: the Convoy Commodore who would sail with them – with *us*, now – to Murmansk in overall control of the merchant ship element. Seventy-three years young, I discovered later. Had retired from the Royal Navy as a rear-admiral two decades before, only to abandon his roses and his gundogs and his Cotswold cottage to volunteer himself again for this most arduous of sea-going appointments. A silver-haired, bluff-looking chap with a presence that immediately instilled confidence, he would keep going, convoy after convoy come hell or high water, until he was either killed by the enemy or died from sheer exhaustion as several of his contemporaries already had.

When he did address us, it was in a manner that made everything seem that little bit better; the coming endeavour a little less frightening. It became evident that both he and his colleague, the escort commander, supported by the Naval Control Service and – yes, I had to concede despite my cynicism – the briefcase-bearing officials at the much derided Ministry of War Transport, had done their jobs to the best of their abilities. Bitter experience and the loss of all too many gallant lives had provided the spur. Every eventuality, every conceivable contingency had been anticipated, and precise plans to counter such setbacks drawn up in minute detail. Storm, fog, mining; surface, air and submarine attack; engine breakdowns, damage caused by stress of weather, encounters with ice, collision in formation, the closing of entry to the Kola Inlet by enemy action, alternative routes, stragglers' routes – even mutiny by crewmen pushed too far.

And inevitably, the action to be taken by individual masters in the event of the convoy being ordered – God forbid that it should happen again – to scatter . . . apart, that was, from emulating my own likely reaction were I ever to find myself involved in such a desperate situation. That of curling into a foetal huddle in a corner of the wheelhouse while sticking a thumb in my mouth.

And then it was time to go.

'Good luck and God speed, gentlemen,' the Senior Naval Control Service Officer called above the scrape of chairs and the clatter of teaspoons in steaming mugs of tea laced with condensed milk. He'd had the grace to refrain from adding, 'Wish I was going with you,' but in that fleeting moment I detected a wistfulness of expression which suggested that, in his case, had he done so, then he would have meant every word.

Personally I'd decided to forego my longingly anticipated char and connie in favour of getting clear of the Admiral's yardarm before my somewhat less than creditable past caught up, but no sooner had I risen to leg it for the exit than The Voice arrested me in mid-flight.

'If you really don't wish tea, Miller, that's up to you,' it said. 'But as I fully intend to enjoy mine, be so good as to wait outside by my staff car while I make my number with the NCSOs.'

'Oh, *hello*, sir,' I said, finally swivelling to meet his granite appraisal. 'What an unexpected surprise.'

'There's something I want you to see,' was all he'd said, motioning me to climb in the back of the camouflaged Humber with him. Already apprehensive, I couldn't help reading further bad tidings for one of the four of us into the way his Flag Lieutenant studiously avoided my eye as he slipped in beside the Wren driver. I decided I didn't like the bloke from the start. He'd already made it clear the feeling was mutual.

Other than that, the Admiral had maintained a stony silence during the short journey along a rutted track towards the loch entrance. Not even a token, 'Sorry I was responsible for getting you blown up again, Lieutenant.' Mind you, as he'd undoubtedly studied the transcript of my *Operation Styx* debriefing, every single lie and fabrication of it, I couldn't really criticize him for displaying a certain shortfall in remorse. Any he'd originally felt must have evaporated while fighting the temptation to have me court-martialled for perjury; dereliction of duty; conspiring with the enemy; conspiring to defraud the British Treasury; conspiring to steal a large boat and lots of other things . . . conspiring with others to conspire against His Majesty the King, His People, and His Dominions . . .

Others . . . ? Oh yeah, there had been others apart from Trapp. Those spectres I've previously touched upon . . . ? The ones that still jolt me wide awake and staring up at the deck-head every night. That foc'sle-full of human flotsam Trapp euphemistically referred to as 'His top-drawer boys: his Internashnul crew' . . . ?

Take his anthropoidal side-kick, Gorbals Wullie, f'r a start. A vertically challenged, pointy-faced, undernourished, thick-as-mince little Glaswegian hard man as inseparable from Edward Trapp as a pet rat from a schoolboy: the main differ-ence being Wullie wasn't nearly as intelligent as your average pet ra— well, not even your dumbest of pet rats, come to that. Trailed after Trapp like one, too: his loyalty to his constant abuser extending far beyond the bounds of stupidity. A sort of love-hate relationship, those two had formed over the years: only in their case it was more hate-hate kept fine-honed by incessant and vituperative squabbling.

But I'm digressing again . . . though it's always a pleasure, pausing to dip one's pen into pure vitriol when it comes to Gorbals Wullie.

'Where to, sir?' the Wren asked.

'Drive up there to the top of the cliff,' the Admiral directed. 'Right to the edge.'

Suddenly even more alarmed, I sneaked a furtive sideways glance at him. He surely didn't propose to throw me *over*, did he . . . ? And no, I wasn't simply giving way to paranoia. I'd every reason to think like that. The last time I'd been in his presence we'd been right on the edge, too: just before the *Charon* sailed off to Mille . . . to *Trapp's* War!

Three merchant ships from *Operation Pedestal* had made it to Malta by then – the *Rochester Castle*, *Port Chalmers* and the Blue Star Line's *Melbourne Star*. The latter's hull and upper-works burned black from steaming over the funeral pyre of the New Zealand Shipping Company's *Waimarama,* one of her less fortunate consorts. They'd entered Grand Harbour without fuss, slipping quietly into their berths where the stevedores had swarmed aboard to begin discharging those incredibly precious cargoes before the Stukas screamed again.

On the following day the gallant *Brisbane Star* had limped slowly into port protected by a screen of warships and fighter aircraft. Her bows gaped wide; her forefoot blown off by a torpedo, but her cargo, too, had remained intact. Four ships safe so far, out of fourteen. The island could eat a little more: the guns keep up their vicious anti-aircraft barrage: there were spare parts for trucks and generators and the Malta-based Spitfires and Beaufighters and submarines and . . . but *still* no damned fuel to allow them to operate.

The whole island had waited: groups of Maltese and service personnel standing in silent watch over an empty horizon. Many prayed, others simply swallowed hard while shielding their eyes from the sun. No one was quite sure whether we were waiting for the tanker, or the enemy. The odds lay with the latter; there seemed little hope for the stricken *Ohio*. Rumour had it she'd been hit so many times she'd been abandoned and was on fire, broken-backed and listing heavily seventy miles off.

I'd gone with Trapp to report progress to the Admiral, just before we sailed. They'd been rushing to get the *Charon* ready – the Dockyard Commander (Planning) had phrased it succinctly that morning. 'I suggest you get ready to sail as soon as possible, gentlemen. Otherwise you may not have time to get away at all.'

And then we'd bumped into that Wren third officer. Her eyes sparkled with excitement. 'Have you heard?' she'd said. 'The good news?'

'The Admiral's had a stroke?' I'd hazarded hopefully.

'*Ohio*. They've gone back on board again. And *Rye* and *Penn* are out there with her. They're trying to tow her in.'

He'd been preoccupied from the start of our meeting, the Admiral. Kept glancing at the phone as if willing it to ring. When it finally did, he'd lunged to pick it up. That was the only time I ever saw him drop his guard, but enough to persuade me that even the least emotional have emotions.

It was a short call. 'Thank you. I'll be down right away.'

After firmly replacing the receiver he'd reached for his cap and turned to us, his expression again hewn from British oak, but his eyes still betrayed him. They burned with a very great pride.

'She was Malta's last hope, gentlemen,' he said. 'The *Ohio* . . . They're bringing her in this very moment.'

She wasn't so much a ship as a mortally wounded hulk, with her main decks almost awash and kept afloat only by being lashed to the destroyers *Penn* and *Bramham* either side of her.

Slowly, excruciatingly slowly, she was nudged and coaxed through the swept channel between the minefields and into the wide entrance to Grand Harbour. Twice abandoned and reboarded: bomb-scarred, her hull colandered by a thousand splinters, her engines and rudder damaged beyond repair, she had a twenty-foot rent in her port side, with the deck above the point of impact curled up and backwards in tattered petals of jagged steel. Part-melted pipework, ventilators and rails sagged amongst a shipscape of fire-ravaged deck housings. The skeletal airframe of a Junkers 88 bomber still sprawled forward of her bridge, having bounced aboard after crashing in the sea alongside. The corpse of a Stuka reared like a dead man's finger from her poop deck.

The cheering began: hesitantly at first as if fearful that the great and gallant event we were witnessing was merely the product of wishful thinking. But then, as the brave *Ohio*'s counter inched through the breakwater, the jubilation of thousands grew to a hysteria of thanksgiving so loud one could barely make out the rousing strains of *Rule Britannia* playing from the end of the mole. Above, only RAF rondels glinted on the aircraft wheeling high in a cloudless sky. It was Malta's day. The enemy weren't invited.

I'd stolen a curious glance towards Trapp in that moment. He wasn't cheering. He'd simply been gazing out at the limping *Ohio* with a seeming air of remote detachment, as if this part of the war bore no relationship to his own enforced contract of service: that the whole celebration was the concern of some other, less profit-conscious authority.

Or had I been wrong in making such a harsh presumption? Because there'd been something more than that, albeit only faintly discernible in those grey, unfathomable eyes. A sort of regretful acknowledgement of something that would be denied to Edward Trapp forever. A sad recognition that those brave moments might also have been a part of his life too.

Once.
Upon a very long time ago.

It was Scots autumn exposed up there on the headland. A
brisk westerly drove the Atlantic-born wind chill clear across
the Minch to snap the Flag Officer's pennant on the staff car
while whipping our greatcoats around our legs. Visibility was
poor, with great scuds of drizzle sweeping towards us on the
coast like curtains drawn over the short, white-capped seas.
The Admiral appeared to be enjoying it, pointing into the
breeze like the frustrated seadog he was. I just felt bloody
uncomfortable, what with the dancing beads of moisture
constantly blowing into my eyes from the peak of my cap,
and the trickling discomfort of water seeping inside my collar.

Waxed Bombay paper, it was. The collar. Came in packets
of ten. An old merchant apprentice's trick – kept the same
white shirt looking spruce for days once anchored securely
with a backstud. A positive boon to peripatetic Flying
Dutchmen such as I'd recently become, who were never
allowed time to catch up with their dhobying. Trouble was,
when they got wet they tended to turn to papier mâché which,
in turn, tended to incur the wrath of admirals on observing
that their junior companion had begun to melt.

I was engaged in emulating a furtive tortoise by telescoping
my neck into the concealment of my greatcoat when the
Admiral stiffened, and grunted, 'Hah!'

'I didn't realize it would be raini—' I'd launched defensively, when I noticed he wasn't looking at me but out to sea.

'There they are,' he added with deep, if somewhat cryptic,
satisfaction.

Then I saw them myself. Two ships approaching from the
west: still wraith-like and strangely insubstantial. There, and
gone. There . . . and gone again as the rain closed around them.
Like . . . like *ghost* ships? I swallowed involuntarily, suddenly
beset by a resurgence of my earlier frame of mind. And then
they came clear of the squalls and I could see them as being
real and substantial, and nothing whatsoever to do with appar-
itions of ectoplasmic origin or a shell-shocked young man's
fevered imaginings.

One was very obviously a warship: the sleek one lying well
astern of the other and maintaining station on her port quarter

like a watchful sheepdog. The leading ship was a merchantman. An old merch— correction – a *very* old merchantman, with slab sides and a drainpipe for a funnel, and upperworks that looked like battered cardboard boxes scattered higgledy-piggledy by a fractious child, and a curiously sloped, overhanging bow that didn't so much carve through the irritable seas as blast them aside with a contempt most shipmasters wouldn't have risked displaying, judging by the inevitably time-eroded condition of her frames.

I'd never *seen* such an antiquated ship. No, sorry. I tell another lie – I *had* seen one ship as ancient as that before. My last sight of Trapp's superannuated privateer was when everything forward of her bridge had detonated in great clouds of steam and fire and rust, predominantly rust, and the *Charon* had begun to capsize as she finally sank, in glorious ignominy, to the bottom of the Mediterranean Sea.

'Well, what do you think of her, Miller?' the Admiral asked, trying unconvincingly to sound as if it mattered to him.

'Destroyer, sir. Onslow Class: possibly HMS *Osborne*,' I answered, sharp as a tack but getting more and more determined to be obtuse an' not be bullied. Again. 'Thirty-four knots: four four-inch guns, eight torpedo tu—'

'Oh, *shit*,' I heard his Flag Lieutenant mutter apprehensively, yet the Admiral merely permitted a wintry smile. But it was easy for him to be expansive; secure in the knowledge he would always have the last laugh any time he felt like it.

'I mean the stuffed, Miller.'

'Stuffed?' I echoed uncertainly.

'Ship Taken Up From *Trade*,' the Flags hissed. 'S . . . T . . . U . . . STUFT!'

Damn Navy. Revelled in unintelligible acronyms: made a positive fetish of them. Why couldn't they just call a Stuffed a bloody cargo boat like everybody else?

'Didn't know there was a ship-breaker in the anchorage, sir.'

Happily he misheard me over the wind. 'Well spotted,' he conceded grudgingly.

'Sir?'

'That she's an ice-breaker, Miller – reinforced bow. Solid as a brick shithouse. Russian built, of course.'

Presumably on the same slipway as the Battleship *Potemkin*, only much earlier, I thought sardonically, but refrained from pursuing that line further. He had a notoriously short fuse and it was a long way down to the sea. And anyway, I was still more preoccupied with discovering what he had in mind regarding my own future deployment – where *I* went from here.

Mind you . . . he *had* brought me up to this desolate headland for a reason. And it seemed plausible that the reason was in some way connected to those approaching ships. Could it possibly be that I'd underestimated his capacity for leniency? Might he, for instance, be trying to make amends in a bluff but basically decent seaman's way? Give me a home posting. Even be about to offer me a . . . a *command*?

No, not the destroyer. Regenerated optimism or not, I didn't think for one minute he would offer me command of a destroyer. Lieutenants, especially former-MN second-mate lieutenants with no sense of ceremony, no tactical training and a history of regularly being sunk, weren't trusted with expensive warships – but they *were* deemed suitable to drive less high-profile vessels. Workhorses of the Fleet like minesweeping trawlers, inshore patrol boats, tenders and landing craft . . . *ice*-breakers?

I frowned seawards dubiously. It wasn't a done deal yet. She still had three miles to cover without foundering before she reached the sanctuary of the loch, and it looked like it would be touch and go, the way her once-upon-a-time re-inforced bow persisted in challenging each short sea to an impact test. But once in calm water and handled like a crate of eggs, she could very well remain afloat for . . . oh, weeks at least. Maybe even another six months before the rust-eater ate her.

But an *ice*-breaker? Wasn't that a leap of faith too far even by the Navy's hard-pressed standards? Careless contact with any cube too large to fit within a pink gin glass could prove terminal, and to me it was evident that somebody on high thought so too. Why else would they feel the need to allocate an escort to five thousand tons of scrap metal, other than to take her crew off in a hurry should the worst . . . no, should the seemingly inevitable, happen?

'It may have slipped your mind, but I *did* ask what you thought of her, Lieutenant,' the Admiral pressed with a touch of asperity. It marked my moment of truth. Blow this, Miller, an' you can forget home postings: you'll be on your way to Russia so fast you'll need water skis . . . and anyway, ice hardly ever forms in Scottish sea lochs, not even in the coldest of winters. Apart from which, even if you *do* happen to collide with something offering a serious threat to what little reserve buoyancy that hulk still retains – like a jettisoned beer bottle, say, or a flotsam cardboard box – then you're never going to be further than a spit from the nearest beach. Merely a leisurely swim ashore. For that matter, you could wear your lifejacket all the time, even in your bunk: make out you're an eccentric, albeit such in-your-face evidence that their new CO somewhat lacks self-confidence might tend to knock the shit out've your crew's morale. But all naval captains have their little whims: hanging, flogging, starvation rations, pot plants on the bridge, an' no one ever dares challenge them . . .

'She's a . . . sound-looking vessel, sir.' I swallowed hard and took a deep breath, resolving to wash my mouth out with soapy water soon as possible for telling such a lie. 'The sort of ship I'd consider myself privileged to serve in.'

'Bloody *hell*,' the Flag Lieutenant exclaimed disbelievingly. Even the Admiral looked momentarily taken aback.

'You *do* realize I'm referring to the Stuffed, Miller: not the destroyer?' he clarified suspiciously.

'Yessir. It's because she *is* a merchantman, sir. And I'm still a . . . well, with respect, sir – still a merchant seaman at heart. I'd feel I was returning to my seafaring roots.'

. . . As long as those roots didn't extend more than a half-mile distant from the pierhead behind us. But I felt I'd pitched it about right. A blend of wide-eyed earnestness tinged with an attractively ingenuous commitment to serving one's country, not as a glamorous naval officer but as a simple seaman. Mind you, the Flags did look like he was about to stuff two fingers down his throat by then; even well used, as he must have been, to watching sycophantic little turds from the bottom of the Navy List barrel attempting to ingratiate themselves with his boss.

On the other hand, the expression in the Wren driver's eyes afforded some compensation for any cynicism harboured by her superiors. A most promising mix of sympathy and the mothering instinct. While probably aware of my having returned from previous conflicts a battle-damaged – but deep down, essentially modest – hero; with a bit of luck she might not yet have gathered I had a lot to be modest about.

'Very well, Miller,' the Admiral grunted, still sounding a tad unconvinced but unprepared, him being a man preoccupied with momentous affairs of war and everything, to sacrifice further valuable time in slotting square irrelevant pegs into round rusting holes. 'It seems we've finally found a niche for your somewhat dubious talents that even you approve of. You have your new appointment. Report aboard as soon as she anchors.'

My short-lived euphoria immediately became tempered by niggling uncertainty. It didn't sound quite right. Report to who . . . ? To who *did* a newly appointed captain report when assuming command of his own ship? Even allowing for my limited grasp of Royal Navy-speak, didn't new captains *relieve* their predecessors, not report to them?

'Report to who, sir?' I asked uneasily.

'Report to *whom*,' the Flag Lieutenant hissed primly in public-school-educated triumph.

'Fuckin' *shut* it, fancyman!' I snarled back sotto voce: reverting to Merchant Navy-speak as anxiety took root.

'Her master, obviously,' the Admiral growled. 'Or did you intend to wander aboard and set up shop as NLO without so much as a by-your-leave, Miller?'

'What's an NLO?' I appealed to my new best friend.

'Naval Liaison Officer, dammit,' the Admiral snorted impatiently, cutting out the middle man.

'But she doesn't *need* a Naval Liaison Officer,' I retorted mutinously, forgetting I was arguing with the man who could have me shot whenever he felt like it. Or worse: shipped off to the Arctic Circle. 'All her old man needs to do is shout ashore if she begi— no – *when* she begins to sink.'

'He'll have to have a jolly loud voice,' Flags sniggered.

'Come off it. It's never going to be *that* far.'

'Sixteen hundred miles,' my ex-new best friend advised maliciously if somewhat obscurely. 'Give or take a zigzag.'

Anxiety turned to outright panic.

'WHAT I – I mean, *where* is?'

For the first time, the Admiral afforded me a smile. But

it wasn't really the kind of smile one might expect appreciative admirals to bestow upon those they consider to be made of the Right Stuff. No. Radiating all the warmth of an Arctic iceberg, it was more the kind of smile they reserved for simple souls far too bloody clever by half, who'd just unwittingly demanded they be allowed to volunteer for hazardous duty.

'Murmansk is, Lieutenant Miller. Murmansk is.'

Four

'*Murmansk*. In *that*?' I'd echoed numbly. For the third time.

'Murmansk, Miller,' the Admiral confirmed gravely. For the third time. All of a sudden he hadn't seemed so much a man pressured by momentous affairs of war as a man determined to set aside quality time in which to enjoy himself. Well, I mean – Christ, I didn't know he'd read my *Operation Styx* apologia *that* critically, did I?

'Murmansk,' I swallowed hard, but it was time to face the specifics. 'In *Russia*?'

'Murmansk. In Russia. That Stuffed out there, Lieutenant – that sound-looking vessel you assured me you'd consider yourself privileged to serve in? She's our NYR previously missing from the PQ convoy plan.'

'Not Yet Report—' the Flags began patronizingly.

'I fuckin' KNOW that,' I snarled, rounding on him. 'If I didn't fuckin' *know* that, clever clogs, I'd've fuckin' ASKED!'

Flags retreated a couple of paces from the edge of the cliff, carefully positioning himself outwith shoving range of a rough merchant service chap. But disregarding that tactical concession to prudence he was a regular: a career-conscious officer clearly made of the Right Stuff. Although of equal rank, he'd made it evident that he didn't intend to surrender the initiative lightly to a hostilities-only interloper like me saddled – thanks to the late unlamented Trapp – with what passed for as good as a criminal record in the eyes of his Admiralty masters.

'Then as you already know everything, one can assume that you're not superstitious, old boy. Not judging by the enthusiasm which you're displaying for your appointment,' he countered sarcastically.

'No I'm bloody not!' I'd already exposed enough of my

inadequacies. 'And anyway: what's superstitious . . . super*sti-tion* . . . got to do with anything?'

'Nothing really. Not as you already know her Convoy Formation Number.'

''COURSE I do!' Inferring I wasn't listening at the conference, was he? 'It's . . . oh, *shit*!'

'Figures wun thuree. Column one, line three,' my ex-best friend pressed regardless. 'Which makes her . . .'

'. . . Number Thirteen, Miller,' the Admiral supplemented. To save me the trouble of working it out.

'Odd,' the Admiral mused as they neared.

I didn't understand what he meant, but most certainly he was spot-on if referring to that Bolshevik coffin ship. Perched some two hundred feet above sea level, we were becoming advantaged by a bird's eye view of the two arrivals now. Or progressively dispirited, depending on whose seaboots one stood in. In my case it was emphatically the latter. Oh, the destroyer looked shipshape and Bristol fashion albeit her forward gun turrets weren't trained as precisely fore and aft as you'd expect, but the merchantman was different. With the merchantman, we were being afforded a plain view of chaos.

Even from half a mile I could tell that any surface that should've been painted, hadn't. Not even the cursory lick of ubiquitous red lead here and there so beloved of British tramp steamer mates as a conciliatory gesture to the owners. Any fender that should've been secured inboard, wasn't. Any rope that should've been coiled down, hadn't been. Any standing rigging that should've been screwed bar taut, sagged. Any deck that should've been hosed down, looked like a ploughed field. Quite simply, I'd never seen such a dirty, untidy vessel in all my li— but hang on – belay that, my last claim. I *had* encountered one other ship as scruff—? But no. No, I'm *not* going to allow myself to be diverted down that route again!

'What's he mean: odd?' I hissed at Flags, suddenly aware that the Admiral was staring at me as if expecting a response.

He shrugged. 'I think he's referring to the way she turned up again after we'd all assumed she'd been sunk, old boy.'

'I didn't know *that*,' I complained petulantly. 'If no one bloody *tells* me what's going on, I can hardly be . . .'

'One minute the Naval Control people were tracking her

progress from her port of loading – Cardiff, in her case – then next they knew, she'd apparently vanished off the plot. Didn't confirm having reached even her first scheduled reporting position off Holyhead, then failed to respond to her call sign.'

'Maybe her radio was down.'

'She was out of contact for over a *week*. They'd had time to post a letter.'

At least it afforded me the opportunity to display the sort of disapproving gravitas proper naval officers with staff jobs ashore were expected to demonstrate for inferior beings. Turning respectfully to the Admiral, I assumed the mandatory purse-lipped expression; happy to be a traitor to my roots if it helped ingratiate myself with the man who had the power to still reconsider my posting.

'Then as you say, sir: damned odd. Typically sloppy merchant service attitude.'

The Admiral frowned irritably. 'What is?'

'The, er . . . the way she disappeared off your plot.'

'Why's that odd, Miller? Ships sailing independently disappear all the time. There *is* a war on,' he growled testily. 'I *meant* the position in which she was eventually found, was odd. Keep up, man.'

I wished my paper collar would. Fatigue and the properties of rainwater had caused it to part from its back stud and its after end had now begun to clamber up into my hairline with a soggy life of its own.

'Yessir. Er, so where was she finally found?'

'Off the Irish coast.'

I blinked uncertainly. I mean, what was particularly odd about that? When you're sailing north from Wales to Scotland, Ireland lies to port most've the way up. It's why they call it the Irish Sea. I felt let down. He should've known that: him being an admiral.

'The Irish *west* coast, old boy,' Flags supplemented, reading my expression. 'The *far* side of the Republic. And even more suspiciously, she appeared to be about to head out into the Atlantic when we apprehended her.'

Apprehended? Like in *arrested*? All of a sudden I'd been offered a clue as to why the escort destroyer's A and B turrets weren't quite trained fore and aft. And why she was trailing, rather than leading, the decrepit Stuffed. It ensured those forward 4-inch barrels remained laid precisely on the bridge of the antiquated steamer. Which, when it came to odd, *really* was. Her being supposed to be on our side and everything.

Getting closer now: much clearer. Near enough to distinguish two figures lounging, seemingly feeling remarkably unthreatened, over the forward rail of that same, slightly skewed bridge. Presumably not originally designed to be lopsided, I mused gloomily. Not unless, by so doing, her long-dead Tsarist builders had intended to compel future generations of pacing watchkeepers, even in a flat calm, to run headlong downhill then clamber back up in order to complete each circuit of the wing. I could only assume it had been displaced by some collision, sometime during the previous century for all I knew, and never realigned on the grounds that the costs of repair wouldn't've been justified.

Smart master all the same, I reflected, not without a grudging tinge of fellow feeling. Had it been me ordered to take my ship to Murmansk – well, *that* ship, anyway – I'd've been sorely tempted to make a break for neutral waters myself.

'The sheer impertinence of the man,' the Admiral growled to no one in particular. 'First giving us the run-around, and *then* cocking a snook at the Royal Navy – His Majesty's Navy, dammit! – like that.'

Like what? Like, how did her Old Man cock a snoo—? I turned appealingly to my interpreter. Riddles had never been my strong point, and I really was fed up.

'*Osborne* had been patrolling outside the Republic's territorial limit. Apparently she'd already steamed well past the bay, a good mile past, when our missing Number Thirteen appeared out of it and crossed her wake, heading outbound. At first they assumed he was making a badly timed run for it. Until he started blowing his ship's whistle to attract attention. Toot . . . toot . . . toot! Short, sharp, impatient blasts. Sounded all irritated, *Osborne*'s captain claimed. Quite put out about that, he was. Took it as a deliberate provocation. That the chap didn't trust his warship to keep a look-out astern.'

'Bay?' I pretended to feign interest. The toot, tooting and ruffled naval feathers bit just went over my head. My sole concern right then was not so much with what the rogue steamer had previously done to earn their Lordships' displeasure, as with what she'd do in the future. To me.

'Droolin Bay. Nothing there apart from a little village called—'

'Not *Droolin*?' I was learning to play the game now.

'Affirmative. Droolin. Droolin Harbour. Lies north of Sodslaw Point.'

'IRA country. Fenians to the last man,' the Admiral grumbled disapprovingly. 'God knows what her master thought he was doing, venturing into Republican waters with a war cargo aboard. Reckless as a blind man pushing an ice cream barrow through an infants' playground.'

'Maybe he wasn't being reckless, sir,' I began in a last ditch attempt to be seen to consider all possibilities, as any model staff officer would. 'Maybe he was planning to sell it to the Fenia—'

I broke off uncertainly at that point. What had made me opt for that fanciful and clearly ridiculous explanation? No Allied master would dare consider perpetrating such an outrageous act of treason. Even should he avoid the near certainty of being hanged from the Admiral's favourite yardarm as a traitor, the chap would be inviting a long jail sentence for barratry – stealing his own cargo – and, particularly in time of war, that was a high risk strategy and implausible to say the leas—?

Wasn't it?

Of course it was! There wasn't a man alive on the high seas irresponsible enough, bloody-minded enough, and greedy enough to ... to ... ?

Now why did that specific phrase immediately spring to mind? No man *alive* on the high sea ... ?

I hadn't known why. Not then. But for no apparent reason, the hairs on the nape of my neck began to prickle despite the clammy stricture of the dissolving paper collar. I frowned uneasily. Narrowing my eyes against the driving rain, I peered harder at the two diminutive figures lounging over my new seagoing appointment's bridge front, but the weather had begun to close in again. Once more appearing almost spectral through the fog and the sheeting spray, she remained too distant to make out detail.

But there I went again. What had made me opt for *that* description? Spectral. As in *ghost*-like?

'Borrow these, Miller,' the Admiral offered generously,

fumbling for the binoculars strap around his neck. 'But handle them carefully. Captured German glasses. Zeiss lenses. Damn sight better that those bottlestop optics our side's issued with.'

... Then added somewhat less benignly, anxious to avoid giving any impression that he might be warming to me, 'Won't get many opportunities to appraise her from a distance, eh? Not once you've sailed for Murmansk.'

I swallowed resentfully. Why didn't he just come out and say it? Treat yourself to a U-boat commander's view, Miller.

I didn't want to take them. Apart from most likely being court-martialled for refusing to obey an order if I did drop them, I didn't want to tempt providence. Seeing is believing, and believing makes it real, and facing up to reality was what I'd spent the past several months in battlefield therapy trying to avoid – but I had little option. My hands shook perceptibly as I ground the rubber eye-cups into place and fumbled to adjust the focus.

Her bow came crisp and clear initially. Damn, it was the secrets of her bridge deck I really needed to face up to . . . but then I hesitated. Of all unlikely things I'd expect to see aboard any ship, was that cement mixer, only partly concealed by the break of the foc'sle. And it was turning.

Why is the cement mixer turning? I mused disconcertedly in continuance of a thought process that was rapidly degenerating into one composed almost entirely of why's and wherefores. Probably because it's mixing fucking *cement*, Miller! But *why* is it mixing fu—?

Abruptly three crewmen, seemingly dressed in fluttering rags rather than oilskins, materialized from the meagre shelter provided by the whaleback. Hunched against the spray the first spun a wheel, the second produced a shovel and the third presented a battered wheel barrow to the inverting maw of the superannuated machine.

Then, gesticulating animatedly to each other while trundling the loaded barrow, they disappeared again like troglodytes into the gloomy recess of the bow structure.

Why are they carting wet cement into the foc—?

Ohhh, shit!

There's only one reason why you'd be pressed to prepare a load of concrete aboard a ship in such conditions. To prevent her from filling with water and, ultimately, conforming to the laws of physics by sinking. *That's* the time when you'd be driven to packing a breached compartment with cement, then praying it sets before you need to start swimming. Invariably such a desperate measure is undertaken as a last resort following a collision or, in extreme cases, to pre-empt total structural failure – like . . . oh, like when your vessel is so old and so flimsy that her corroded below-water plates have begun to open of their own volition, for instance? Deep down in the forepeak at the foot of the bow, say; where the stresses imposed by constantly butting into head seas are greatest. Or in the case of a former ice-breaker, through having spent the thick end of the past century constantly butting into . . . well . . . ice?

Of course, any other master would reduce speed to a prudent crawl as well; maybe even turn his ship to present her stern to the waves. But this captain hadn't even eased back from full ahead, judging by the volume of smoke still pouring from her spindle-stick funnel. Toot, tooting irritably at one of His Majesty's warships . . . ? That lunatic out there was putting two fingers up to God Hisself.

My own index finger, fast numbing with the cold, had to be persuaded to refocus. The vertical unpretty slab of the Stuffed's centrecastle fused into sharp relief before the lenses. Seven-times magnification confirmed precisely my diagnosis of poor long-term maintenance compounded by sheer incompetence: the last caring paint brush stroke *that* corroded area of scabrous steel had benefited from, I reflected bleakly, had more than likely been administered by some long dead Bolshevik bosun to celebrate Lenin's birthday. Angling the glasses further aloft I scanned up past the splintered teak boards lining her skewed bridge front: rising yet higher to surmount the wildly flapping remains of a canvas dodger boasting so many threadbare patches it had long ceased to fulfil its original purpose of providing a windbreak until, finally, assisted by the ocular magic of Herr Zeiss, two pairs of arms swam into view; each brace comfortably crossed to take full advantage of the leaning facility afforded by the rail. One pair sported the four gold rings and diamond of a supposed merchant service captain, verdigrized with age: the other terminated in the frayed wool cuffs of an oil-grey seaman's jersey that may have been white thirty years ago.

I blinked disconcertedly. How laid back can a bridge watch get? Only the peaceful, the conscience-free, the mad or the . . .

Or the . . . the *already* dead could relax so completely as that while navigating five thousand-odd tons of good-as-foundering ship, still steaming full tilt towards what was a perilously narrow entrance carved between vertical, spray-hazed granite faces, while at the same time doing so under point-blank threat from four precisely laid and already deliberately antagonized 4-inch naval guns. It was almost as if Number Thirteen's old man was egging his RN counterpart to shoot or keep up. A bizarre game of maritime chicken between skippers: first to lose his nerve's a girlie.

But what responsible shipmaster would be so perverse? So awkward, so contrary as to challenge a warship to a headlong race to disast—?

No. No, don't even think of pursuing that train of thought, Miller. *Don't* be so silly . . .

Ohhh, DO it! I grated to myself. Mind over matter . . . all right – mind over *ectoplasmic* bloody matter if you must. *Make* yourself tilt these lenses that extra fraction. *Force* your eyes to confront the impossible and thus assure yourself, once and for all, that it can't exist.

So I did.

It was a brave if somewhat reckless decision on my part, though I still maintain it seemed perfectly logical at the time. Face up to what cannot be, Miller, and, by so doing, prove it isn't – if you, ah . . . well; if you see what I'm trying to get at?

OK, so I concede I'd been flying in the face of medical advice. That RAMC colonel in the desert hospital had told me as much: had warned me not to try going down the self-help reality route. Precisely the opposite in fact. Remember he'd said 'I can't cure you,' before he'd finally lost the place himself and started yelling? 'The great Professor Freud himself couldn't have *cured* you, Miller, but I *can* help you embrace the therapeutic last resort of self-denial: lay the Captain's ghost as of now.'

But, because reckless bravery can occasionally go hand in hand with stupidity, I'd overlooked the fact that, as with every gamble, there can be a downside. In my case, the penalty one invites for ignoring the counsel of a professional mind pilot is that one can just as easily aggravate, rather than resolve one's particular psychosis. I only discovered that potential pitfall once I'd tilted the binos a fraction higher in order to put logic to the test.

It marked the moment when the Colonel proved he'd earned his rank, while my bold experiment fell apart along with the remnants of any hope I'd so far clung to that I couldn't *be* that crazy. One stunned glance was enough to discover that Miller's Theory of do-it-yourself psychobabble had been precisely so, and that all those ill-disciplined, constantly arguing ghosts of pirates past who'd long gone down to the bottom of the sea inside an indisputably sunk parody of a warship were still there; still squatting inside my head. I'd known that much because they'd immediately resurfaced through my subconscious to jostle and elbow and flail at each other as persistently as ever, competing to occupy the high ground of my scrambled psyche with the tenacity of a clan of Cairo street photographer's monkeys.

All except two, that was.

The two out there on that ship's bridge. The same two who'd always managed to force their way to the front of that spectral queue, hell-bent on invading my sleeping moments. In their case they didn't need to compete. Every bloody night they contrived without effort to shove their way to the fore: those Zeiss-sharp images who now stared amiably back at me in close-up through my own . . . ohhh, *all right*! BE pedantic if you must – through the soddin' *Admiral's* lenses.

Every *night* that pair had done it to me.

Every bloody night since . . . since they'd died off the coast of North Africa.

An' *now* they were even at it during the DAY!

I felt at peace for the first time since Hitler declared war on me. My step was positive, my resolution absolute.

The Wren driver, on the other hand, sounded most disquieted. She hadn't uttered a word, and quite properly so, since we'd arrived at the top of the cliff, yet there she was, all of a sudden, revealing a state of solicitude for me verging on hysteria.

'Sir – Lieutenant Miller! I think he's going to . . .'

'Jump, you reckon?' Flags speculated, more interested than concerned.

'Then *tackle* him, man. Stop him for GOD'S sake!' the Admiral bellowed. 'Fellow's still got my damn glasses.'

I'd moved close enough to the brink by then to frown directly into the maelstrom. Two hundred feet below and driven by the onshore wind, sea after boiling sea erupted against black saw-toothed rock; instantly atomizing into a fine mist which, in turn, became snatched and whirled aloft to taint my lips with salt.

You should *never* have put this bloody paper collar on this morning, Miller, I reflected petulantly, irritated by such lack of sartorial foresight. No sense of occasion. The first thing to come off, even before your hat, arms an' legs do, once you plummet into that hydraulic meat grinder.

But other than that I harboured no doubt I'd opted to take the correct course of action. Straightforward, quick, easy; even exhilarating . . . well, the first three an' a half seconds would be anyway, whereas, courtesy of the Admiral, the alternative was too awful even to contemplate. Being ordered to sail in a Russian convoy I'd been prepared to accept. Many far more worthy than I were making ready for departure in the anchorage behind me, and the majority of those otherwise ordinary men, because they *were* ordinary men, would be equally apprehensive if not downright frightened of going. Yet they'd still go. As I would have done, right up to that disbelieving moment when I'd gazed through the lenses to test a theory but had, instead, gained absolute proof that I really was insane confirmed before me.

He was dead. They were *both* dead. Yet there I was: actually *staring* at them. Which suggested that if I did submit to the Admiral's demand, and reported aboard that approaching coffin ship – in this instance, a classic case of seafaring gallows humour suddenly assuming deeper meaning – I wouldn't be joining as her Naval Liaison Officer so much as some sort of Necromancy Liaison Officer, and that was *not* going to happen. I'd no intention of acting as go-between for a grumpy admiral on one hand and a crew of squabbling, incompetent spooks on the other.

Christ, I mean: even when *alive*, serving under Trapp had been unbearable thanks to his stupid conviction he was immortal. Now he was one of the already dead and thus, by definition, indestructible, he'd be bloody impossible to sail with.

So get it over now, Miller. You won't end the voyage with all your bits and pieces working anyway. Not with him as your Old Man f'r a second time, along with his monstrous ego an' his greed and his. . . his sheer bloody-*mindedness*. Whereas this way you can at least look on the bright side of dying. For a start, you won't have to put up with the cold and the icebergs an' the torpedoes an' the Luftwaffe an' . . . an' the constant *arguments* before he finally gets you killed. No more than with the being bawled at; the being unjustly accused; the being resented, unappreciated, unloved . . . I mean, *think* about it. What's the point in delaying the inevitable? You won't even be able to bloody *hit* him: him bein' a ghost an' everything.

Philosophically I lifted one foot to take my final step into oblivion while, at the same time, deliberately retaining the Admiral's precious binoculars in a vice-like grip. Yeah, OK: so I concede it was a childish, spiteful reprisal and hardly one I wished to be remembered by, representing my very last gesture on earth as it did, but do bear in mind I'd just been forced to accept how eminently qualified I'd become for volunteering to join the Fleet Air Arm without an aeroplane. I'd been officially diagnosed as psychotic remember? Incurably mad in fact, with the proof positive out there before me.

Apart from which, I have to confess that the expression of horror on the Admiral's face, allied with the desperation betrayed by that supercilious Flag Lieutenant's lunge to rescue his boss's glasses before I, the Zeiss, and probably his career went for the deep six, did make it all seem worthwhi—?

Yet, perversely, that was the moment when I hesitated.

And frowned thoughtfully.

Sorry to break off so abruptly, poised literally between hell and high water as I am, but I'd just come up with another theory. Well, the same theory actually: still Miller's Theory but, in psychiatric terminology, simply turned bum over tit. I mean, just suppose my fundamental premise *had* been valid – all that stuff about forcing myself to confront the impossible and by so-doing, proving it couldn't exist? Except that with Miller Mk II, let's hypothesize that the impossible – my assumption that it was the spirits of the dead who'd been plaguing me – were to be reversed. In essence, that those images out there weren't spooks at all but real, existential, flesh and blood beings, and that I – *and* that clever clogs Colonel, I reflected triumphantly – had misdiagnosed my obsession in the first place.

The downside of *that* possibility being, of course, that the situation would then prove even more dire than previously feared. That my 'ghosts' weren't so much a symptom of madness as the products of wishful thinking on my part. Even more depressingly: if it *were* to prove the case that other members of HMS *Charon*'s appalling complement had actually survived her sinking without my being aware of it, I wasn't entirely convinced I'd want to continue living with the disappointment anyway. The realization that the one silver lining I'd desperately clung to despite shot, shell and an admiral's spleen, would no longer afford me solace.

. . . Yeah, yeah, I know: all a tad last minute and frustrating for anyone reading this; especially for those of you desperately egging me to prune back on the cod psychology and bloody *jump* f'r God's sake – turn this account into a proper ghost story penned by a genuine ghost writer. But do please wait: indulge me that little bit longer and I can promise you it gets worse. After all, it's not a *lot* to ask, is it . . . ? Not bearing in mind I'm balanced precariously on one foot by now, teetering on the edge of eternity while attempting to think my future through beyond the next three and a half seconds.

For a start, the superannuated merchantman itself had to be real: no question about that. There's nothing ectoplasmic about five thousand-odd tons of slowly sinking steel: no more than there was about His Majesty's disenchanted Ship *Osborne* following doggedly in its wake.

I knew it was real because not only could my companions see it as well – which they couldn't have done if it really *was* an apparition conjured by the disordered brain of an official lunatic – but also because everybody knows a ghost can't go rusty. It's a simple matter of physics or, in this case, metaphysics. Rain and sea spray can't stick to it for a start.

Ergo, if the ship was real, then *someone* real had to be

driving it . . . well, maybe not *driving* it exactly, because the verb 'to drive' suggests some degree of forward planning and control, whereas that hulk out there was ploughing on regardless. But nevertheless she was managing to maintain a reasonably straight course for the entrance, and everybody knows a ghost can't grip the spokes of a ship's wheel no more than it can read a compass.

So there had to be a real helmsman still shielded from view within the renegade STUFT's wheelhouse, physically holding her to that course. Someone particularly thick in this case, considering what they were steering towards although, to be fair, they might just have been absorbed in concentrating on the compass card without thinking to look out of the window. But either way, thick or not, to know what course to steer requires an order from someone in command – someone equally existential, because everybody knows that while ghosts can clank and moan all they like, they can't interpret charts or give ord—?

'I'm *not* mad,' I said with slowly dawning realization.

'The Admiral is,' Flags muttered apprehensively, still inching forward with hand outstretched to retrieve the Zeiss. 'He's fucking furious.'

'No, I mean I'm not crazy. Not an incurable lunatic like that colonel said.'

'Everyone's entitled to an opinion,' Flags retorted acidly: not the most diplomatic comment to make considering I was still holding his career in my hand.

'Could you do something for me?' I asked.

He nodded cautiously. My collar finally gave way as I passed him the Zeiss, but I didn't care anymore. He accepted them gingerly. 'Something like what?'

'Take a look at the Stuffed's bridge. What d'you see?'

Flags focused quizzically: still giving me a wide berth in case I sidled up close and personal: decided to take him as well as the glasses. 'Not much. Two blokes out on her port wing.'

'But you *can* see them?'

He gave me a strange look. 'One appears to be her master: rough looking type. Got a funny hat on.'

'It got chopped near-enough in half by a Chinese pirate. In 1929.'

'The other's a runty, weasel-faced sort of chap. Some kind of engineer. Or more likely a stoker, judging by the state of him.'

'He's not a stoker,' I said. Then smiled in recollection. It was an unexpectedly warm smile considering. Almost nostalgic, in fact. 'He's not got brains enough to be entrusted with a whole shovelful of coal at once.'

Absent-mindedly Flags returned the glasses to me, then looked horrified.

'It's all right. You'd better give them back to the Admiral,' I reassured him, sane as you like. 'I've got another nightmare to report to.'

Five

I'd cherished no illusion it would last: that inexplicable surge of warmth which had assailed me on discovering they were still alive. Furthermore I was bleakly aware that the relief of discovering I hadn't been possessed so much by demons as pursued by idiots during the past few months, was unlikely to provide adequate compensation in the long run. Even in an uncertain war-torn world some things remain the same. My constant was writ large in stone. It decreed with absolute certainty that everything would go pear-shaped from the moment *he* became involved again.

I could even predict how long it would take. I just knew that given, say, twenty-four hours max, I'd be staring yearningly down into the sea once more. I'd even made a mental note to dress appropriately for topping myself next time. Lashing a couple of cast iron firebars to the soles of my boots suggested a good starting point, with sporting a decent linen collar coming a close second. One that wouldn't come apart quicker than the rest of me.

Because, yes: it *was* him this time. Trapp: shipmaster by profession, buccaneer by inclination, and unsubtly protesting reservist by blackmail. Edward Trapp lounging shoulder to grumpy shoulder with his unsanitary familiar, Gorbals Wullie, and undoubtedly he in the curmudgeonly flesh, so to speak. Because that tableau out there just *had* to be real. Not even the most disordered mind could make it up and, anyway, everybody knows no ghost, not the most resentful of spectres, could have matched Trapp's bloody-minded commitment to causing total chaos within his despised Senior Service . . . this time it seemed he'd achieved it even *before* the Navy had finished rounding him up an' shepherding him into his allotted convoy.

But then, what had the Admiral expected when he'd put

them together? A Bolshevik boat which refused to sink, commanded by a bolshie sea captain who refused to die . . . ? They were made for each other.

And so it was, then, that I tentatively began to accept Trapp's whole resurrection thing, albeit with mixed feelings. I couldn't really make up my mind about whether I was glad, or sad. On reflection I'd probably been more dazed than euphoric at the shock of it. Either way I'd decided on balance to give life another go: resolved to milk some benefit from my respite from paranoia while it lasted . . . especially from the first part. The bit where all I needed to do was watch from our vantage point on the cliff top and enjoy the response of Convoy Number Thirteen's crew to her pell-mell landfall.

I hadn't required the facility of *Herr* Zeiss any longer. She'd been close enough by then for the Mark One Eyeball to make out detail perfectly well.

The previously unseen helmsman broke first. I'd been right about his concentrating on his steering so intently he hadn't thought to spare a glance at what lay ahead, or appreciate how close the assembly anchorage's spume-hazed cliffs had become – probably filling the window before him by then: certainly near enough to have compelled him to crane his neck right back to even catch sight of us looking down from the top of 'em. Either way, I watched with satisfaction as a frantically gesticulating figure shot out've the wheelhouse door like a cork from a popgun to tumble head over heels down the port bridge ladder, legs still going like pistons so's he'd be ready to hit the deck running, then continuing to pound aft in search of sanctuary as far from the bow as possible.

I suspect it wasn't so much the wheelman's Olympian-standard gymnastics display as his screaming that alerted the ragged trio of seamen-cum-concrete-shovellers still sheltering out of sight under the break of the foc's'le. An enquiring head poked in leisurely fashion around the side plates; took one look and worked out sharp as a tack that, should their suddenly unguided vessel veer as much as two degrees either side of the narrow entrance, then he and his shipmates would be located precisely at the point of impact between five thousand tons of careering steel an' several billion cubic metres of Scotland . . . whereupon he instantly joined the ex-steersman in a shrieking duet. All three of 'em broke cover, the last out having completely forgotten, in his panic to evacuate, that he was *still* carrying a cement-filled bucket, and legged it for the aftmost well deck ladder while all the time each man grabbing and snatching an' clawing to hold his oppos back so's he could climb its shaky rungs first.

'My top-drawer internashnul crew,' hadn't Trapp vainly attempted to sell them to the Admiral as, all those months before? Yeah, right. Though I did have to concede that, while those I was observing may well have been replacements for the piratical crowd he'd managed to get blown away in our HMS *Charon* debacle, they were still good: I gave him that. Give 'em squeegee boots, red flashing noses an' a clown-mobile that blew up, they'd have provided top drawer entertainment in any internashnul circus.

While, speaking of Trapp . . . ? I switched my attention back to the ice-breaker's bridge. He was still there, still out on the wing; still playing the chicken card with typical theatrical overkill; ostentatiously slumped over the rail in poker-faced determination right up to the second when *Osborne's* captain finally lost his nerve and ordered his man-o'-war into a skidding starboard turn that took her parallel to the coast while heeling a good thirty degrees with the momentum of it. One could only admire that commanding officer's enormous self-control for resisting the temptation to place a full broadside into Trapp as he whizzed across his wake: a sort of parting shot, so to speak. Well, either his self-control or the fact that all the guns he could have brought to bear had been pointing down into the sea at the critical moment.

Barely a half-mile to go now. Stay over-confident another two minutes, Trapp, I found myself urging optimistically, and I won't need a waterproof collar. I won't even need to pack woolly socks for your voyage to Murmansk. I might even get a job with the salvage team.

Wullie? Gorbals bluidy Wullie . . . where had Trapp's unsanitary side-kick got to all of a sudden? I found out when, somewhat to my chagrin, Trapp finally reacted. Stooping, he hauled his now petrified aide-de-camp from whence the little rodent had hurled himself into the corner of the wing, hands clamped firmly to cover his eyes. A grubby plimsoll applied to the backside, the same one I swear he'd been wearing

when the *Charon* went down, propelled the anything-but-able
seaman into the wheelhouse to replace the former helmsman
who, judging by the abruptly fastidious way he was running,
had relieved himself twice already: the second time somewhat less formally, en route along the boat deck.

With carefully measured insouciance Trapp sauntered back
to the wing telegraph and yanked its handle astern. The jangle
of bells carried clearly over the moan of the wind, as did the
subsea echo from the engine room repeater. With a bit of luck,
I speculated hopefully, you've pushed the cocking-a-snook bit
too far. Knowing the quality of flotsam you sign on as crew,
your engineers won't respond: they'll have abandoned their
harbour stations as well, to join the rest've the crowd on the
poop. But then it struck me that was too much to hope for.
They wouldn't have portholes in the engine room to give early
warning, largely on account of its being situated below water
level. Her Russian designers had got that design detail right,
at least. Well, either that or Trapp had blocked them off with
cement, too.

Nothing happened. She just kept coming. This was good.

Trapp yanked the telegraph handle again; a tad anxiously.
Ringle, dingle!

Still nothing happened. This was even better.

Beginning to get agitated now, Trapp lost his cool at that
whereupon, snatching his already decimated cap from his
head, he wasted a further ten crucial seconds by throwing it
to the deck and jumping up an' down on it in choleric frustration before grabbing the handle for a third go, furiously
working it back and forward like a bilge pump lever. This
time the prolonged carillon of bells that carried to the top of
the cliff made her sound more like a lopsided cathedral than
a ship . . . mind you, she *looked* more like a lopsided cathedral than a ship anyway, come to think of it. And best of all
from my point of view, a cathedral playing not so much even-
song to call the faithful to prayer, but more of a swan song
calling the salvors to don their diving helmets.

Less than four cables; eight hundred yards and *still* continuing to push a white-water bone in her teeth while, as a bonus,
heading ever more erratically for the gap since Wullie had
been put in charge of the steering; probably still with hands
clamped firmly over his eyes.

Catastrophe loomed. I was about to experience a shipwreck without actually being aboard the bastard for once. Most importantly, Miller's prospects for thus finding himself a superfluous Naval Liaison Officer from the instant the tolling of bells merged into the screech of compressing rust, were about to take a quantum leap.

I was *so* happy. For the first time ever I found myself in a position to witness Trapp's natural-born aptitude for planning, command and control without wishing to fault his level of incompetence.

Regrettably, such duplicitous euphoria was only to last a half-minute longer.

You know, I *still* can't get my head round how that bloody man always contrived, invariably more by luck than design, to snatch victory from the jaws of idiocy. I can only assume her chief engineer had been more terrified at the prospect of bringing Trapp's wrath down upon his oily pate than of meeting his Maker wearing a shroud of superheated steam. It's the only motivation I can think of to induce a spanner jockey who'd been caught cat-napping in blissful unawareness of the imminence of land, to break every rule in the marine engineer's book: achieve the almost impossible, and throw an already over-pressured coal-fired reciprocating compound engine of indeterminate vintage into panic-accelerated full astern mode despite the odds-on risk of blowing his whole bloody ship up.

Every shiny connecting rod and rocker arm and piston rod and slide valve must've frozen instantaneously in mid-cycle when the unfortunate denizen of that otherwise rust-dank, ill-lit and cacophonic cavern below decks threw himself blindly at the reversing lever.

'*Coal* – more f&**%$* COAL . . . !' he'd've been bawling to the sweating, black-encrusted stokers of the watch. 'We gotta better f&**%$* idea, Chief,' her black gang would've been screaming back. 'Wot about we puts *you* in the f&**%$* FIRE box?'

Three cables to go . . . DAMN! Abruptly a great cloud of soot jetted from the careering STUFT's spindle-stick funnel to hang somewhat uncertainly before being dispersed by the wind, not quite sure of why it was there or, indeed, why it had been so rudely disturbed after decades of being left in peace. *Chuff*, the tortured con rods would've been gasping by then: *chuff, chuff* CHUFFIN' *chuff* as slowly, painfully slowly at first, they began to ease from their top dead centre paralysis and recycle astern.

Two cables. Only four hundred yards lef—?

CHUFF, chuff chuff CHUFFITY, chuff, chuff . . . Chuffity chuffity CHUFFITY rumble-*chuff . . .* ! More smoke and soot and glowing embers whirling aloft. The base of the funnel beginning to glow red-hot; almost as incandescent as its by-then panicking captain. A great blister of turbulence revealing itself now: welling from under the antiquated counter as, ever so reluctantly, her propeller finally began to turn the other way.

Have faith, Miller. Do not despair. Only one cable now, and *still* closing.

But then she slowed. And I mean, like, she *really* slowed. If she'd actually run smack on to the rocks beneath me, she couldn't have slowed much quicker. She slowed so abruptly that the three evacuating cement mixers fell all the way back down the well deck ladder while I caught a satisfying glimpse of Wullie's cloth-capped head rebounding from the window in front of him, which was lucky for Wullie because, had he been catapulted clear over the wheel backside foremost, he could've suffered serious brain damage.

It was all about pitch: the angle of the blade . . . What's that – you don't give a *shit* about pitch? You want to skip the technical stuff an' just get on with the consequences . . . ? Oh, excuse *me* for being so pedantic; for assuming you might *just* have managed to muster a flicker of passing interest in why a vessel built for ice-breaking would be able to stop quicker'n your average steamer running amok on account of the ice-breaker having a propeller coarse enough to drive her through ice and push bloody icebergs out've the way . . . which also helps her stop faster, even when in inefficient astern mode, and *especially* when she's commanded by a vituperative chancer and chief-engineered by a *jelly*fish . . . !

. . . No, look: I do apologize. I'm sorry. It's just that I still suffer the flashbacks. I can't help reflecting on how, if Trapp had run into the cliffs and got himself drowned – and I mean *thoroughly* this time so's I could have viewed the body; ideally furnished with a wooden stake and a mallet – then none of what follows would have happened, and there would have been no Russian convoy for me, and I could have finished this journal – *Miller's* War, remember? – on a happy note without ever having been forced to return to the Colonel for supplementary treatment.

While talking of the Colonel . . . ? I think I'd be well advised to take another short break at this point: the memories have become too distressing, suddenly. He's in private practise now. Just around the corner, actually. I might even give him a call.

Again.

When Trapp sailed his . . . well, his *ship* I suppose, were I to stretch such description to the point of derision, into the assembly anchorage at a sedate five knots, we – the Admiral, Flags, the Wren bird an' me – were still blinking, stunned, almost directly down on him.

The first thing I noticed about her in close up was the name under her bow, particularly as it had been applied in a most curious script. I hate to admit it even now but that still recognizable, albeit ham-fistedly-corrupted legend brought an involuntary lump to my throat . . . or maybe I'd simply been resisting an overwhelming temptation to gag. Where the actions of Trapp's crews were concerned, they've always induced a confusing mix of nostalgia and nausea.

Either way, СИДЯОИ II it proclaimed, disregarding the fact that the sailor who'd inscribed it had known sod all about the Cyrillic alphabet, bless him, but had still engaged in what I later discovered to be an attempt to make the ship appear even more Russian, and thus more friendly, by virtue of the Reds being rumoured to be trigger happy up in the Kola Inlet: being inclined to shoot first and identify a blown-away foreign flag merchantman after the burials at sea.

The effect of transcribing *Charon II* was further undermined by the fact that the downstroke of the last numeral was roughly fifteen feet long and trailed a vertical smear right down to the waterline, suggesting that whoever did it had broken the first rule in the ship painter's handbook . . . taken a step back from Trapp's no-doubt shaky staging to admire his finished handiwork.

Meanwhile Trapp, being Trapp and irrepressible, had reverted to show-off mode once more: lounging ostentatiously over the bridge rail looking totally unfazed as if he'd *always* intended to make his grand entrance with the finesse of a panzer division arriving at another nation's border. An ill-dressed, pugnacious parody of those genuinely loyal shipmasters with whom we would embark in convoy upon the coming voyage to Murmansk, he'd glanced aloft at that point and seen us observing his appropriately designated Number Thirteen pass between the Heads. If he recognized me he gave no hint of it, which was bloody typical, but I suspect he'd identified the Admiral because, quite unexpectedly, he suddenly straightened up, came to a sort of attention, and saluted.

I frowned uncertainly. Such military pleasantry was totally at odds with the insubordinate reprobate I'd known and hated, but of more immediate concern – wasn't that a mutilated hand that Trapp saluted with . . . ? Maybe I'd been a bit hard on the chap. Might he, by chance, have been wounded after all during the former *Charon*'s last battle? Might he, for that matter, have met up since with the same disgruntled Chinese pirate who'd partially severed his cap in 1929 and had now finished the job by chopping three fingers an' the thumb of his fancy Navy saluting hand clean off . . . ?

I think the Admiral must have noticed Trapp's solitary, stiffly extended middle digit being flourished at him too. Because only then did he break his silence.

'Remember I gave you a medal, posthumously as we believed at the time, on Lieutenant Commander Trapp's behalf, Miller?' he said in a carefully controlled voice.

I did remember. It had been presented at a ceremony to celebrate . . . well, *mark* might be a more respectful way of putting it . . . the loss in action with all hands – except me – of His Majesty's Armed Merchant Cruiser *Charon*. The parade had taken place overlooking Malta's Grand Harbour and the empty, part-submerged wreck of the gallant tanker *Ohio*. The Admiral had hefted the medal thoughtfully for a moment before handing it to me.

'The Commander would have been pleased with this,' he'd whispered before, to my astonishment, winking conspiratorially. 'It's worth nearly two quid. Cash price.'

. . . But then, I've often wondered if he hadn't always understood Trapp almost as well as I did.

'Still got it, sir,' I confirmed. 'In the bottom of my seabag.'

Together we gazed down at Trapp's hand. The extended middle finger had company again. Miraculously he seemed to have regrown the others.

'I want it back,' the Admiral growled.

Six

Two hours later I joined the СИДЯО— No, dammit: the *Charon II* . . . and made ready to sail to war with the worst captain and most inept crew there ever was. Apart from the ones I'd sailed with on my previous mission, anyway.

Strangely it wasn't the apprehension of what must come that preoccupied my musings while the Naval Control launch neared that now-anchored and seemingly abandoned hulk.

No, it was more a case of pondering the mystery that had niggled at me since I'd first observed her from a distance.

'Cocking a snook at the Royal Navy,' Flags had dismissed it as. Trapp's all-too-convenient emergence from a back-of-beyond bay in the Irish Republic, then blowing his whistle to attract the attention of a warship he'd already successfully eluded.

I didn't buy the thesis. I rather suspected the Admiral hadn't either, though why he'd apparently been prepared to go along with it only created another riddle, and I'd more than enough to go on with. But we both knew Trapp's penchant for Machiavellian skulduggery only too well. I've already referred to his deplorable capacity for emulating Will-o'-the-Wisp prior to his first arrest, remember? The ease with which he'd continued to slip invisibly between the Allied and Axis fleets for months on end, loaded to the gunnels with contraband cigarettes, whisky, Dutchman's gin, tinned salmon – dear God, I'd have given *anything* for just one of his smuggled tins of salmon while I'd been cowering in my custom-dug hole on Malta – but anyway, the very suggestion that he'd been caught by accident a second time was ludicrous in the extreme.

No, in my admittedly prejudiced view, Trapp had *wanted* to be arrested. Which, in turn, begged the question of why he'd gone AWOL from his route to join this embryo convoy and diverted to Ireland in the first place, only to turn himself in once he'd got there? Why successfully evade his duty to the King by going to ground in neutral waters where the Navy couldn't touch him, only to change his mind at the last minute and leave . . . *Why*, for that matter, had he placed himself and his new command – and I really do abuse that adjective even in its loosest sense – at the Ministry of War Transport's disposal, knowing full well they'd send him to somewhere unprofitable, like Russia, with her? Even in war, Trapp never lost sight of the bottom line accounting-wise.

Come to that, how had he come by her, this latest СИДЯОИ II or whatever? Though on second thoughts, maybe I was better off not knowing. I was aware he'd acquired his first *Charon* more by default than deliberate intent. I'd gleaned that much while on watch during a unusually placid Mediterranean night, meaning one of the very few when we weren't being shot at, when Trapp, in an unguarded moment, had not only been nice to me but had suspended lying in his teeth f'r five minutes. And naturally, as was inevitable with Trapp, the tale just had to involve a Boys' Own Paper mix of avarice and duplicity and betrayal: of Middle Eastern crooks and blunt instruments; of gun-running and murder most foul and the *Légion Étranger* and strongly held principl—

Oh, look: my trying to summarize, in one paragraph, the contrary, prickly, grasping, grumbling, intractable and yet occasionally, *very* occasionally, likeable . . . OK, so I'm grudgingly prepared to admit it now the medication's taken effect and I'm still in an expansive mood – the illogically *likeable* rogue that constituted Edward Trapp, would be akin to attempting to paraphrase the entire works of Shakespeare in a sentence.

So despite my already having taken one stab at doing so in *Trapp's War* perhaps, to help facilitate a better understanding of what made the Captain tick, you may feel the circumstances which had led to his becoming a shipowner in the first place might just bear repeating?

Or skipping, of course. If you don't give a damn either way.

Having survived the Great War, the erstwhile Midshipman Trapp RN, blissfully unaware that he still *was* Midshipman Trapp RN because, typically, he'd loftily disregarded the paperwork involved in resigning, had found himself bound for Shanghai aboard a listing, rusted old freighter . . . sound familiar, does it? Exactly so. Because not only would sailing in vessels long past their scrap-by dates become the norm throughout Trapp's seagoing career, that berth in his first coffin ship was to prove a seminal experience for the man-child who'd only managed to stay alive long enough to see his fifteenth birthday by the fortuitous suicide of a pop-eyed fish.

One might have thought the appalling living conditions he'd endured on that, his introduction to the rope's end of the tramp steamer trade, would have persuaded any grown man, never mind a mere youth, to abandon all aspirations of going to sea. Not so with young Trapp. Perverse as ever, his first voyage before the mast as a merchant seaman had only served to reinforce, by his reckoning anyway, that the life he'd embarked upon was indeed the true path to fortune.

He'd jumped ship in Hong Kong. She'd gone to the bottom the very next morning like a lead-weighted bag of confidential books, dragging all remaining hands down with her. Yet again Fate had steered Edward Trapp on a safe course around sudden death. It had been enough to seal his already growing conviction that he could always rely upon the one priceless gift that elevated him to a higher plane than other, more vulnerable, beings.

That his destiny, no matter what he did or even to whom he did it, was undoubtedly to survive.

By hook or, offered a preference, by crook.

. . . Which was precisely what Trapp did become, shortly after side-stepping his second premature demise within a corroded tomb that had simply proved too tired to stay afloat any longer.

It had been only a short sampan passage from Hong Kong to Macao. And Macao during that period had afforded a spawning ground for international crime: a magnet for gun runners, opium dealers, gold smugglers and every other low-life drop-out fleeing post-war retribution. The settlement had become the symbol of the exciting, adventurous, inscrutable East: the very epitome of those robust, romantic, disease-ridden days of the Tongs and the China Pirates and the river gunboats.

And Edward Trapp had become, in turn, captivated by the lawlessness of it. Utterly intoxicated in fact. To him Macao represented his golden land of opportunity where the survivor became king and the meek became dead.

He didn't die. Yet he never quite became a king either. Perhaps that was because too many good things still stirred into occasional wakefulness deep inside him. He'd even discovered, much to his chagrin, that he harboured principles. For instance he could never bring himself to have any truck with supplying drugs or engaging in white slavery. He stuck to his word – until the other guy broke his, an' then God help him. To cap it all he was to discover, albeit with a sense of deep frustration, that he simply couldn't kill a man in cold blood and without reason: a fundamental handicap for any young get-up-an'-go executive aiming to make it big in Macao society.

He also tended towards a sometimes self-destructive irreverence which didn't exactly attract patronage from those who might otherwise have assisted his career. Like the time when he'd won a ten-ton cargo of weed killer from a down-and-out Lebanese ship's captain in a game of mah-jong, only to find no one gave a shit about their garden in Macao. Unfazed, Trapp, reasoning one chemical had to be much the same as another, had simply stuck *Fertilizer* labels over the originals and sold it on to a local Fu Manchu to dress that gentleman's opium poppy fields with.

Fortuitously as ever for Trapp, the great Poppy Blight descended on China that year. Everybody's poppy fields emulated the Gobi Desert during a dry spell, and Fu Manchu had been temporarily fooled for just long enough for Trapp to realize the true enormity of what he'd done. It was the only thing that saved the budding entrepreneur from the severe discomfort of having his skin peeled from his still-living torso in one inch strips before the rest of him was slowly converted to mince. Not that having been granted such a Heaven-sent reprieve taught him a lesson, mind? It had merely served to further convince the idiot he was destined to survive.

. . . Though he still got the hell out've Macao in plitty damn quicktime, chop chop. Just to make bloody sure he did.

Which proved just as well. Within an hour following his departure, Fu Manchu had vented a small part of his oriental annoyance at Trapp by kidnapping the blameless Lebanese ship's captain, Trapp's current Chinese mistress and, for good measure, a visiting commercial traveller from Birmingham whose only link with Trapp was that he'd had a drink at the pier with a chap who'd given the impression he was leaving in a hurry.

Their dismembered remains were dumped from a truck on to the front garden of the British Consulate the next morning. 'Smack in the middle of my croquet lawn,' the Consul had fumed, 'an' damn uncivilized, even for a blasted yellow blighter.'

Depressingly, things never again seemed to work out quite as smoothly for Edward Trapp. During the next few years he'd drifted aimlessly, clinging petulantly to a succession of berths aboard clapped out old tramps until their mates finally tired of his intractable bloody-mindedness and dumped him back ashore for someone else ter argeyfy with. Between engagements he'd continued to hone his skills in smuggling, conning, small time wheeler-dealing and, as ever, simply surviving.

By the mid-1930s there was nothing left of Trapp's dream. There remained only a burly, penurious, hard-as-nails loner with a chip on his shoulder against the whole rotten world an' a tongue rough as a moored hulk's bottom.

It was then that his last chance had arisen. Born by avarice out of mistrust.

When Captain Trapp, as he then called himself, received the offer of his own command.

The offer had come from a seedy syndicate of three Egyptian business gentlemen who had a ship and cargo but no one to drive it since their last skipper had suffered a fatal collision with a firebar wielded by an anonymous member of her crew.

Their vessel was the *Charon* – the original *Charon*, RIP. And that presented the first snag, although Trapp never quite saw it that way. To him she was the most beautiful ship he'd ever set eyes on, notwithstanding he'd never before come across such a run-down, shored-up, rust-scaled monstrosity of a maritime scrapyard since the time he'd plundered an 1897 wreck off the Taipan coast – an' he'd had to do *that* wearing a diving suit.

The second snag promised to be the *Charon*'s port of discharge, to say nothing of her cargo: a beach in North Africa and a consignment of fourth-hand guns which could still kill anyone they were aimed at.

The third snag took the form of the French Foreign Legionnaires who patrolled that particular area just waiting for gun-runners like Trapp. A thoroughly uncouth lot, they were far too disposed towards shooting first an' jumping on your bullet-riddled corpse later, just to make sure.

While the *fourth* snag was the . . . well, the frankly deplorable attitude of his bosses, the Egyptians. To further aggravate those other flaws that held him back from becoming a fully-fledged, truly black-hearted pirate, one of Trapp's inflexible principles had always been that of loyalty to his employers. So it was understandable he'd taken offence at the way they'd insisted on his staying aboard while they took the gear ashore and received their final payment from the local sheik. Almost as if they didn't trust their own captain to return with the money. Even inferring that he, Edward Trapp, might shanghai his own *cargo*, f'r cryin' out loud.

And it was then that Trapp got his Big Idea.

Naturally it ensured, above all, that the cargo would be perfectly safe. There had never been any question that he'd fully intended to land both his bosses and their guns in any part of the Mediterranean they so directed, an' he would've been keelhauled rather than purloin so much as a single round of .303 ammunition in the process.

But the way Trapp saw it, it seemed only reasonable that he should derive some small gain from the transaction too, wasn't it?

Like, well . . . like, stealing their *ship*, f'r instance?

So he did. Just as soon as the first fusillade of rifle fire carried across the still waters from that distant beach. Which, to be fair to Trapp, did suggest that his late employers were unlikely to be returning for dinner that night anyway.

. . . And more crucially, were extremely unlikely to lodge any subsequent claim as to the legal ownership of the SS *Charon*.

So thus did Edward Trapp, survivor, become a man of substance: a self-employed master mariner with allegiance to no nation and the whole of the globe his oyster. He'd even acquired a ready-made crew and, while he never could prove it had been a certain vertically challenged and *very* ordinary seaman, albeit one who cherished ambitions to rise above his natural station and graduate to the status of cretin – one known as Gorbals Wullie – who'd retired the *Charon*'s previous skipper with a blunt object administered from astern, he took bloody good care to ensure the same fate never caught up with him.

But anyone familiar with Trapp's subsequent and on-going squashing of Wullie by a combination of vituperative camaraderie and utter derision, would have anticipated *that* much already. Within weeks they had become, within the seafaring community, the Laurel and Hardy of the high seas.

Remarkably, things were happy and successful in a sordid kind of way aboard the bad ship *Charon* as she shuddered tentatively from one illicit destination to another with only the occasional stabbing or shooting or splash in her wake during the middle watch to disturb the harmony of her crew. While Fate, as ever, steered Trapp on a safe course despite himself, to avoid retribution at the hands of the authorities.

Until Adolf Hitler sent his Wehrmacht into Poland, and the one event Trapp had sworn long before that he would never, ever become involved in, occurred.

The world went to war.

Again.

. . . Apart from the not-in-the-slightest-bit-patriotic crew of the *Charon,* that was: who unanimously declared themselves neutral and simply carried on cruising as before, although, in fairness to them, most of that particular crowd of international dead-beats would've had great difficulty in remembering exactly whose side they should've been fighting on anyway.

And you've got to admit, that policy of non-involvement *did* have a certain logic to it. As Trapp himself reasoned, 'Either way, we gotta steer clear of warships, lads. So we might as well be doin' it on our own account an' puttin' a bit o' profit aside at the same time.'

But Trapp's principles still held sway as rigidly as ever. Nothing he did must jeopardize the Allied war effort. Any black market spirits or chocolate or butter he picked up from his shadowy contacts along the African coast would go straight into British hands . . . for a price. So even the morality of it was undisputable. From a renegade expatriate's point of view, anyway.

And that was why the island of Malta, brought almost to her knees by the Nazi blockade, woke up regularly to discover yet another consignment of luxuries being bartered from a ship's boat that had spent the previous night waiting off a little cove just down past Vittoriosa. While any senior British officer who may have been privy to a little more intelligence than Trapp would have liked to think, only glanced tolerantly at the faces of those who needed every spark of cheer they could get, and then had deliberately turned away.

. . . And so Trapp's non-involvement in World War II had proceeded. Until a certain admiral conceived a cunning plan to press-gang such an eminently qualified ghost ship in order to redeploy her on more destructive duties; and so had despatched his long grey seadogs of war to find and apprehend her while, as part of the package, recalling a by-then Lieutenant-Commander Trapp, RN, back into the service of his King.

I'd almost felt sorry for him. The Admiral, I mean: not Trapp. His whole strategy of using the *Charon* as a Q-ship could've worked a treat if he hadn't gone a clever-clogs too far and blackmailed Trapp into continuing to captain her . . . but felt sorry only briefly. I stopped wasting sympathy on admirals the moment that bloody Messerschmitt started machine-gunning me before I'd hardly had time to clamber aboard Trapp's *first* wreck!

. . . So you can hardly blame me for experiencing a dispiriting sense of déjà vu as the naval control launch bumped against the predictably rickety accommodation ladder of his second, whereupon even that slightest of impacts served to dislodge a rust scale big as a dustbin lid from the blacked-out hull towering above me.

'D'you think you could go round again, PO?' I asked the coxswain.

'Sorry, sir,' the PO said defensively. 'Didn't reckon I'd come alongside too hard this time.'

'That's what I meant,' I retorted.

He craned his head back to look up, then shook it disbelievingly. 'When d'you want me to come back for you, Lieutenant?'

'I don't,' I said. 'Well, I do . . . but I can't.'

'Christ, you're not *sailing* with her, are you?'

His expression told me everything. Now I knew what the

faces of a kamikazi pilot's ground crew must've looked like while they strapped him in and screwed down his canopy.

I didn't insist on his having another go at sinking her by accident. Just asked him to wait alongside a few minutes in case he had to retrieve me after I'd fallen through the rotting treads of her ladder, and left it at that.

Listless I felt, by then. Mentally exhausted. An' that was *before* I'd met any Germans.

But I hadn't been able to get it out of my head. That most vexing question. Why *had* Trapp, who'd never done anything in his life without a profit-driven, usually self-destructive and invariably devious motive, spent time and coal on embarking upon a mystery tour to some back-of-beyond bay in neutral Ireland, only to put his hands up at the last minute and toot a British warship?

Presumably *something* had happened during the few days he'd been missing from the Navy's plot that persuaded him to change his mind. But what . . . ? What conceivable reason could Edward Trapp have chanced upon to make him suddenly and uncharacteristically keen to put himself and his sole commercial asset, the *Charon II*, in harm's way?

To *want* to be returned to a high-risk convoy that was going to have to fight for every sea mile on its way to Russia?

Seven

There was no one to greet me at the head of the *Charon*'s ladder. I wasn't surprised. They'd probably figured a gangway watch was unnecessary as no potential boarder was likely to survive the climb. I only achieved it because, having sailed in the Captain's previous death trap I'd learned from bitter experience never to rely on any handrail or safety rope because it would only convert to dank mush at the slightest touch, and to never, ever place my foot on the middle, weaker area of a tread unless I really wanted to go bathing through a puff of woodworm dust.

There were no lights either, not even low-intensity red-shaded ones, partly because of the wartime blackout regulations but mainly because Trapp had always been environmentally aware at heart. Not, I hasten to add, that he'd been ahead of his time as an advocate of the risk posed by global warming. No. It was simply that the old skinflint had never been able to bring himself to waste costly auxiliary boiler coal on helping to ensure crew well-being . . . apart from which, most of 'em would've been used to feeling, rather than seeing, their way past rotting gaps in the bulwarks on account of the professional necessity for smugglers to observe darken ship routine, even in bloody peacetime.

Cautiously I toe-tapped my way around missing deck planks and rusted ringbolts to the deserted foredeck where I hesitated for a moment, listening to the creak of an unsecured derrick swinging in the wind interrupted only by an occasional *plop* as another piece of the ship fell off. Such lack of urgency to prepare for the coming voyage – *my* coming voyage too, dammit – was disconcerting, to say nothing of eerie. Less than an hour to go before the Commodore's lead freighter began to weigh and every other vessel in the anchorage had become a hive of pre-sailing activity. Lashings undergoing final inspection by shaded torches beneath deck cargoes of light tanks, army lorries – even railway engines ... to starboard the outlines of two aircraft tail fins projecting above the after well deck bulwarks of a tramp steamer that had seen better days and a previous war ... unusually pensive seamen griping lifeboats tight into the rails: davits already swung outboard in war configuration to facilitate immediate launching should the *Please God, no* moment occur ... more silhouettes, this time of DEMS gun crews – yet another obscure, and all-too-often derisory Navy acronym meaning *Defensively Equipped Merchant Ship* – moving quietly and methodically on each poop: breaking open ready-use ammunition lockers; sponging out, degreasing, and making last minute checks on the only serious armament most STUFTs carried: a solitary 4 or 4.5-inch stern chaser harking back, in many cases, to the same era of that venerable trampship; at least one war out of date but still pressed back into service ...

Thank the Lord they haven't given *him* a gun this time, I reflected gratefully. Give Trapp a gun, even an old one as a sop to his show-off tendency, an' he'll lose all sense of proportion again: want to take over the worl—?

What was *that*? A shuffling sound accompanied by a ... a *movement*, was it? From over there by the forward contactor house? I swung nervously: didn't I *say* it was eerie out there all on my own? An' then it got eerier still as wind-torn clouds parted fractionally to allow a melon-pale full moon to light what could easily have doubled as a theatrical backdrop to some penny-dreadful drama set in a shipbreakers' graveyard.

Jesus! A flutter of ragged clothing ... a black cut-out form rising from behind a steam winch. Then others, cautiously revealing themselves and beginning to shuffle forward to surround me. Ten, fifteen shambling figures barely distinguishable in the sallow moonlight, making it all too easy for my by-then bow-taut imagination to make comparison with those pre-war films of Boris Karloff that had terrified me as a child. The Monster Men; the Things; the Unspeakable with hunched shoulders and slime-tendrilled hair an' gobs of rotting flesh melting from dead cheekbones like ... like the ... ? *Damn*, there I went again: me an' my bloody paranoia ... like the undead rising from the coffins of a *coffin* ship?

I noted a length of chain-stopper lying on the deck beside

me. Stooping urgently to retrieve it, I wound a couple of turns around my fist. It chinked as I did so. Even providing your own supernatural sound effects now, Miller, I reflected wryly as I prepared to lash out at the nearest approaching ghoul.

My size of ghoul.

A small ghoul.

A *very* small ghoul indeed . . . ?

'No need to hit 'em, Mister. This crowd, they're more a bunch o' girls' blouses than cut-throats,' a gratingly familiar voice boomed from the heavens. 'It's just they never seen a poncy Navy uniform this close before. They wus hiding in case you was a revenue man.'

So much for the *Welcome aboard, Miller* . . . ? I craned to glare aloft. He was slouched over the bridge rail, wind-buffeted cap bob-bob-bobbing in the moonlight while grinning down derisively.

'Don't call me Mister, call me Lieutenant,' I snarled. 'This time I'm only here as supercargo, Trapp. Reporting as your Naval Liaison Officer; not your do-this, do-that First bloody Mate.'

'In that case, remember what you was told in Malta. Call me *Sir*,' he beamed angelically. 'Me bein' *proper* RN an' your superior officer an' everythin'.'

The very small ghoul just had to butt in then in a crucified Glaswegian patois: him saying the wrong thing in the wrong way at the wrong time being in his nature. ''Allo, Mister Miller sir. It wis me put you on that hatch cover last time an' saved your life, so it wis. So's at least youse'll be pleased tae see *me* again, eh?'

I wasn't, actually. If Gorbals Wullie had left me to drown I wouldn't be having all this hassle now. I debated whether to banjo the ingratiating little rodent with the chain stopper anyway, just for the satisfaction I'd gain, but reluctantly decided against it. No doubt he'd give me another excuse to settle old scores. Probably within ten minutes tops, judging by past form.

But I had to do *something* to establish my authority before the rest of those shambling deadbeats from Trapp's foc'sle interpreted Wullie's over-familiarity with an officer as a bench-mark for the future. Whipping my cap off, I threw it to the deck then pointed at him.

'You, sailor. For exercise – unexploded *bomb*!'

Grinning slyly at his shipmates, Wullie, who'd never quite been able to grasp the philosophy that every action invites a consequence, kicked it clear over the side into the water.

'F'r exercise . . . *bomb* made safe!'

I grabbed him, carried him kicking and screaming to the rail and dropped him after my hat. He went down on the end of a howl abruptly terminated by a splash.

'Man OVERBOARD – hands to the emergency boat! This is NOT a drill!'

The order's effect, while gratifying in terms of the crowd's speed of response, did give rise to some concern within me as to their competence as seafarers. They all started to run about aimlessly and in different directions. One appeared particularly panicked: an elderly, somewhat angular gentleman wearing odd bits of what had once been a uniform, who kept shouting, 'The boats: the boats . . . where are the *boats*?'

'Try the fuckin' *boat* deck, mister!' Trapp hollered back, face suddenly suffused with embarrassment at being shown up like that, then catching sight of my expression.

'*Mister*?' I queried pointedly.

'Oh, all right – so *he's* me chief officer, smarty pants,' Trapp conceded grudgingly, then rallied. 'But lissen, that man's a gem, see? A real seadog. Wasn't that long ago since he held command hisself. *And* of a whole fleet, come to that.'

'Fleet? What fleet?' I asked.

He mumbled something I didn't quite hear. It could have been the wind, but I knew evasion when I heard it.

'I didn't quite catch that, Trapp,' I pressed enjoyably. 'What *fleet*?'

'Ohhhh, Birmingham Municipal *Council*'s fleet, if you must know,' he exploded angrily. 'On every pond in the city, mind? Two hundred an' eighty rowin' boats, sixty inflatable giraffes an' forty paddle floats in all.'

The СИДЯОИ's gem of a chief officer whizzed past me on his third questing gallop around the contactor house. 'The boat deck's that way,' I said, pointing to the ladder. 'Two flights up and hard a starboard.'

'Don't confuse 'im with technicalities,' Trapp cautioned anxiously. 'Jus' tell 'im keep to the right.'

Welcome aboard indeed, Miller, I thought.

Yet, do you know . . . ? I felt strangely at home as I checked to make sure my seabag hadn't been stolen.

'. . . But what about Gorbals *Wullie*?' I hear you ask. 'He's still down there drowning, isn't he?'

Well, it would be true to say I did find myself in something of a quandary on that count, albeit one brought about by my own doing. At a rough estimate I calculated that Wullie could doggie-paddle for at least thirty minutes before hypothermia or one of the already waterlogged lifebuoys they were throwing at him, killed him. On the other hand, it threatened to be a close-run thing unless someone with at least some vague idea of which end of an oar to stick in the water took charge. With that in mind, and despite my just having stressed to Trapp that I wasn't part of his Merchant Navy complement – that I didn't do first mating – it seemed the onus had to fall squarely on me. But we *were* talking urgency here. Life and death. *Wullie's* life and death.

Soon as I'd finished my cigarette I strolled up to the boat deck.

To my surprise there appeared to be an empty space between the davits where the emergency lifeboat should have been: a space even larger than that which existed between Wullie's ears on our previous trip. I was impressed: maybe I'd underestimated them. It seemed they'd managed to get it lowered within a time scale that even a warship captain would have been satisfied with.

Which made it seem all the more odd why, instead of speeding off like a dysfunctional water-beetle in the pursuance of their mission of mercy, the crowd were still clustered around their ever-more agitated Chief Officer, all peering with Neanderthally furrowed brows at something he held in his hand.

'You forgot to *board* the boat before you put it in the water, didn't you?' I speculated accusingly.

The old guy waved it at me vaguely. In the moonlight I could see it was a dog-eared copy of the MN's standard tome, *Nicholl's Seamanship and Nautical Knowledge*: possibly the actual 1912 edition I'd assumed had gone down with the *Titanic*, judging by the state of it.

'Chapter Four, Section One,' I offered wearily. 'Under Ships' Boats.'

'We 'ave to wait, sir. For—' he began querulously.

'There could be a man drowning down there while you do,' I reminded him helpfully.

'Fuck you,' he concluded somewhat obliquely.

'There's no need to be like that,' I retorted defensively.

'No, he means they gotta wait f'r Fuk Yew, me chief steward,' Trapp advised from the after end of the bridge having, by then, sauntered to collapse over the rail at a new vantage point for a change.

'Why so?' I asked reasonably. 'Are they planning to have a picnic on their way to the casualty?'

''E's the only one can read,' Trapp explained, equally reasonably and with the sort of irrefutable logic that already threatened to prove as much the norm aboard this *Charon* as her predecessor. 'Mind you, seein' he can only do it in Mandarin an' doesn't speak English, that might not be a lot o' help to Wullie.'

I lit another cigarette and pondered the problem. Something had to be done to raise the crowd's level of commitment to their new life-saving role from inertia to casual interest.

'Look, see that big roundy pile of rope and wooden slats under where the boat was?' I explained laboriously. 'It's called a boarding ladder. You just kick it over the side; it unrolls as it goes, and then you all climb down it into the boat.'

'Notta lotta point in doin' that, sir,' the Mate said anxiously.

'Oh, don't always be so bloody *negative!*' I growled before placing my foot on the roll and shoving it hard over the edge. It ejected a protest of abruptly evicted wood-masticating creatures as it unwound. The last I saw of Trapp's emergency boat's emergency boarding ladder was its inboard end snaking downwards to follow the rest of it to the bottom of the anchorage.

'You *also* forgot to secure it to the ship when you rigged it, didn't you?' I deduced with the merest touch of asperity. But then, my official status aboard – my merely being a sort of honorary seamanship advisor to the *Charon* and even that only out of necessity – did tend to inhibit me from acting like a fully integrated bucko mate and beating them pleasurably about their particularly thick skulls with a rope's end.

'It's not *that* either, sir,' Trapp's Seadog persisted, moving to peer uneasily down over the ship's side. I frowned and followed him curiously.

Below me the lifeboat hung vertically from its after fall, its lower bow section completely submerged. Around it floated a random selection of survival gear which should have been firmly lashed in place before launching: such emergency equipment being generally deemed useful to those who find themselves sunk in the middle of an ocean, possibly hundreds of miles from land, and thus called upon to complete their voyage in an open craft. Handy cruising accessories like, well . . . food and drink, for instance. Wooden barricoes filled with fresh water that, in this case, obviously hadn't been seeing they were currently skittering across the surface like cork balloons under the press of the wind. And once rock-hard ship's biscuits getting mushier by the second, plus already dissolving Horlicks tablets and atrophied tins of condensed milk that had burst from corroded, originally watertight lockers to expand in a high calorie ring around the dangling boat.

Oh, and the lifeboat's oars, of course. As well as its rudder. *And* its mast an' its lugsail and its bottom-boards and that little screw-plug thing we sailors use to keep the sea out . . .

I took my first decision of the voyage then. Remember that earlier sense of inhibition I'd felt, due to my being aboard only as a Naval Liaison Officer? Sod it, I thought.

'You *also* forgot to lower both ends at the same time an' *together*, didn't you?' I finally erupted at Trapp's gem of a chief officer. 'If for no *other* reason, Mister, than to ensure the fuckin' *boat* stays fuckin' *level* when it fuckin' *hits* the fucking WATER . . . !'

Someone elbowed unnoticed through the crowd and came to stand beside me, frowning down. The new arrival was dripping wet.

'Somethin' up, Mister Miller sir?' he queried with enormous interest.

I turned to look hard at Gorbals Wullie. I gained the impression he'd been back aboard for some time but hadn't thought to mention it to anybody.

It was fortuitous for him I'd asked the anchorage launch's coxswain to hang around awhile.

In the grey half light of dawn we sailed in company with the real merchantmen to join Convoy PQ Whatever-it-was off Iceland.

Trapp's Seadog did not sail with us. Oh, not because Trapp had bulleted him ashore as incompetent following the rescue boat debacle. Were Trapp to fire every incompetent crew member he'd previously boasted was a gem he'd finish up sailing the bloody ship hisself – an' *that* only by special dispensation. And anyway, you don't lightly dismiss a man who'd once commanded sixty inflatable giraffes and even supplies bits of his own uniform.

No, it was more because, even before the *Charon* had begun to edge one inch towards the direction of Russia, and while she was still weighing anchor, the poor old fellow had fallen victim to a slight misunderstanding between himself, the Bosun and . . . an' I cringe at the thought of bringing him up again so soon – and Gorbals Wullie.

I'd completely divorced myself from the actual departure process, having firmly resolved to dig in on the bridge wearing full uniform complete with brand new linen collar and shiny shoes, loftily ignore Trapp's pointed references to cruise ship lounge lizards an' brassbound lead swingers, and do absolutely nothing more than perform the duties of a convoy NLO: duties which, seeing nobody had thought – or had considered it a pointless waste of resources to brief me on what they might be – promised to leave quite a lot of time on my hands to hear all, see all, and bite my lip 'til it bled.

Actually it had gone well considering it had turned pitch black out there since the moon had been smothered by more cloud . . . or at least, it went well at the start, anyway. The anchor party had turned up on the foc'slehead not more than ten minutes late, and even our Mate managed to find the front end of the boat eventually. After a few explosive hiccups the windlass had begun to turn slowly, albeit to the accompaniment of various hisses, pops and splutters of steam leaking from unpacked packing glands, and when Trapp gave the order *Heave away* through his megaphone – not that he generally needed help in the volume control department, but he'd been issued a naval one for free an' it had been like giving a fractious child a new toy – we on the bridge could clearly detect the clank and grumble of rusted cable dragging up through the hawsepipe, although we couldn't actually see what was happening.

And so it had gone. A touch ahead on the engine to take

the strain off the asthmatic windlass: an eruption of incandescent soot from the funnel; a sudden, gritty sensation inside the band of my previously pristine but already trampship-grey collar . . . *clank, clank, clank* from the foc'slehead until the chain began to heave vertically, meaning the anchor was just coming clear of the bottom . . .

'Cablesupandoonmistermillersir!' Wullie's self-important shout carried above the sigh of the wind. Like he and the Mate knew what were they doing. Like anybody would be able to interpret the thrust of Wullie's communication in the first place. Like anybody bloody well cared. Especially like Mister *Miller* sir bloody well cared.

'Why don't 'e report proper?' Trapp snorted, clearly jealous of Wullie's inexplicable and, considering I'd just tried to drown him, apparently indefatigable allegiance to me, before bawling back, 'Lissen, rat face: *I'm* the bloody Captain – not 'im with the poncy uniform. An' from now on, report the cable is up an' DOWN – not *doon*. Doon's a place in Scotland what's got a bridge innit. So if this wus a haggis-basher's ship, then you could say *doon*. But as it ain't, then it's up an' bloody DOWN!'

Clank, clank . . . wheeze . . . silence! Broken eventually by Wullie's aggrieved complaint again from out of the darkness ahead.

'It's mebbe no' a Scots ship, Captain, but it's sure as hell a bluidy *Disney* ship, so it is!'

'Disney . . . *Disney*? What's 'e mean now. What does he mean?' Trapp fulminated.

'This disnae work: *that* disnae work,' the invisible Wullie filled in for him. 'Now the bluidy anchor's come up arse aboot tit and winnae go intae the thingy hole.'

Meaning, presumably, that the anchor had swivelled on the cable so that its flukes – or, as Wullie would describe them: the pointy ends that digs intae the bottom – had turned inboard and were preventing the stock of the anchor from entering the hawsepipe. Continuing to heave away would only risk puncturing the plating of the bow or, more than likely in our case, ripping the whole front of the boat clean off. The only way to clear it was to . . . ?

'It's a'right, Captin,' Wullie called reassuringly. 'The Mate's climbed ower the side wi' a boat hook tae lever it round.'

The anchor weighed approximately three tons. He'd have been as well taking a toothpick with him. And anyway, on what . . . I swallowed anxiously then as a disturbing thought began to take shape . . . on *what*, precisely, did Trapp's Gem propose to *stand* to afford him purchase?

'Bring him back aboard,' I yelled frantically into the dark void, breaking my own self-imposed *omerta* before we'd even got properly under way. 'But f'r God's sake, take the boat hook off him first, so's he can hold on with both hands. An' above all, DON'T . . .'

'You heard Mister Miller, Grandpa. Gie's it then: gimme the whatsit . . . *Leggo*!' Wullie could be heard arguing as, presumably, he tried to retrieve the boat hook in slavish obedience to the first part of my order before I threw him over the wall again.

'. . . let him stand . . .' I persisted urgently.

'Leggo, dammit!' Wullie was demanding furiously now. 'Let GO!'

'Aye, aye – LET *GO*!' the Bosun's throaty confirmation followed instantly: a purely reflex response which – as it was he who controlled the windlass and, most pertinently, the cable brake – would normally have been commendable but which, in this instance, turned out to be somewhat less so. Not when considering that Wullie's irate demand to 'Let go' wasn't actually intended for him but directed at our elderly chief officer balanced precariously under the bow.

'. . . stand on the ANCHOR!' I concluded too late. Not that the specifics mattered by then; my horrified appeal being drowned out by the rumble, roar and splash of the *Charon*'s 3-ton hook rocketing back to the seabed again.

And by the wail of incomprehension plummeting with it.

I have to admit it did feel good to finally be heading for sea again. Standing up there on the foc'sle as we *chuff wheeze chuffed* outward between the cliffs guarding the loch entrance: sensing the bow begin to rise and fall beneath my seaboots even despite its being stuffed with concrete to help us stay afloat; feeling the salt-laden wind tugging at my oilski—

'But *wait*, Miller,' do I hear you say? 'Only a short time ago, weren't you hanging out on Trapp's bridge resplendent in pusser's rig with shiny shoes, resolutely claiming you intended to have absolutely nothing whatsoever to do with the actual management and running of Convoy Formation Number Thirteen . . . ? Yet now, all of a sudden, you're wearing seaboots and oilskins while indulging yourself in overly lurid Boy's Own Paper romanticism up forr'ad in the eyes of the СИДЯОИ II; a location which – forgive me for being nit-picky but, as I'm taking the trouble to read this bloody journal of yours, I expect you to get your facts right – is surely that part of ship where any vessel's *chief officer* should rightfully be present on duty at the time of her leaving harbour?'

Ah . . . true. And well spotted. There's nothing an author appreciates more than input from a bloody armchair critic. But I'd been a bit busy in the interim, you see. What with helping eyeball Trapp's half-drowned gem of a mate through the darkness, then directing the NCS launch to where he whirlpooled slowly like a spluttering, disoriented starfish amid the gear jettisoned from his earlier lifeboat disaster . . . and me all the while assuring the launch's increasingly truculent coxswain that, 'No, I really *don't* expect you to follow us all the way to Russia, Chief. Not just so's you can recover the steady stream of Tom, Dicks and Wullies we tend to keep losing overboard.'

And then had followed the aftermath. The reckoning. But not directed at those parties who properly deserved to be censured. Oh no. No, that wasn't the Royal Navy's way of doing things. Applaud the incompetent, disregard the guilty, an' punish the innocent: *that* was their style. I mean, Gorbals Wullie an' the Bosun – Trapp himself, for that matter, who should never have entrusted them with any task involving seamanship or requiring a brain . . . *they'd* been the ones responsible, yet here I was again, once more the helpless butt of all the unpleasantness and criticism just as the psychia— just as the *Colonel* had pointed out in that desert hospital.

The way things had kept going wrong on Trapp's previous *Charon*? None of *them* had actually been my fault either, had they?

The hastily summoned Duty Boarding Officer had . . . well, *boarded* us, I suppose.

He'd managed to do so safely, albeit only on account of my having cornered Trapp beforehand and pointed out that

drowning Royal Naval officers by economizing on the cost
of providing a sound rope side ladder, could well come back
to haunt us. That his topping one of their brethren as a direct
result of criminal negligence might tend to disenfranchise our
future convoy escort commanders who, in turn, might very
well leave us hanging out to dry as an undefended target when
the fuckin' *Germans* attacked!

I even made sure I secured it to the ship personally. If you
want a job done . . . ?

A decent chap, the DBO. A reservist like me. It was his
job to sort out any last-minute hitches, although even he had
his limits. Performing miracles like arranging for lightning to
strike Adolf Hitler before Friday week or, albeit rather more
demanding, getting Trapp's crowd to depart on time, didn't
enter into his remit. He came; listened with increasingly glassy-
eyed incredulity to Trapp's tirade about how the Admiralty
wus puttin' his top-whack sailors at risk through ignorin' the
health an' safety rules laid down by the Board of Trade f'r
merchant seamen by expectin' them to work in the dark, an'
that in his, Trapp's view, there wus a solid case f'r compensation, payable to him, Trapp, by the way, on account of the
stress he'd suffered from losin' his much-prized chief executive – not to our waterlogged chief executive himself – then
departed shoreward again shaking his head. I was left with
the impression Boardy hardly considered it worth the NCS
people trying to produce a replacement mate from God knew
where at that time of the morning because, as we hadn't even
managed to clear the anchorage before taking a casualty, he
didn't reckon we had a hope in hell of making it to Russia
anyway.

But it was then that everything really started to go downhill when, half an hour later, my earlier adversary, that pompous
little turd of a Flag Lieutenant, turned up. Had I known he
was coming I'd've arranged for Wullie to re-tie the knots
securing the new boarding ladder.

'The *Admiral*,' Flags informed me, genuflecting as he
mentioned that seven letter word, 'is displeased with you,
Miller. Without putting too fine a point on it, he's had enough.'

'You mean I'm fired already?' I prompted hopefully. 'That
he won't, ah . . . *allow* me to go to Murmansk after all? That
I'm no longer this fine ship's Naval Liaison Officer?'

'I mean you're no longer *any* kind of naval officer, Miller,' Flags retorted, the regulation purse-lipped expression making it eminently clear he felt I'd let The Side down for the very last time. 'In fact the *Admiral*,' he crossed himself again, 'personally countermanded your recall to the Reserve fifteen minutes ago.'

I was disconsolate. Rejected by the Royal Navy? Not being permitted to sail in even *one* Russian convoy? Never having to salute anyone ever again. Or use a fish knife? While above all, no longer under *Trapp's* command . . . ? It was like finding I'd suddenly won the Irish sweepstake.

'Oh, *no*,' I protested. Very faintly.

'Oh yes, Miller. You have already reverted to being,' he appeared to find the very definition distasteful, 'a *merchant* service, ah . . . whatever it is you people call yourselves on Stuffeds.'

'Oh dash and oh dear,' I sighed. 'I suppose that means I'll just have to find myself a trampship berth again.'

'No need to.'

I frowned. 'You mean I can stay ashore for the rest of the war?'

'I *mean*,' he retorted heavily, 'you've already been allocated a new berth.'

'Who by?'

'By *whom*,' he corrected, proving he never learnt nothing . . . or should that be *learned*?

'Lissen you, if I'm back to bein' Merchant Navy, then I'll fucking stick with *who*,' I snarled, getting irritated. Plus starting to feel a tad uneasy at the way the conversation was shaping. 'So who arranged this new berth for me?'

'The Ministry of War Transport. As you are now technically a civilian seafarer, your deployment for the remainder of this war will henceforth be at their disposition, Miller.' He hesitated then: evidently a man of precision. 'Unless, of course . . .'

'Unless?'

'Unless you opt for the alternative, which is your privilege by law. You are perfectly entitled to refuse point blank to serve afloat in any capacity the Ministry so orders you to.'

'Oh, that's all right then,' I said, mollified. 'I'd rather choose which ship I sail in anyway.'

'. . . in which case,' he finished smoothly, 'you will immediately be conscripted into the army. You'll be eating tomorrow's lunch as a private soldier.'

I thought about that for a minute. Those itchy-rough serge uniforms. The impolite way the sergeants shout at everybody. That *bloody* hospital tent. The prospect of being left with one leaky sandbag between me an' a German tank. Their limited verbal skills which, as I've already recounted, tend to consist solely of *Incoming* an' *Take cover* an' *Medic – where's the fucking MEDIC . . . ?*

'I'll get my seabag and you can give me a lift ashore,' I decided. 'They can put me on the next train to wherever she's lying.'

'To where what's lying?'

'My next *ship*, dammit!' I snarled, fighting my growing sense of anxiety.

'No need to,' he demurred enjoyably.

'You keep *saying* that: sayin' no need to. Whaddya *mean* – no NEED to?'

Flags smiled as he turned away. Smiled for the very first time.

'Because you're already aboard her. *Mister* Miller!'

'Look,' I'd appealed desperately after his departing shadow. It had become a bit like trying to hold a conversation with the Cheshire cat in *Alice*: slowly disappearing until only its smile was left hanging in the night. 'He was hardly damaged. Pump him out properly, stick a plaster cast on his broken leg, an' he'll be perfectly fit to continue sailing as mate.'

'Fit?' Flags came back derisively. 'The sick bay PO reckons he won't even be able to speak for a week.'

'With Trapp as old man, he won't get the bloody *chance* to!' I exploded.

'The *Admiral*—'

'Don't cross yourself again, you sycophantic little prick. Don't even think about it.'

'—has decreed that either you sail as Captain Trapp's relief chief officer or he will take your case up personally with GOC Allied Land Forces.'

'Meaning?'

'Meaning he will ensure the army issues you with the

dirtiest, most antiquated rifle they've got before posting you to Russia anyway . . . while talking of Russia: this ship should have sailed two hours ago. You'll already have a struggle to catch up with your convoy. It's make your mind up time, Miller – freezing seas or freezing mud?'

He'd hesitated then, peering about him through our over-the-top blackout, courtesy of Trapp's economy drive. 'Now, remind me: which is the, ah, least hazardous route back to your boarding ladder?'

It was as well for Flags I've never been one to bear a grudge; malice being an emotion totally foreign to me. Instead I merely checked to make sure the NCS launch was still on emergency stand-by: *putt-putting* aimlessly in circles by then with her coxswain morosely scanning the length of our bulwarks, trying to anticipate from which part of ship the *Charon*'s next man overboard might jettison himself.

'No, please,' I demurred solicitously having decided that, in Flags's case, it would be well worth risking the withdrawal of all escort protection from the *Charon*. 'Shinning down vertical rungs can be damn awkward when a chap's rigged out in best staff uniform. Do feel free to use the ship's own accommodation ladder starboard side.'

I'd withheld my parting shot until Flags had actually placed one mirror-polished shoe on the first tread.

'Remember to hold tight to the safety ropes, old boy . . . Oh, and by the way; considering you've spent the last few hours consistently undermining my position as Naval Liaison Officer with the Admiral, then ask yourself how come I've managed to break *one* convoy record already?'

I hoped I'd allowed enough time for him to register the punchline. I had to talk fast to complete it before he actually hit the water.

'This has to be the first tramp in the Allied fleet –' I'd followed him triumphantly all the way down – 'to become a straggler even *before* she's left bloody harbour!'

Eight

We cleared the assembly anchorage and set course for the main PQ-whatever-it-was rendezvous north of Iceland without further trauma.

Mind you the *rest* of our feeder convoy got attacked in the interim. It didn't affect us. Typical Trapp luck; spawned entirely by accident and not design. By then we'd been lagging so far astern that the three hit-and-run Dornier bombers never even saw us when they strafed the main body just north of the Minches.

Well, either they didn't notice, or misinterpreted the dense pyre of glowing ash generated by our cheapest-on-the-black-market bunker coal as indicating we were already on fire following some earlier raid and that, for us, the war was good as over anyway. Trapp's unmerited salvation yet again; this time born out of penny-pinching avarice. To save a few bob he disregards every warning in the *Make Smoke, Sink Ships* war-at-sea manual, leaves a long swirling trail of soot-laden give-away like a bloody great marker leading directly to the *Charon* saying *Bombe hier* . . . whereupon *they* – the Luftwaffe – assume some other Hun, some previous pilot, has been there, seen it, done that one already.

It was over in less than a minute. We watched them on the horizon: eleven ships steaming steadfastly through a flurry of water spouts in their four rigidly adhered-to columns with the escorting corvettes scurrying around the perimeter like anxious sheep dogs. Under a fluff-puff pelmet of ack-ack bursts, the briefly hanging plumes of spray caught the setting sun and twinkled mischievously before they collapsed. Quite pretty really. From five miles away.

'Is it safe tae come oot yet?' Wullie probed tentatively from under the chart table as the drone of aero engines subsided.

'Them Jerries. Couldn't hit a barn door,' Trapp snorted contemptuously.

'Just as well,' I said. 'Seeing you've just described this wreck of yours to a T.'

A funny thing happened on our way to Iceland.

Well, quite a few funny things happened – or didn't, if you consider the term 'funny' as meaning 'funny peculiar', and that it can just as appropriately be applied to a journey when the anticipated actually fails to materialize . . . such as no one else having fallen overboard; our managing to stay afloat for the whole leg, and our not having collided with anything en route. But after all I *was* aboard the *Charon II*, spawn of *Charon I*, so, having long resigned myself to a fatalistic acceptance that even the most insignificant Trapp-generated action must invariably escalate into a Trapp-mismanaged crisis, I'd felt grateful for as many negative outcomes as Fate was disposed to afford me.

Although having said that, one incident – no, two incidents really: the second following hard on the heels of the first – were to give me grounds for uneasy conjecture in the middle of each subsequent night.

OK, so I concede it was to be a different sort of unease: one which made a change from cowering sleepless in a hole in Malta or lying wide awake on a dune-strewn battlefield brooding, as on those previous occasions, over the ghost of a pirate past. Instead I could look forward to lying wide awake, staring hollow-eyed up at the mildewed, rust-encrusted deck-head of my potential steel sarcophagus, while mulling on the worrisome evasions of a pirate present. Not that the prospect was all bad. At least I wouldn't be stuck for choice of night-mares this time: confined solely to pondering the nature of the next fine mess Trapp would inevitably get me into . . . Lord, no. No: on this trip I could always take a break from that particular anxiety attack by turning my thoughts to other preoccupations. Like waiting for the first ship-buster bomb to penetrate our eggshell-thin deck plating, or some undetected floating mine to erupt under our conveniently concrete-filled bows, or the explosion of a torpedo in the engine room directly below my berth heralding a U-boat hello and goodbye.

. . . But again I digress. It had been Trapp's increasingly furtive behaviour from the moment we sailed that first began to ring alarm bells. I could always tell when he was holding something back: something he knew I knew he knew, but was damned if he was going to admit to because *he* knew I'd only get hysterical an' start kicking things, usually Wullie, in childish pique just because then *I*, too, would know f'r *certain* he was plotting to put us in harm's way yet again – and I don't mean just the Murmansk run level of harm: I'm talking Trappageddon harm. As I've already said, from the start I'd been convinced there was no way the old skinflint would voluntarily offer to charter his pride and joy to the Allied cause for such a perilous voyage, and certainly not at bog-standard Ministry of War Transport rates. Not without harbouring some tortuous hidden agenda aimed at maximizing the bottom line.

Yet how, in God's name, might even Edward Trapp, skul-dugger extraordinary, possibly hope to manipulate a whole Russian convoy – forty-odd merchantmen plus their ring of fighting escorts – to serve his own ends . . . ? Which took me back full circle to questioning the reason for his turning up in Ireland in the first place? And even more mystifyingly, to the riddle of why he'd deliberately got himself arrested and frog-marched back to face the coming battle when he could easily have lain low in that safe and neutral haven . . . Dribblin, was it? No: *Droolin*. Droolin Bay: a destination which – equally worry-provoking – seemingly represented the heartland of an Irish dissident faction not exactly noted for its allegiance to the British Crown.

There was only one way to find out. Confront him. It would demand finesse. Prizing a totally alien concept like the truth from Trapp entailed meticulous preparation. I resolved to broach the matter obliquely during the small hours of the morning when his defences were at their lowest ebb, then go in for the kill.

Having tossed and turned sleeplessly throughout the first three of my precious four-hour watch below, and during that misery become ever more paranoid, by the time I'd trailed up to the bridge well before I'd been due to relieve him my own defences had collapsed to ground zero and I'd decided Sod the subtle approach.

Thus: 'What the hell made you leg it to Ireland instead of Scotland from your port of loading, Trapp?' I'd accosted soon as my eyes had adjusted from the 25-watt gloom of my single cabin light bulb to the blackness of the night.

Immediately he looked shifty. Well, even more shifty than his normal shifty. I could always tell when he was being shifty. There was something about the way Trapp's partly severed cap lid bobbed ever more agitatedly in that . . . well, that shifty sort of way.

'You're a minute late relievin', Mister,' he countered weakly, caught off guard.

'No he's no', Captin. Mister Miller's fifty-nine minutes early,' Gorbals Wullie corrected punctiliously from his slouch across the wheel before his brain caught up with his mouth too late to avoid a pointy elbow in the ribs.

'So don't try changing the subject,' I growled. 'Why *Ireland*?'

The cap bounced more violently. It's not only weasels that resort to aggression when cornered. 'Never mind that, Mister. What I wants to know is . . . is . . .' He searched desperately for a nit-pick. 'Is why you 'aven't corrected them new Arctic charts the NCS people put aboard yet?'

'Because they *are* new. Meaning up to date. Which not only makes 'em unique for this ship but also quite irrelevant considering there's no one else aboard can understand a chart except you and me, and you won't bother to. And anyway, as we're highly unlikely to even make it as far as Russia, your concern is somewhat academi—?'

I broke off abruptly. The cap lid was beginning to wallop faster; shifty had escalated to uneasy shifty – but *why*? I mean, all I'd said was we were highly unlikely to make it as far as *Russ*—?

'Trapp?' I probed uneasily. 'Trapp, you're being devious. You *are* hiding something, aren't you?'

He started trying to shout me down then: the last refuge of the guilty. 'It's time you understood *I'm* Master afore God of this vessel, Mister; not you. An' that means I don't 'ave to stand 'ere to be questioned by . . . by CREW!'

'I'm NOT crew!' I yelled back, stung to the core at being lumped together with the other subnormal flotsam comprising his gang. 'Well, all right: I *am* crew – but only thanks to some ill-informed admiral an' that bloody man with the brown suit from the Ministry . . . so if you *don't* bloody like what I say then you, bein' Master before God, can, without having to ask so much as a by-your-leave even from *Him*, go take a runnin' jump over the fuckin' WALL!'

I trailed to a halt yet again. The cap had vanished. Either I'd been right all along about him being a ghost, or he'd taken my advice and topped himself – which was too much to hope for – or he'd stomped off the bridge in pique.

'An' you – shut *up!*' I rounded on Wullie.

'I havenae *said* nuthin',' Wullie protested.

'In case you do.'

OK, so I accept I should have been more alert to the respon-sibilities I'd inherited. I could have shown greater alacrity about assuming the watch following Trapp's inexcusable deser-tion of his post without giving a proper handover – *any* handover, for that matter – but, apart from having registered from the now looming black-cut silhouettes before us that we'd nearly caught up with the convoy by then, I again sought solace in self-denial, quite forgetting we were steaming flat out with no one looking ahead.

. . . Until Wullie started muttering from the wheelhouse.

'Say again?' I demanded irritably, annoyed that my wallow in self-pity was being disturbed.

No response. He kept his eyes fixed obstinately on the compass in petulant refusal to acknowledge my existence. Just continued to mutter darkly under his breath.

'Dammit: report when I order you to, sailor!' I ventured experimentally.

There persisted an even longer silence. Finally:

'Make up yer bluidy mind,' Wullie retorted, all aggrieved by his role model having turned on him so hurtfully. 'A minnit ago ye wis telling me tae shut up.'

'I'm sorry,' I gritted, suddenly weary of confrontation. 'But I'm your chief officer and I'm allowed to be cruel. Apart from which I've been, well . . . preoccupied with keeping a weather eye cocked for any hostiles approaching.'

Yeah, right. The foul mood I was in, the only hostile I'd been preoccupied with was my own captain. But it was only a *little* white lie. I mean, I did have a reputation for infallibility to live up to, even though the Admiral hadn't quite seen it as such.

'Then ye've done a lousy job of it,' Wullie grumbled, refusing to be placated.

'Job of what?'

'Keepin' an eye cocked.'

'Oh? And pray tell me why?' I entreated with heavy sarcasm.

Wullie triumphantly extended a grubby arm. Virtue had finally routed the Evil Officer Class, and all had come good again in his minuscule world.

''Cause there's been a whole warship steaming less than a heaving line's throw aff our port quarter for the past five minnits.'

The escorting corvette had dropped astern to check we were all right. Obviously they hadn't yet heard about my little prank on Flags, or Trapp's two-fingered tooting episode, otherwise they might have been more tempted to illuminate us in the beam of their searchlight on the off chance that some so-far undetected U-boat might be cruising for a bruising.

'Good morning, Captain,' her Tannoy crackled soon as her bridge party had finished assessing our state of seaworthiness and regained the power of speech. 'Welcome to the Iceland Express. Please begin manoeuvring to take up your convoy station in position Wun Thuree.'

Not in the mood for tolerating irony from some . . . some *ex*-employer, and already furious at being caught unawares, I rushed out to the wing clutching Trapp's shiny new loud hailer. 'I'm *not* the bloody captain f'r a start, pal,' I roared back, stung to the core at being so insulted. 'I wouldn't *be* captain of a rust-bucket like this.'

'Wot you got that for?' Trapp's voice grumbled over my shoulder, having been tempted by the commotion to resurface like some over-curious squid. 'The Navy gave *me* that hailer, Mister. It's not to be used willy-nilly by . . .'

'Say 'crew' again, Trapp,' I promised darkly, 'And you *will* go over the side.'

'. . . unauthorized personnel,' he concluded amiably – rather too amiably. *Far* too amiably . . . ? Not that I was given opportunity to challenge him on why the happy face? I wasn't granted time to.

Being fully preoccupied by then with also wondering why the *Charon*'s engine had suddenly stopped?

Boasting the underwater profile of a concrete post office, and being built not dissimilarly, Trapp's Queen o' the Seas began to slow immediately: so abruptly in fact that the corvette, taken by surprise, overshot us before she engaged full astern and began to fall back. In the interim I allocated a few moments of quality time to panicking while trying to remember where I'd last seen my lifejacket which, considering it bore an expiry date immediately following the First Great War, promised to prove something of a misnomer in itself. But I hadn't been joking about the possibility that a U-boat might just have been watching from just outwith depth charge range, and every little might help.

'Oh, botheration. We seem to 'ave developed engine trouble,' the voice at my shoulder exclaimed mildly. Disconcertingly mildly, to say the least. Then, even more disturbingly, 'What a wretched nuisance.'

'You sure you're all right, Captin?' Wullie probed warily through the darkness; conditioned to expect Trapp's bog-standard volatile reaction to stimuli such as his boat being broken. 'Usually you'd be tryin' to kick seven bells oot o' me at this stage.'

'I'm perfectly well, Able Seaman,' Trapp assured him politely. 'But thank you f'r asking.'

Right – that was *it*! Him being courteous to *Wullie* . . . ? I just knew we were heading for deep trouble then. That hidden agenda of his . . . ? He'd started on it.

By the time my second half-panic subsided, we'd lost all way: lying dead in the water with the funnel *putt-putting* quietly and the ash from it speckling down to crunch underfoot in the absence of any dispersing wind of passage. Yet still Trapp displayed no sense of urgency. Almost as if he *wanted* to underline our predicament to the Navy?

'As you keep harping on ad nauseam: *you're* Master afore God, Trapp. So bloody *do* somethin'!' I snarled, rounding on him. 'Get on the voice pipe to the Chief and find out what's wrong.'

A bad mistake, catching Trapp unprepared like that. It allowed me just enough time to register him hurriedly erasing a blatantly smug expression. Hardly the kind of reaction one might expect from an old man who suddenly finds his ship placed in jeopardy.

'Can we assume you've developed engine trouble, Captain?'

the corvette questioned tinnily: this time without the slightest trace of surprise which, in itself, was hardly surprising. They'd probably opened a book on her mess decks from the moment we'd sailed: betting on how many hours we'd keep going before our first breakdown. With double your money for the *Charon* cutting straight to the chase and capsizing.

'You can indeed, sir,' Trapp hollered back while ostentatiously holding his shiny megaphone up for everyone to admire. Including any stalking periscope watcher, should the moon choose the wrong moment to glint. 'A busted over an' under thingummy. No need to baby sit us. Me Chief's a gem. Have it fixed in no time.'

'He's a *what*?' I stared incredulously. 'The guy's even less of a gem than your last mate was. According to the Bosun, before you signed him on for buttons, the nearest he'd got to an engineering career was valeting motor cars in a garage.'

'Rolls *Royce* motor cars, Mister,' Trapp supplemented; skilfully turning the main thrust of my criticism. 'Top of 'is profession, that makes him.'

'Apologies for leaving you as a straggler yet again, Captain, but orders and the greater good call,' the corvette acknowledged with the white water already threshing under her counter as she made to head back to those of her charges really deserving of protection. 'No U-boat activity presently reported in this area so hopefully you'll stay lucky. Make for Seidisfjord once your repairs are effected. You have twelve hours grace to play catch us if you can. Until then, *au revoir* and *bon voyage*.'

Trapp watched them go and chuckled. 'Them RN lads. Real cards. Always a quip, eh?'

Trapp had *never* chuckled over anything to do with the Royal Navy before.

'More to the point,' I challenged, 'how can you possibly know it's an over-and-under whatever without checking? There's no one able to diagnose an engine fault withou—'

The instant his cap began to tremble I realized that extracting an explanation remotely verging on the truth would prove as productive as attempting to collect fog in a bucket. My only small achievement was that I now knew where our

Master afore God had disappeared to during his temporary flight from the bridge. He'd scuttled below to the engine room. I could tell that much by the shiny new blob of oil on his hat and the fresh smear of coal dust across the front of his reefer jacket.

But Sod's Law, being Trapp's ally and my adversary, was to ensure I'd gain little satisfaction from having figured that particular mystery. Come to that, all I'd actually done was to burden myself with yet another riddle. Because *why* had the old schemer contrived to go down to the engine room in the middle of this particular night just as we were about to overhaul the convoy and, even more suspiciously, only minutes before our main engine mysteriously broke down?

Assuming it *had* broken down, of course?

I mean, perish the thought, but some voyager more cynical than I might just have been tempted to wonder whether Edward Trapp hadn't ordered our so-called Chief to, well . . . stop it on *purpose*?

A funny thing happened during our brief respite in Seidisfjord . . . no, I've explained that non-event stuff already, so you'll know what I mean. Suffice to say that nothing catastrophic took place. Meaning we managed to leave again in much the same condition as we'd arrived. Parlous: in no fit state to risk sailing to the nearest breaker's yard, never mind skirt the ice barrier, and with everyone's morale apart from Trapp's at rock bottom.

In actual fact Iceland hadn't provided so much a respite as a pit stop: the *Charon* only arriving in time to find the motor ships among our consorts topping up bunkers from a waiting fleet tanker, and again making ready for sea in preparation for the final long haul. But we were able to drop anchor briefly and without incident due, largely, to my repeated exhortations to the foc'sle party not to bloody *stand* on it next time we let it go. Less than an hour later the same thing happened – or didn't happen – when we weighed. No one contrived to immolate himself, not even to lose a minor extremity out of sheer stupidity . . . and anyway, I'd made a special point of hiding the boat hook.

. . . But wait. I tell a lie. One funny thing *did* happen while we were there. An incident so funny unexpected and, indeed, so funny peculiar that it almost passed me by without registering.

Once anchored, and with Wullie despatched to make marmalade sandwiches – a rare breakfast treat only sanctioned by Trapp when in one of his expansive moods, meaning hardly ever – we'd found ourselves leaning together over the bridge rail in silent contemplation of what was revealing itself to be a land of magic in the early dawn.

Layer upon layer of mist had begun to dissolve as the sun burned through: each melting wisp disclosing yet another joyous vista. To port, starboard, and astern crowded the blue Icelandic mountains, still wearing fluff caps of autumn snow with more cotton wool balls hiding in the gulleys. It seemed every pink-roofed chalet, dotted at random above the tiny settlement, overlooked its own special fairy stream cascading by the door. Seidisfjord itself was but a line of simple wooden houses built on stilts along both sides of a dirt track road leading to a picture postcard fishing harbour. Smoke from a hundred cosy fires rose straight aloft from chimneys as crooked as the *Charon*'s funnel, into what was promising to become a cloudless day.

Ideal conditions for convoy-spotting aircraft; a prayer fulfilled for the wolf packs. But we still had eighty miles to steam before we moved beyond the range of our own Allied air cover and in those latitudes, even in autumn, the weather could turn manic in a flash.

Overcast and fog, I prayed for nervously. Please God, send us fog. And seas as high as those mountains out there.

There came a *plop* and a swirl in the water just below the downside of our lopsided wing.

'I 'ad a fish once,' Trapp was stirred to reminisce.

'I know, you told me,' I reminded him unkindly, still discommoded by his earlier recalcitrance. 'You ate it alive.'

'After twelve days adrift without water or vittles, Mister, it was either that or tucking into me shipmate . . . well, my half shipmate,' Trapp pointed out reasonably. 'And anyway, that's not the fish I'm referrin' to. I'm talking about the goldfish I kept as a pet.'

'Thought you kept Gorbals Wullie as a pet,' I retorted,

resolved to remain grumpy. 'Mind you, one *would* be able to hold a more intelligible conversation with a goldfish.'

He didn't seem to mind. In fact his eyes had gone a bit misty. 'Horace, his name was. Won the little mite at a fairground in Constantinople. 'Ad a little glass bowl he'd steam round an' round in. Full of tricks, 'e was. Sometimes he'd even turn, then swim the other way.'

'Wullie can do that. It's what he did last time I threw him overboard.'

'Used to feed 'im crumbs of hard-tack biscuit.'

'Wullie?'

'Horace. 'E used to love the weevils in 'em. They was his . . . his . . .'

His voice faltered then. Frowning surreptitiously I registered, to my disconcertion, a tear trickling ever so slowly down one leathery cheek. '. . . his *special* treat,' Trapp concluded sadly.

'What happened to him?' I asked kindly.

'Gone f'r marmalade sandwiches.'

'I meant *Horace.*'

'He died.'

I hardly dared ask. The words *sympathy* and *Trapp* had never before sprung to mind as likely components of the same sentence. But I couldn't resist the impulse.

'Died of what?'

Trapp uttered a long, shuddering sigh.

'Seasickness,' he sniffed.

It would niggle at me later: that conversation. Caught unawares, I'd actually found myself growing to respect Edward Trapp. Even to *like* him for the previously unsuspected marshmallow concealed within that usually flint-edged carapace.

OK, so I wasn't persuaded to like him all *that* much. And certainly not for more than a few minutes. But the incident would, nevertheless, prove enough to make me view his coming antics with a slightly more tolerant eye.

A fatal error where Trapp was concerned. For therein lay weakness.

And in weakness, germinated the seeds of madness.

. . . So thus it was that our twelve-ship feeder group sailed for a desolate cross on a chart roughly sou'west by west of Jan

Meyen Island and just north of the Arctic Circle. It was to be at that secret position that we would rendezvous with the main body of PQ whatever-it-was.

From that point on, nothing funny would happen to us on our way to Murmansk.

Not in any sense of the word.

Nine

I'd never seen so many ships seemingly jostling for posses-
sion of much the same area of sea when the two elements
met up. Together we virtually filled the horizon. Forty and
goodness-knows-how-many-more merchantmen: a fleet
carrier; cruisers; destroyers; corvettes – two ack-ack escorts
bristling like sea-hogs with the multiple barrels of pom-poms
constantly tracking what had now become a leaden, threatening sky.

'I hope the rest of them masters knows 'ow to keep a proper
course,' Trapp grumbled without a trace of irony as we
approached.

'Yes, Trapp,' I said, eyeing Gorbals Wullie at the wheel.
His little pink tongue already protruded from the corner of
his mouth. Obviously Wullie's helmsmanship skills were being
stretched to the limit, and we hadn't even begun our manoeuvre
to slot into station within the main body yet.

'What's our thingy number again?' Trapp muttered, staring
with furrowed brow at the convoy plan. Even he was showing
signs of strain at joining what was increasingly shaping to
become the maritime equivalent of a stock car race between
deep-laden juggernauts all heading for the same spot; an
apprehension hardly eased by our being half the size of most
of 'em.

'Thirteen,' I said wearily for the umpteenth time. 'Our
formation number's bloody thirteen on this leg too.'

'Then we're lucky it's no' a Friday, eh?' Wullie chipped in
jauntily, determined to earn some much-needed kudos by
playing the chirpy chappie joking in the face of being squashed
like a fly between two colliding flat irons.

'It *is* a bloody Friday!' I snarled. 'So jus' watch your heading
an' SHUT . . .'

Wullie fixed me with a reproachful, expectant stare and I

recalled his counter-attack following the corvette incident. I couldn't cope with being sent to Coventry again quite so soon. Not considering his instant response would be vital when a change of course was ordered.

'. . . your mind to the possible hazards we are about to encounter,' I concluded lamely.

A flag hoist suddenly broke out above the Commodore's bridge ahead: gaily coloured bunting bright above the sombre grey freighter, fluttering and snapping in the wind.

'What's he saying, Mister' what's 'e *sayin'*?' Trapp agitated as I thumbed hastily through the signal book. Yet another unanticipated turn of events: him betraying nervousness like that. Not at all his usual reaction to authority, particularly when it wore a military hat. Two fingered toot-tooting was more his style.

All joiners wheel in columns twenty degrees to starboard . . .

Abruptly the Commodore's hoist dropped like a stone. 'Execute!' I snapped.

'St'b'd ten the wheel,' Trapp ordered tensely.

'Which way's starboard?' Wullie asked.

Five minutes later the blood from his nose had reduced to a trickle.

'Ah wis only joking,' Wullie sniffed. With difficulty.

'Flawless, Mister. Told you she wus a Queen, di'n't I? Slipped into station smooth as a jelly slid on a plate,' Trapp said an hour later, with two ships ahead and two ships behind us making up the port outer column of that new entity now sprawled across something in the order of a six-mile frontage, with a perimeter in excess of . . . say, fifteen?

I sneaked a covert glance. I couldn't get used to the way he'd continued to surprise me since our brief sojourn in Iceland. First a tear for a fish, then his uncharacteristic nervousness – and now *this*? Trapp looking . . . well, looking almost *proud* of doing something worthwhile.

Because it *was* pride, you know, though he'd have died rather than admit it. The pride of belonging, of coming together with his peers in a great and heroic endeavour. It was the one emotion that Edward Trapp the renegade, the archetypal loner, had abrogated all right to experience until then. Remember how I described the last time we'd been privileged to watch

a momentous event together – back in Malta on the eve of
our first enforced contract of service for King and Country?
About how the rest of us: the Admiral, the generals, the gunners
and matelots and airmen, the women, the children; everyone
on that beleaguered island had welcomed the deliverance
against all odds of the near-foundering tanker *Ohio*, yet how
Trapp had declined to cheer in company with the rest of us?
How he'd simply held himself aloof from it all as if the whole
celebration had been the concern of some other misguidedly
patriotic society.

But I'd also added, if you'll recall, that even then I'd questioned whether making such a harsh observation had really
been justified. Because there *had* been something more than
detachment, albeit only faintly discernible in those usually
unfathomable eyes. A sort of regretful acknowledgement of
something that, at the time, Trapp had assumed was to be
denied to him forever. A rueful awareness that had he followed
a less impulsive, less self-serving course, then such a brave
moment might also have been a part of his life too.

Yet now, as ever, the wheel of Fate had taken a further
unlikely turn for Edward Trapp. This particular brave moment
did involve him notwithstanding his earlier and still unexplained
attempt to evade it. A moment made even more stirring by the
traditional naval ceremony of Sounding Off when, as the two
elements of Allied escort vessels converged to work as one,
so every bosun's pipe began to keen and every man-o'-war's
siren began to shriek, while those of their complements who
weren't stood-to at action stations lined each forecastlehead to
salute the senior ship.

A half-puff later and even normally phlegmatic merchant
captains were sounding their foghorns, lowing sombrely like
the herd of sea cattle war had forced them to become, while
many of them . . . especially the American vessels – that
brand new tanker out of Frisco; those Liberty ships we
derided as having been built by the mile an' cut off to length
but still impressed us with their sea-keeping qualities nevertheless; the *Sam* boats whose gum-chewing, tobacco-spitting
crews really knew how to project pride in their origins – a
lot of *them* hauled down smoke-grimed, wind-tattered sea
ensigns before temporarily replacing them with their best
Stars and Stripes kept clean for very special occasions. And

then others followed with their own bright maritime ensigns. Within my own range of vision I sighted a Pole; four Dutchmen; three Norwegians and a Dane; a Frenchman, a Finn, two Canadians and more British Red Dusters than you could shake a marlinespike at.

Yet therein lay the enigma that was Trapp. He didn't do any of those things. Not hoisting an ensign I understood because, being an international outcast belonging to no port of registry, the *Charon* never flew one anyway, although she did carry a handy assortment of illegal bunting side by side with the false cargo manifests and forged bills of lading held ready in Trapp's cabin to produce for any customs cutter or inshore gunboat uncharitable enough to suspect she might be a smuggler.

But the whistle? Now his reluctance to join in the cattle chorus *was* a bit more difficult to explain. I'd even reached for the foghorn's lanyard myself when he curtly ordered me to leave it. Almost as if, well . . . as if Trapp, for all his po-faced pride at having miraculously completed the joining manoeuvre, didn't wish to be *too* closely associated with that grand argosy. As if he felt slightly ashamed at being counted in the company of heroes. As if . . . as if . . . ? Oh, I dunno. Or more specifically: I didn't know what he was planning to do at the time. Either way, in the end I dismissed the unease that briefly assailed me by assuming Trapp's being loath to blow our steam whistle had been down to his usual reason for not doing anything. Steam used coal. An' coal cost money.

Later I was to regret not having pressed him more closely. And by later, I mean too late.

But apart from that, only one note of real Allied discord was struck. There had been three Soviet ships in that PQ convoy. Genuine USSR, I mean; not our own clumsily counterfeit СИДЯОИ still masquerading as a sheep in sheep's clothing. Not one of those vessels made concession to the near certainty that, during the coming nine days or so, fellow seafarers speaking a multitude of foreign tongues would die in the process of carrying succour to their own hard-pressed Mother Russia. Not one crewman or, as was often the case, crew woman, could be seen on deck observing that haunting ceremony. Not one whistle blew; not one scrap of Hammer and Sickle bunting flew. Brothers in arms . . . *Comrades*? Their bosun-commissars had ensured they took refuge behind an iron curtain of fear long before there ever was an Iron Curtain.

So it had been a poignant moment, but a slightly disheartening moment as well; being one that further served to increase my niggling sense of guilt at having judged Trapp too harshly over the *Ohio* incident – or had, indeed, allowed his constantly trying to get me killed to unduly influence my opinion of the bloody man. Because I couldn't help wondering whether my pirate captain with the wobbly hat might just have been right all along in his bloody-minded determination to refuse to pay homage to any party or state . . . and that was a *very* dangerous frame of mind to adopt – to concede there might be *any* logical justification for Trapp's appalling behaviour throughout his life.

But the Soviet attitude to this convoy alone demonstrated that war does all too often demand a forced alliance between mutually mistrusting bedfellows. And I didn't doubt such cynical manipulation of the world's cannon fodder had proved to be the one game that Edward Trapp, seemingly perceptive even as a boy marooned on a sliver of wreckage with nothing but a part-corpse and a fish to sustain him, had determined he would not play.

. . . At that point I gave up reflecting on the enigma that was Trapp, and went down to my foetid cabin feeling angry with myself. Three times in as many days, I'd done it – allowed myself to think benignly of the man. Three *times*, dammit!

Get a grip, Miller. Be like those Russkis – no concessions. Let mutual hostility and suspicion remain your credo. Always be on your guard.

Or next time you could be dead quicker'n that bloody goldfish of his, before you twig he's dropped you in it once again.

Some way north of Jan Meyen Island, with Iceland a fond memory astern and Greenland over two hundred miles off our port quarter, Gorbals Wullie was first to sight it.

'Is yon an albatross aboot a mile off?' he frowned, pointing ahead and slightly to starboard.

I fumbled to focus our only visual aid: a pair of Yokohama binoculars which Trapp persisted in maintaining were perfectly adequate despite one eyepiece having fallen off some time around 1933 and the other being taped in place with Elastoplast. Where was my ex-Admiral when I needed his glasses?

'It's a Condor. A good seven miles away,' I said, suddenly concerned.

'Ah thought condors wis vulture birds that lived on mountains,' Wullie frowned with a rare flash of awareness that surprised me. God help us, I thought despite the dispiriting news he'd just delivered: now I'm even thinking kindly of *Wullie*. You're losing it, Miller. Losing all contact with reality.

'I mean a Condor with a capital C. It's a Focke Wulf.'

'No it's no',' Wullie insisted, reverting to type. 'It's a fuckin' bird.'

'I mean a Focke Wulf Condor *aircraft*. FW 200 long range recce . . . it hasn't taken them long to find us.'

It flew around the convoy, occasionally disappearing behind cloud but always rematerializing a little while later. Already it would be radioing back to its Norwegian base logging details of our course, speed of advance and the composition of the convoy. Sometimes it would turn and fly anti-clockwise for a change, just as Trapp's late goldfish Horace had been wont to do, the ingenious little bugger. Some claimed that was to stop its aircrew getting bored, others swore it was through a Teutonic sense of chivalry – to prevent us watchers from becoming dizzy. *Snoopy Joe* the regular Murmansk hands called it as if it were a singular companion. There were a lot of Snoopy Joes in fact, despite such familiar personalization: sometimes the long lean FWs, more often the ubiquitous Blohm Voss bat-winged jobs. As soon as one ran low on fuel it would be replaced by another, but all with one common task: to help vector the bomber squadrons on to us while giving early warning of our coming to the wolf packs marshalling in the more distant north east. More immediately they would save fruitless hours of periscope scanning for any lone hunter-killer already searching this area: help its Kapitanleutnant short-circuit the wasteful sizzle time so to speak, and concentrate on pricking the sausages.

In some ways it was a further non-event, albeit not at all funny: a mutually agreed stand-off almost, in that the escorts didn't fire a shot because Snoopy stayed just out of range, while Snoopy didn't try to bomb us because his payload was represented by additional fuel tanks. Occasionally our own Seafires would launch from the carrier to chase it away – just to let Jerry know not to get too complacent – but as soon as they'd returned, so would it.

'I'd better let the Captin know,' Wullie said, predictably unenthusiastic.

'Why bother?' I said, still kindly disposed towards him. 'He's a devotee to the principle of killing the messenger. You'll only get shouted at when he blames you for the Luftwaffe spotting us. Come to that, all he'll do is shake his fist at it and make it angry.'

Trapp turned up anyway. Any trouble looming and he'd inevitably materialize just in time to aggravate it. Two minutes later he appeared at the head of the ladder red in the face, exhibiting a light dusting of flour, and grumpy. I was familiar with the symptom.

'Had another row with the cook, have you?'

'That bloody cook. I told 'im to bake loaves o' bread: he went an' done pancakes.'

'Those pancakes *were* his loaves of bread.'

'*Bloody* cooks!' Trapp repeated. But he didn't have the same enthusiasm for it. He'd never really enjoyed a proper vein-bulging, head-to-furious-head argymint in the galley since he'd got his former Greek cook killed. Now *those* domestic dramas really had been barneys to cherish, I reflected nostalgically. The last one they'd had was world class. It had escalated from Trapp's default position of demanding mince an' chips f'r dinner while the Cook, who could've given *Trapp* lessons in bloody-minded obduracy, had finally dug his heels in, insisting he was only prepared to do cheeps wit' da meence: not the other way round.

Whereupon Trapp's face had suffused with rage. 'So forget mince. I wouldn't '*ave* yer bloody mince. You can't cook decent British mince anyroad an' . . . an'. . . .'

He'd hesitated then, trawling pleasurably to dredge for the most devastating insult he could devise. 'An' I'd order you ter do spaghetti instead, except yer spaghetti's *worse* than yer mince. I mean, *anyone* c'n cook spaghetti better'n you. The ship's *cat* could cook spaghetti better'n you . . .'

'But we havenae *got* a ship's cat,' Wullie had interjected, mystified.

'Thass because Olive Oyle 'ere turned it into ragout three nights ago.'

'Oh aye,' Wullie had mused appreciatively. 'I thought yon stew wis tasty. Mind you, ah did wonder aboot they whiskery bits.'

Well, by then the Cook had become incandescent. 'Spaghetti? *Spaghetti . . .*? You theenk I looks like a bluddy Eyetie, hah? 'Ow many times I 'ave to tell you I am GREEK gentlemans, you terrible Captin. An' Greek gentlemans never *ever* cooks the spaghetti. No one even dare ask me to cook the spaghetti all the time I 'olds the post of 'Ead Commis Chef at the 'Otel Majestique in Salonika, I bluddy tell you.'

'*Chef*?' Trapp had bellowed back incredulously. 'CHEF is it now? When I hired you, Fatty, you wus second assistant bloody DISHWASHER, you was – an' *that* wus only in Georgie Kyriakopoulos's bug-ridden doss 'ouse next door!'

Dead now: that most fondly recalled culinary adversary. Shot by the Afrika Korps, he'd been. Mind you, Trapp *had* contrived, albeit by accident, to arrange a place for him in history. Not many Greek ships' cooks could claim to have been topped by the German *Army*; especially when still aboard their own boat.

But that's another story.

'Recce plane's found us,' I reported. 'The carrier's just launched a chaser.'

'Whereaway?' he said curtly, still smarting over the flat-bread. Or rather, flat bread.

'Two points on the starb'd bow at the moment: flying right to left.'

'Wish we 'ad a gun,' Trapp muttered resentfully. 'They should've given us a gun.'

'He's too far away, and it's just as well they didn't. Give this crowd access to a gun and they'd cause more destruction to the convoy than a wolf pack.'

'Too early for the wolf packs. That Admiral Donuts is a crafty sod. He's already been pushing us further an' further north. He'll wait to corner them once they gets their backs up against the ice barri—'

He broke off abruptly and seemed annoyed with himself. Immediately my earlier suspicions flooded back. Was that an unconscious slip of the tongue? What was it about his reference to the ice barrier that had caused him evident discomfiture? And even more disturbingly: what did he mean by 'they' ...? Surely *we* were just as much a part of 'they' as *they* – those other merchantmen – were, so ...?

Oh, Lord, I noted despondently, his cap's begun to bob already. I still tried.

'Who's *they*, Trapp? Your saying *they* like that makes it sound as if you see this trip as being *them* and *us*. And anyway, why did mentioning the ice barrier make you look guilty?'

But he'd had time to regroup. And Trapp dug into defensive mode was unassailable.

'Dunno what you mean, Mister: all that they an' them stuff. All I said was she wus a *nice carrier*.' He jerked a thumb in the direction of a second Seafire taking to the air like a disturbed wasp from its grey sea nest. 'Very comforting.'

'No, you didn't.'

'Yus I did.'

'*No* you bloody di—' I saw the way it was going and decided to save my energy for dodging the Germans. I wasn't going to give up entirely, though. He wasn't the only one entitled to a childish moment.

'All right,' I grated. 'Then they'd do as much damage as a *single* U-boat would.'

'Don't be daft, Mister,' he jeered, still determined to have the last word. 'It's 'ardly likely there'd be any U-boat lucky enough to find us this early in the voya—'

I wished he hadn't said that. As soon as Trapp made a prediction, events inevitably conspired to prove him wrong. There came a long, rolling *booooommm* from the other side of the convoy and our first casualty, one of the big flush-decked freighters in Column Nine, began to veer out of line while falling back with smoke already pouring from her fore-deck hatches.

'... though I grant yer, it *is* still possible,' Trapp concluded. Shaken.

We'd maintained our current speed and heading as required by standing orders, albeit somewhat erratically given the state of our steering gear. Other vessels in convoy had been briefed to act as rescue ships. Happily for any potential survivors, Trapp's *Charon* wasn't one of them.

We walked through the wheelhouse to the starboard wing and watched the torpedoed ship slip remorselessly astern. The flag hoists began fluttering as the Commodore's vessel ordered the remaining merchantmen of Column Nine to close up while the small steamer nominated as rescue vessel turned about to tend to her first client. For the next hour or so she would be self-electedly vulnerable to a second torpedo attack herself: the equivalent of being a straggler while she delayed on her mission of mercy, and to her crew it would seem a very long hour indeed. Two of the sleek grey destroyers and a tiny corvette had detached from the main escort group and were homing in on the U-boat's estimated position, ASDICs pinging hollowly as they sighed through a rising sea. She would have dived deep and turned hard; her commander maybe even brave enough and cheeky enough to try to run under the convoy itself to claim another victim. Meaning his next target could be a vessel on our side.

'Keep a sharp watch for torpedo tracks, you,' Trapp called back to the port wing lookout, conceding not one whit to the man's limitations as an early warning operative considering he had one eye blanked off by a black, albeit admittedly highly professional-looking, pirate's patch: an accoutrement which, by itself, wouldn't have been too disadvantageous had he not been further inhibited by the sight of his other requiring assistance from a sort of monocle. I say 'sort of' because it had been fashioned from one lens of a broken pair of spectacles stuck to his eyebrow with Trapp's ubiquitous Elastoplast.

Dead-Eye Alf, the crowd called him – no, don't ask . . . oh, all right; I'll tell you anyway. It was to save confusion I'd gathered, because we already had a Dick on board: the Bosun . . . Dick Head *his* name was. According to Trapp, at least.

The casualty lay dead in the water now; drifting broadside across the convoy's line of departure. I was relieved to note she appeared to be sinking only slowly by the head suggesting that, with her having been torpedoed forward in the region of number two hatch, there was a sporting chance that few, if any, crewmen would have been caught in the immediate area of the blast. With the sea state still moderate, plus a fair chunk of luck and no second torpedo, they'd get them all off before she took her final plunge. Hopefully even the watchkeeping engineers below would have time to clamber from her remorse-lessly filling bowels.

But don't get me wrong: such dispassionate assessment doesn't take account of the shock, injury and sense of loss they'd already suffered. Every man had lost his shipboard possessions: that tin box of watercolour paints; the especially thick wool scarf knitted by the wife and saved for the day you sighted your first iceberg; the spare set of Hong Kong dentures in case you lost your originals overboard; the well-thumbed pocket Bible given to you by Mum and Dad with All Our Love, Dear Son, on the eve of your first trip; the second mate's sextant; the deckboy's comic; the lamptrimmer's darning kit . . . all those personal items that helped make the rigours of a seagoing life that little bit more tolerable and which represented, in many cases, everything you owned in the world. Some wouldn't have had much even before the torpedoing. The stokers and trimmers, mostly poor as church mice, might only have begun the voyage with fifty-four pieces of kit – their Merchant Navy discharge book, sweat rag, an' a dog-eared pack of playing cards.

But the greatest loss of all would be their loss of faith: the sudden realization that being just one tree hidden in a whole forest doesn't help one jot if you're the one the woodcutter selects for the chop. To each survivor now dazedly scrambling to abandon, the explosion would have come as traumatic proof that the hope of invulnerability – the determined conviction we all cling to that sudden death only takes the next man – that it won't happen to you – was, after all, an illusion. That brutal confrontation with reality would haunt those seamen throughout every coming day and every sleep-disturbed night for the rest of the war and even after it.

Should, please God, there *be* an after-the-war to look forward to?

''Bout nine thousand ton gross, would you say, Mister?' Trapp mused thoughtfully, one eye screwed ferociously into a squint against the remaining lens of his perfectly adequate binocu-lars. 'Tanks, trucks, bulldozers under her hatches; hospital equipment; four aeroplanes on 'er well decks . . . probably enough vittles to feed five 'undred Russky families f'r a year?'

'Plus eighteen months in the building; the pride and sweat

of two thousand shipyard workers invested in her,' I reflected bitterly. 'All bloody wasted now.'

Of course he misunderstood me. But to me, war would always be an unmitigated foulness: to Trapp, an opportunity.

'That's what gets me too,' he grumbled, shaking his head sorrowfully. 'Them U-boat commanders: they don't have no thought for the commercial implications. At least in the old *Charon* we was able to salvage a few trinkets from them Axis supply ships afore we sank the bastards.'

I eyed him with distaste. Yes, OK: together during those sweltering days and gunfire-shattered nights off the North African coast we'd watched a lot of ships die, sunk most of those ourselves, and you do get hardened to it. You *do* keep repeating to yourself that, in the final analysis, it's them or you. For the first few weeks we'd borne a charmed life: kept our armaments concealed, put false Axis Colours and two fingers up to the Luftwaffe while pretending to be one of their own, and created havoc within Rommel's Mediterranean supply routes – crumbling coasters almost carbon copies of ourselves; dhows loaded to the gunnels with arms and Wehrmacht ration packs; even those tiny Arab caiques working for the enemy which all went to prove that, even then, the Afrika Korps was being forced to scrape the bottom of the logistics barrel.

It had become almost a job of work. Some we boarded and, before we scuttled them, left no doubt in the minds of their terrified crewmen that they should've stuck to the red, white an' blue path of true British Righteousness. Others – those we suspected of carrying radio, who could have compromised our cover – we'd just opened fire on from the night, without any warning at all. It was what they were trying to do to us – already *were* doing to us, dammit, in the middle of the Atlantic and down in the Pacific . . . what they were about to do to us on this Russian convoy, come to that.

So we'd killed a lot of merchant seamen in that hellish period, though probably in no greater numbers than more conventionally delivered Allied bombs or torpedoes would have done. It was war – *Trapp's* bloody War! – and whether Arab, German, Italian or even Vichy French, they were the enemy while they sailed those covert routes.

Or so I'd kept telling myself, anyway.

But that was where I'd drawn the line: not so Trapp. He didn't have a line. Just a profit motive. Because there had been a steadily-accumulating trove of cheap Arabian silver and tawdry bits and pieces in Trapp's cabin, while I and my Royal Navy gunners got sick of eating Wehrmacht-bound sauerkraut and bratwurst ration packs retrieved under the open sights of our 4.7 from ships already with the mark of death on them; all in order to save Trapp a few miserable extra pennies on buying decent vittles . . . and that was what had made it seem a dirty war. Even dirtier than it needed to be.

Almost a trade, in fact. The trade of the privateer. Certainly not a patriotic crusade for the Allied cause as was, say . . . sailing voluntarily in a Murmansk-bound convoy when you could have remained safely hidden behind a neutral flag?

And *that* seeming about-face on Trapp's part was what worried me most. Especially as we got nearer and nearer to the ice barrier.

What dark intention HAD he nearly let slip, by his unconscious reference to *them* and . . . *us*?

Ten

The temperature began to drop like a stone later that afternoon. The Day of the Bombers we called it later. Among other expressions.

Well, torpedo bombers specifically, in the first wave. Heinkel He 115 seaplanes. Six of them in Arctic camouflage: fuselages long, slender and seemingly far too fragile to support the weight of their cumbersome stepped floats.

There wasn't much warning. A sudden urgent flutter of flags and me taken completely by surprise: running into the chartroom to rummage for the code book. 'Five enemy aircraft approaching from . . .'

'The sou' east,' Trapp finished for me triumphantly. 'An' there's six of 'em at least, Mister, but what do them bells an' whistles Royal Navy blokes know?'

'He can be very pedantic, the Captin,' Wullie commented.

'Oh I *do* wish we 'ad a gun,' Trapp fumed predictably.

'See whit I mean?' Wullie confirmed.

'Shurrup and concentrate on remembering which side's port an' which is starboard,' I entreated. 'You may need to employ that knowledge very quickly indeed should, perchance, a torpedo track happen to head our way.'

'Yon wee airyoplanes – they carry *torpedoes*?' Wullie stammered, suddenly unsettled.

Thank God, I reflected gratefully. Thought for a minute he was being brave. And, right at that moment, the psychological equilibrium of my increasingly cartoon-like world was balanced far too finely to cope with a shock like that.

The first puffs of flak appeared above the starboard side of the convoy. *Bang*, *bang*, *bang* the Oerlikons were saying in welcome: *pom-pom-pom* snarled the . . . well – the pom-poms. A vicious flat *crack* from one of the DEMS merchantmen's poopdeck-mounted 4.5s: loud enough to trigger a paroxysm of unbridled jealousy from Trapp. Onwards the black-crossed float planes came, barely two hundred feet above the surface now in the classic approach of the torpedo bomber: so low we only caught intermittent glimpses of them between the staggered ranks of ships. Thank Christ they're on *that* side, the far side of the convoy, I thought, and felt ashamed of myself the instant I'd done so.

'They got one,' Trapp shouted grudgingly even as I watched. One moment a most elegant firefly with clubbed feet; the next a long thin alloy coffin for three men, still carrying forward momentum but arcing with a bizarre grace towards the sea its tail fin and clumsy floats shot clean away. Three . . . no – four . . . distant splashes as some released their lethal munitions and began to pull up and bank away. The remaining Heinkel trailing a stream of smoke from its port engine, stuttering and coughing and maintaining an undeviating course right across the convoy with what was presumably an already-dead pilot at the controls and every ship that 'ad a gun – even a bridge-mounted Lewis gun . . . even a bloody revolver – blazing up at it.

There wasn't even time to duck your head, never mind throw yourself prone as it rocketed twenty feet above our spindleshank smokestack with a white face staring down from the air gunner's blister, dazedly savouring his last few seconds of life. Poor bastard, I thought with a surge of enormous sympathy; the very last image he'll take down to the bottom of the Barents Sea being a close-up view of our *Charon*. Then the seaplane had faltered, begun to dip nose down, descended just low enough for the waves to get all excited and reach up with snatching fingers until one float caught the tip of a particularly voracious, particularly athletic one, whereupon the whole bloody aircraft began to disintegrate in skips and bounds with a terrible rending of men and metal until all that was left was a foam-swirling patch fading slowly astern.

The guns suddenly stopped firing and all went quiet apart from someone aboard a ship half a mile away nervously loosing off a valedictory burst at what must have seemed a particularly threatening seagull. The *torpedoes*, I remembered abruptly . . . they must've hit *some* . . . ?

But seemingly they hadn't. Quite incredible really. These

serried ranks of ducks in a shooting gallery, yet not one had been stroked by death.

'That's sorted the bastards,' Trapp observed with satisfaction, watching as a single wingtip broke surface momentarily on our port quarter, then submerged forever. 'Jerry won't be back f'r a second 'elping now we've shown 'im whose boss.'

'NO, Trapp!' I appealed desperately. '*Please* don't make any more predic—!'

The drone of desynchronized airscrews from the horizon, barely perceptible at first then grumbling louder and louder. More flags bursting out in rainbow warning: *25-plus hostiles approaching* . . . our flakship escorts, dazzle-painted white and black, *whoop-whooping* in a race to form a barrier across the angle of approach . . . the carrier turning hard into the wind to allow her counter-wasps to take off yet again from where they waited aft on her flight deck, propellers spinning impatiently . . . the bloody Cook stomping up the ladder to the bridge and marching aggressively over to glare at Trapp: completely disregarding the commotion. 'An' *another* thing, Captin. Seein' you wus too mean to take on stores in Iceland, we've run outa spuds. All you left me wiv is sprouty ones that 'ave greeny bits stickin' out!'

And there they wus . . . *were*, dammit! Like a swarm of bees homing on a pasture of honey flowers: all the way from Northern Norway and directed straight on to us along the beam of Snoopy Joe's radio direction finder.

'Fuckin' *'ell*!' Wullie muttered, shocked.

'No – fucking Junkers this time,' I snapped. Shocked.

Low level, full frontal they came. Three hundred feet, flat out and spread out. The shrapnel curtain went up as every ship that could bring a weapon to bear opened fire. The sky between us and them became criss-crossed by lines of tracer, pockmarked by black-hanging ack-ack bursts, but *still* those aircraft came; pressing home their attack with a determination that had me thinking ridiculously: *If we were all on the same side we could pacify the bloody world.*

Less than a mile from Formation Number Nine One, their nearest target vessel, and the first aircraft exploding in a giant ball of flame. Then *another* . . . and another streaming smoke! Some of our ragged crew had congregated on the forr'ad well deck like theatregoers in the dress-circle and began cheering although, like I've already said, half of 'em didn't know which side they were supposed to be cheering for. Trapp got apoplectic furious and rushed to hang over the wing. 'Get below an' under COVER! I 'aven't paid out good wages to get yer this far, jus' so's you c'n get killed enjoyin' yerselves at my expense.'

Economics. It was always economics foremost with Trapp.

'Sprouty ones – s*prouty* ones you say?' He raced back, invigorated, to re-engage the Cook. 'Lissen, you: them sprouty bits is nutrition, see? Green-growin' means *fresh*, right? An' as Master afore God I won't tolerate no vittle-vandal accusin' me of feedin' my lads with stale grub . . .'

Quarter of a fast-closing mile to go.

'Excuse me,' I broke in tightly.

'Wait yer *turn*, Mister!'

'Just thought you might like to know . . .'

'WHAT?'

'We're about to be bombed.'

He took one look at the bees which had, by now, grown to fair-sized pterodactyls, and bellowed, 'Then why di'n't you *tell* me? That's what you gets *paid* for, Mister – to tell me we're bein' bombed.'

'Except I 'aven't . . . *haven't*!' I snarled back, finally losing it somewhere between rage and outright terror.

'Haven't *what*?'

'Got paid.'

'Yes you 'ave.'

'*No*, I . . .'

'Orl right, I'll DO the fuckin' sprouty bits then,' the Cook bellowed above the swelling cacophony of gunfire: evidently an adversary who was, much to Trapp's delight, proving himself a worthy successor to our late-departed Greek gentlemans. 'But on the menu I ain't callin' it *Boeuf Surprise* ett Spuds *à la Maritimes* . . .'

Thud . . . the first waterspouts rising, spray-white against the overcast and ever so briefly hanging high above each masthead. *Boooom, thud* . . . some aircraft peeling away now, their pilots unable to bring themselves to face that devastating rebuttal, but the rest, the majority, holding steadfastly to their bomb runs while we – the targets themselves . . . ? Each merchant ship maintaining course with equal determination because where *can* you run to at ten cumbersome knots to evade an enemy doing two-fifty-plus? An' come to that, which way *do* you turn to dodge the stick of high-explosive intended for you, when most of you have a tramp or a tanker or a sluggish freighter to port, starboard, ahead *and* astern? And on top of all *that*, remember: each of our ships, laden deep as we were, would take a full, seemingly endless minute even to *begin* to answer the helm: four or five to even slow appreciably . . . a good half-mile at least, to bring to rest. Even the slightest weakening of resolve on the part of those tight-lipped masters could lead to collisions every bit as destructive as any enemy action and God help each one of us should the vessel ahead suffer catastrophic damage, break all the rules, stop virtually dead in the water because its bows have been blown clean off or its ammo cargo has erupted, leaving its next in line with no choice but to swing hard over to avoid combining with her.

'. . . on the menu it's gonna be Bully an' Green bloody *Salad* – so THERE!' the Cook decreed with gravelly imperiousness before primly turning about, straightening his grimy apron with a Mrs Beeton flourish, and marching from the bridge watched by an admiring Trapp.

'Now *there*, Mister,' Trapp said, dead impressed, 'goes a *proper* ship's cook. Can't boil a dishcloth: makes porridge so watery you can drink it out've a teapot; while the Chief could replate a busted boiler with 'is omelettes. But 'e'd still rather be keel-hauled than admit it.'

He turned briskly to face the remains of the day.

'Now what wus that you was sayin' about bombers?'

The raid happened so fast, yet took so long to happen so fast!

More near misses: more and more ships still bearing a charmed life, straddled by bombs detonating so close alongside that their engineers must've been left with ears echoing like gongs while great cascades of explosive-tainted sea thundered and hissed across the exposed decks above them. There was no aerial formation now; only a pandemonium of snarling grey aircraft weaving like boxers with palsy through that forest of mastheads with little black tadpoles streaming and tumbling end-over-end from gaping bomb bays. Surely it couldn't last – our luck? And then it ceased to. Two columns over on our

starboard beam, a steadily climbing roll of fire-tinged smoke
indicated that one ship had been hit. A doggedly steaming
tramp piled high with deck cargo, far as I could make out,
although she seemed to be continuing to hold her course. A
British Seafire spiralling vertically into the drink with no
chance for her pilot to bale out: another Luftwaffe plane
exploding in a red an' black-starred puff-ball . . . a further
Junkers trailing smoke, corkscrewing through the web of aerial
shrapnel shedding whirling, silvery strips of airframe and
losing height fast – an image which didn't last for more than
a few seconds seeing she was only a hundred feet up when
they took her. A *second* freighter hit by two bombs with the
tell-tale smoke billowing and her foremast keeling sideways
and . . .

More flags from the Commodore. *TWENTY-plus Heinkels
approaching low level bearing two thuree FIFE.*

'Shit!' I muttered.

'*Shit!*' Wullie yelped.

*Fifteen Stukas approaching high level bearing wun seven
zero degrees . . . !*

'SHIT!' even Trapp was moved to exclaim.

Pom-pom-pom . . . Slam! Slam! Slam . . . every AA gunner
in the fleet hanging back in their harnesses by now: steel-
helmeted, duffle-coated, eyes screwed hard into gunsights
juddering like road drills and the white anti-flash hoods drawn
tight around smoke-grimed faces . . . far below them the
ammunition supply numbers, blind to the outside conflict,
surrounded by high explosive within claustrophobic steel
magazines located below the waterline and offering no way
out should the worst happen; stripped to the waist with the
sweat pouring in rivulets and their POs and leading hands
snapping them on; handling and heaving and loading a continuous supply of shells on to pulley hoists which would take
them to the upper decks . . . a desperate moment later and
those same missiles would be reduced to empty, hot-clattering
brass cases ejecting around each gun position to present a
sparkling, ever-present danger to the unwary boot sole. Then
it was handle and heave and hoist even faster . . .

BROOOOoom . . . the roar of twin Junkers *Jumo* aero-engines
– JESUS! Ducking involuntarily, to say nothing of somewhat
belatedly, I stared up in time to glimpse a massive winged

silhouette roar feet above our masthead with little winking red lights saying *Goodbye britisches Seemann und gutes Glück wenn Sie sinken* from its rear-mounted gun: the *good luck when you sink*, Luftwaffe style, arriving in company with a stitch of 7.92-mm machine gun rounds that chopped away a corner of the chartroom abaft the wheelhouse: further ventilated two ventilators: compelled Wullie to shriek '*Kamerad*, I surrender – an' when ye's get back ye can tell yon Mister Goring ah never agreed wi' this bluidy war onyroad . . . !' and caused Trapp to explode with outrage louder than the single bomb that landed close alongside the *Charon's* number three hatch, deluging us with corpse-grey, HE-tainted Barents Sea, while the old hulk shied ten degrees away to starboard with the shock of it.

There hung a slight delay while we made sure we were still connected to our various body parts. Then: 'I thinks I sees an aeroplane comin', Mister Miller,' our spotter-expert, Dead-Eye Alf, finally warned with a glint of pride in his patch.

But better late than never.

'You there! Get back on the wheel an' hold your course,' I snapped at Wullie who'd begun to tip-toe sneakily towards the wheelhouse door – although under which part of ship he planned to take cover that was any safer, eluded me – while Trapp launched into a tirade directed after what had already become a fading hyphen on the horizon: a straight from the wallet homily that covered a comprehensive range of criticisms based on Internashnul Law in general, through quoting each individual clause of the Geneva Convention relating to illegal attacks upon unarmed merchant vessels, and concluding with 'ow he intended to pursue the Third bloody Reich f'r reparations an' damages no matter '*oo* won in the end – not even if it meant 'im, Trapp, *personally* havin' to haul Hitler hisself inter the DOCK . . . !

And he will, I thought wearily. He bloody *will*, you know.

Then the Stukas arrived. Oh, those *bloody* Stukas! If there was ever a war contrivance that so befitted the description of a bat out of hell, it was the Luftwaffe Stuka – the Junkers Ju 87. Even mention of the acronym, derived from its type category Stur*zkampfflugzeug* or falling combat aircraft, is enough to engender in anybody who experienced the blitzkrieg on France and the Low Countries, the Mediterranean sea war, the English Channel convoys, the Libyan campaign, a chill of recollection that courses clear from the nape of the neck to the tail of the spine.

And considering I could tick three out of four boxes on that list, you can imagine how much I looked forward to their targeting me yet again.

It wasn't so much the destruction they caused; other Axis bombers were faster, carried greater and bigger payloads, as the accuracy of their attack combined with the psychological terror they induced in their selected victims. Tiny and, to the unwary, seemingly innocuous specks in the sky above you at first sight, they'd begin their dive from fifteen thousand feet: their pilots literally rolling the aircraft upside-down while pushing the houses lever forward to nose it into its div—?

. . . Sorry, what's that you say? Oh, yeah; right – *why* did I unconsciously refer to the joystick as a houses lever? Ah well, I'd once had a most interesting conversation with a captured Stuka pilot they'd brought into my desert hospital for refit and repair, although, regrettably, sticking his leg back on hadn't proved possible. Nice chap, all the same. Bore no animosity towards the two hulking military policemen permanently stationed by his bed in case he . . . well, hopped it, I suppose. Never been a Nazi, of course, and had never wanted to fight anybody – a bit like Gorbals Wullie in a way except his, my pilot's, English was better.

. . . Anyway, I'd asked him about flying the Stuka he hadn't wanted to fly and he'd told me all about how marvellous it was as a killing machine. About its remarkable technology whereby, once he'd coaxed it into its near-vertical plunge, red tabs would lift from the upper surfaces of its angled gull wings to actuate the automatic dive recovery system should he temporarily lose consciousness by virtue of the 6-G force imposed as the aircraft pulled up at around 350 miles per hour after dropping its lethal cargo. The dive brakes would then be retracted, the throttle opened, the propeller reset to climbing pitch and it was hands around the houses lever before zooming up, up and away into the wild blue yonder in search of other refugee columns.

'I joke, Tommy,' he'd added hastily at that point. 'But we *Stuka Flieger* have always invited a bad press.'

'That houses lever you refer to?' I'd asked, mystified.

He'd grinned a bit at that. Enough to make the duelling scar across his cheek go all crinkly. 'You pull it back, the houses get smaller, *ja*? Push it forward, they get bigger.'

. . . But I digress as ever: seizing on any excuse to delay returning to my self-imposed penance as chronicler of Edward Trapp's first, last, and only concession to the spirit of patriotism and selfless service under the Allied flag.

Or that's what I'd still *thought* he was committed to, even at that stage of the trip. That selfless service to the Allies thing?

But then a fundamental belief in the innate goodness of man, loyalty to one's superior officer, and, above all, a failure to learn from one's previous experience because you're a particularly naive bastard, can ultimately prove a terrible affliction.

Ah, well . . . regrettably I can't afford to hang around any longer, dwelling wistfully on where life might otherwise have taken me in an idyllic, Trapp-less world.

Not now. Not considering the Stukas are just about to peel off over PQ Whatever-it-was.

Die Trompeten Von Jericho: the Trumpets of Jericho, Junkers had christened them; those wind-powered sirens affixed between the Stuka's fixed undercarriage struts. Not all mounted them: some pilots were of the view that the added drag further hampered the performance of an aircraft already slow and vulnerable other than when you kicked its legs from under it and were hurtling groundwards relying entirely on the stress calculations of a designer who wouldn't have to *fly* the fucking plane, reinforced by the conviction that *Gott* really *ist mit uns* like your *Stukegeschwader* padre assured you . . . unless, of course, your wings sheared off or the dive brakes didn't operate according to the manual, at which point you had around one an' a half seconds left to reappraise both your faith in God and your future career path with the Luftwaffe.

In our case it seemed, most of them had opted for the trumpets. Jericho was about to become a very noisy place.

'At least *those* wee ones up there haven't seen us,' Wullie announced with relief, screwing his neck around to look up through the wheelhouse window at the dots. 'They'll be well past in a minnit.'

I squinted skywards too. 'Where was it you were thinking of hiding when you ran away last time?' I asked levelly, beginning to count down.

Six.

Five . . .

'Onywhere, Mister Miller sir,' Wullie frowned, mulling over his options before his expression cleared. 'China, preferably.'

Four . . .

'Well, that's the worst over,' Trapp pronounced, thereby sealing our fate while he watched the last wave of bombers depart leaving a wake of ack-ack bursts astern of them. Quite cheerful, he seemed. But when all was said an' done, a bit chipped off the chartroom plus a couple of holes though a ventilator wouldn't cost *that* much to repair.

Three . . .

I double-checked my former RN-issue steel helmet was screwed securely on my head, making only a slight concession to setting it at the sort of rakish angle favoured by Noel Coward in last year's propaganda film *In Which We Serve*, then firmly tightened its chin-strap watched by an envious Gorbals Wullie. 'Wish I had one o' they tin bonnets,' he observed wistfully. 'But the Captin said they wis too expensive.'

'Never mind,' I offered consolingly. I could risk being nice to him: we were unlikely to have any further conversations. 'When a two-fifty kilo bomb lands on you, the kind of hat you're wearing really doesn't make much difference.'

. . . two . . .

Abruptly Dead-Eye Alf, who hadn't even *seen* the last plane even though it near as dammit hit him on the head, suddenly craned his neck back and trained his patch on the clouds. 'Fourtee . . . nay – *fifteen* Ju 87 Stukas above us, Captin. Long Range Variant R, if me eye don't deceive me.'

'Well would you believe it?' Trapp beamed at me, dead impressed. 'Di'n't I tell you my lads wus the cream, Mister? And 'ere I was thinkin' they was insects – them Huns I mean: not our crowd.'

. . . ONE . . .

'Do you really *have* to keep using the past tense, Trapp?'

I snarled, then instantly regretted my rudeness. Noel Coward would never behave like that.

ZERO!

The screaming began right on cue. Not from me – well, not at first anyway – but from the Stukas. More a mournful dirge at first, barely audible whilst high aloft but growing in intensity as their airspeed built up. Peeling off, wing tip over wing, tail over nose; dropping one by one by one they came, a near-vertical column of black carrion birds following in their leader's prop-wash; diving down through fourteen ... ten ... eight ... *four* thousand feet and hurtling ever faster; wailing like banshees and plunging with enormous gallantry into and through the canopy of shrapnel laid directly above the convoy, MG81 machine guns beginning to wink along each wing, while each escort increased to full speed and took evasive action violent enough to heel them hard over with every gun elevated to its maximum; yammering and banging an' spitting fury.

We, the STUFTs, just kept steaming in resolute defiance along our straight and predetermined lines, two of those already hit by the previous wave of Heinkels billowing smoke yet still holding course; the third pulling out of formation and gradually, ever so wearily lying over to port with her main decks already awash.

'They're goin' for the flat-top,' Trapp says. All of a sudden the irreverence has gone. His voice is tight now the moment has arrived.

I did wish he hadn't adopted that tone. Trapp irrepressible in hazard, I can handle: even draw an equal mix of courage and irritation from it. But when Trapp gets grim-serious, then I *know* we're in trouble.

I watch her out to starboard: a utility, or Woolworth carrier – a flight deck and tiny island constructed on seemingly spindleshank legs built over a former merchantman's hull, her largely graceless lines softened by the mist with the two flak escorts barrage-nursing her ferociously as she ploughs long, slow, undulating swoops through the increasingly irritable sea. Ugly duckling or no she will, nonetheless, always present one of the prizes most sought by the enemy on this hellish voyage for they know that if they can deny us air

cover, we'll then be totally blind as well as impotent outwith
the range of our armaments. They'll concentrate first on her,
then the American aviation spirit tanker, then the ammunition ships located at the heart of the convoy to afford them
some marginal protection from the U-boats waiting ahead.
Happily there was no requirement for troopships on the
Russian run: if little else, the Red Army already had an inex-
haustible supply of cannon fodder.

The leading Ju 87 hits the nadir of its curve. Even from this
distance I can clearly see one bomb separate from the fuselage
and head straight as a supersonic die for the flat top, whereupon it – the Stuka, not the carrier – pulls up and comes straight
across the forest of masts towards ME, dammit, with wings
rocking crazily and its pilot struggling against the G-forces to
control it . . . then, just when I can't endure the prospect of
watching my own death approaching at three-hundred-odd
knots, my eye is drawn to the rolling ball of smoke and flame
rising above the carrier's flight deck as, suddenly, there are
black Stukas everywhere: a lunatic air pageant of whining,
screeching, snarling aircraft plunging seawards before zooming
up and across: breaking away left an' right, with the climbing,
hissing columns of bomb bursts mushrooming right through
the convoy.

By now the sky has erupted like a Brock's benefit fireworks
display accompanied by a literally continuous percussion of
gunfire. One Stuka explodes – *boooom*! A second loses a
wing, twirls just above the surface like a spinning jenny for
a good three hundred yards, then smashes straight under with
barely a splash. Mix with that high explosive musical score
the dull *crump* of falling bombs, the higher altitude chatter
of aerial machine-guns and the ever-closing, ever-more-shrill
wails of the still-committed dive bombers; further savage your
eardrums with the blast waves radiated by a thousand detonations a minute; sting your eyes with the acrid, wind-borne
miasma of cordite and burning oil and white-hot steel and . . .
and . . . ?

And, all of a sudden God help us – burning MEN?

Because that lead Stuka – the one I thought had *my* name
on it – has jettisoned his secondary, wing-underslung bombs
just a fraction too early to reach our *Charon*: just a luck-of-
the-draw chalk box on a Naval Control Officers' blackboard

too early. Instead, the time-worn Greek tramp stationed one ahead in Column Two to starboard has suffered a direct hit on her bridge and is beginning to veer out of line; swinging from lying broad on our bow to cutting directly *across* it. The safety margin is closing so fast I can already distinguish two crewmen, one without a head and his shipmate without any legs, strewn like tiny rag dolls across her boat deck in company with a third who very evidently *does* have legs but I don't want to imagine what else because the blast has compressed him, shoulders first, into the maw of a big bell-mouthed ventilator . . . while yet *another* of her watchkeepers, this one ablaze from head to toe – maybe even her captain – deliberately flings himself from her shattered wing to land, gratefully sizzling, in the sea . . . !

Whereupon, suddenly, Trapp is roaring to Gorbals Wullie, 'Go starb'd. Hard a STARBOARD *dammit* . . . !' and Wullie's desperately spinning the wheel with the spokes a blur an' not offering any backchat at all 'cause the imminent fear of collision has made his little rat face go bleach-white at the prospect of finishing up on a Carley float in the Barents Sea should he be so lucky as to avoid being smeared into jam an' thus make it even that far, only tae find hissel' stranded with a bunch o' Johnny Foreigners who cannae speak proper English tae help shout '*Save* wis!' in the very few minutes they'll have left before they freeze to death.

This isn't fair, I'm thinking numbly. This simply isn't *fair* and shouldn't have happened to her either because she's nearly as old as we are . . . yeah, OK; I exaggerate – nothing can even remotely approach being *nearly* as old as Trapp's *Charon* . . . but nevertheless, wasn't I just telling you how the Stukas'd go for the carrier first then all the other high-value vessels, whereas we – the Greek and us – are hardly worth the price of a bomb by strategic comparison?

. . . But hang *on* a minute: something's wrong?

Nothing's happening. Nothing's bloody *happening*! Christ, just when we need it most our steering gear's failed . . . Wullie's spokes are hard over: knuckles white to screw an extra inch out've them, and we're *still* holding a ruler-straight course for disaster.

While *she*, our punch drunk consort, keeps closing: bruised white water rumbling and leaping and parting under the bluff

bow and her name *Λουλούδι* . . . Flower, is that? Some bloody
flower – now plainly discernible cut into the rusted plating,
with the smoke pouring from the cavity where her wheelhouse had been less than a minute ago, to roll and trail aft
along her decks and, mercifully, shield those dreadful images
from view.

Finally the *Charon*'s head does falter, starts to come round
ever so slowly – *too* damn slowly – as her antiquated rudder
finally bites. *Maybe that'll teach you a lesson, Trapp*, I think
with savage, albeit somewhat self-disregarding satisfaction.
Those first panic-stricken turns of Wullie's wheel had merely
taken up the slack in pitted chain and rusted wire steering
linkages that should've been properly maintained – tightened
and greased years ago, ideally replaced altogether – but then,
that managerial irresponsibility, further aggravated by Trapp's
Scrooge-like nature had, if memory serves, been largely the
reason why he'd nearly written off bloody SCOTLAND less
than a couple of weeks before!

Yet again I take refuge from reality: finding I can't bring
myself to gaze ahead a moment longer. I'll feel it soon enough.
Probably be catapulted clear over the bridge front when we
meet, merge, and crumple. I've no desire to spend my last
few seconds in this world bloody *watching* for that moment
of contact. Nevertheless I was to wish I hadn't decided to opt
out of the full benefits offered by that front row seat for my
own likely demise. The instant I drag my eyes from impending
catastrophe they are greeted by a panoramic over-view of
carnage. Two further merchantmen have been successfully
targeted apart from our still fast-closing Greek. One, a brand
new Liberty ship, already sinking fast. Presumably one bomb
at least has penetrated her upper deck, continued down through
every level to finally explode in her double-bottoms, blowing
apart her keel and breaking her back. Numbly I watch as her
bow and stern rise steadily to the sky then, with a great hissing
and boiling and gouting of foam, both ends slide below the
surface in tandem while only a few pathetic dots mark those
very few survivors that had made it to the upper deck in time.

I turn away, sickened. There but for the Grace of God . . . ?
Almost inconsequentially a movement aft distracts me: notable
because any of the *Charon*'s crew still caught on her upper
decks have thrown themselves flat as frogs after a tractor's

gone past. Not so Trapp's now favourite adversary, the Cook. *He's* just stepped blithely over the galley coaming on to the exposed poop, cigarette dangling from his lip and carrying a bucket of slops. He slows for a moment, takes a long, leisurely glance around at the gunfire and mayhem: observes with close interest another Ju 87 streaking, flat out and MGs winking to leave a spouting track of mini-fountains right down our port side not more than a boat's length ahead of him . . . then ambles to the rail, empties the slops overboard, takes a last satisfying draw before flicking his fag end after them, and wanders back inside his galley.

. . . What the hell am I *doing*? My life hanging on the turn of a ship's wheel an' I'm overawed by the sheer insouciance of its bloody *cook*?

Hurriedly I turn my attention outboard to seek the carrier. She's still afloat, still making headway, although the smoke pouring from her flight deck has become even more dense and tinged with orange flame. God help them if that's from her hangar, I reflect dully. Men, aircraft, bombs, depth charges, aviation spirit – all will be scrambled together in a potentially lethal, steadily over-heating omelette . . . I don't need to call on imagination: I've been there myself, albeit in a Stuka-stricken destroyer. The scene aboard will be of tightly controlled chaos: discipline transcending terror; heroism and hysteria stalking her lower decks hand in hand. Her damage control parties heading down into the pits of hell hauling their shores and their props and their clamps an' their wedges while all the time fighting against a tide of stumbling, blinded, terribly shocked survivors attempting to make it to the upper decks. Her firefighting numbers rigged in unyielding white asbestos suits and unwieldy, lung-sucking breathing apparatus: clawing and dragging hoses – if such essential aids haven't already been cut to ribbons by splinters; connecting them to hydrants *if* such equally essential terminals haven't already ceased to deliver more than a trickle . . . *Right, lad, nobbut a scratch,* her sick berth attendants will be grinning tightly to men who've lost legs, arms, half their bloody entrails. *'Ave you out of 'ere in a jiffy . . .*

There comes a slight jolt . . . hardly even a kiss, but enough to re-instil the fear of God into me and compel my addled concentration to switch back to the incident ahead. She, the

Greek whatever-it-is flower, blanks out the horizon as she slides ponderously across, *СИДЯОИ* 's nose to *Λουλούδι*'s tail so to speak, yet miraculously making only brief contact, the stricken ship's counter merely brushing our own still shying bow, generating little more than a screel of tortured plating and a hazing of powdered rust.

I watch her go as if in a dream. She's listing slightly yet still steaming ahead. Either her engineers are all dead, all incapacitated, or they've evacuated the engine room without screwing down the steam valves. Through the smoke I can distinguish a group of crewmen now clustering around her remaining port lifeboat, scrambling and pushing to climb aboard with shock and fear taking charge of the deck and prudent seamanship abandoned.

F'r Christ's sake don't lower away YET, someone's shouting across the intervening sea and it takes a second to realize it's ME yelling. *Launch while she's still under way and you'll be swept astern an' smashed to bloody PIECES . . . !*

They do. And they are. I avert my eyes.

She continues to steam off into the distance, an ever more lonely coffin ship getting smaller and smaller while heading more or less due north. She might even reach the ice barrier before the remaining coal in her fireboxes burns itself out. Maybe those poor devils on her bridge had the best of it after all. Crushed to death, burn to death or freeze to death? It's not much of a choice for anyone left aboard and they won't spare an escort or even a rescue ship to chase fruitlessly after her. The soulless mathematics of the Murmansk run dictate she's a write-off, and only the wolf packs lying in wait can profit from any diminution of our already weakened defensive screen.

Trapp stays aloof from it all though I suspect, deep down, he's as shocked as I am. 'Port ten the wheel . . .' he growls expressionlessly as if it's all been a bit of a nuisance, the raid. Then adds a somewhat perplexing footnote.

'Just as well we didn't chance it on our own then, eh Mister?' he says.

I frown at him. What the hell does he mean by that? Try *what* on our own . . . ? Is that him harping on again about *us* and *them*? But I'm too tired to press him further.

We swing back into formation as the flags begin to flutter.

Close up on next ahead. It's like stepping into dead men's shoes.

The barrage dies away. The last Ju 87 has departed for Norway, its compatriot Blohm Voss continues to circle the horizon ahead of us, continuously broadcasting our position. Brave men, all of them. Or very scared men like us, which makes them even braver.

The carrier has fallen well astern and turned her tail to our determined argosy, with two destroyers fussing around her and the smoke forming a funeral pyre above. It seems we *are* blind now. If she makes it back to Iceland it'll be a bloody miracle. But the Royal Navy's good at miracles when grit and seamanship are crucial to the mix.

'Midships . . . Steady. Steady as she goes,' Trapp calls then turns briskly to me. 'Well, Mister. Seems that's the wors—'

'No, Trapp, it isn't. The worst is only beginning,' I cut him short hurriedly. But I don't need his help to hasten it.

It starts to snow.

Eleven

Snow's a funny thing at sea. Funny peculiar, that is. It's good and it's bad. The good phase generally comes first; especially in war when you know your best chance of living through it a little longer is to become invisible, and thus snow, as with fog, helps you achieve that ambition. One minute you're steaming along, a target clearly seen; the next you're that bit safer, concealed behind a scudding veil. There's rumour of a new device called radar that some claim will render such anonymity an outmoded advantage but it's all very secret and only capital ships of either side are fitted with it – certainly not U-boats – though my own view is it's just a gimmick anyway; as much a propaganda as a practical weapon, put about to sap a merchant seaman's morale almost as much as sailing under a master like Trapp can.

It's also quite pretty, is snow. It softens lines, turns the mundane into the magical, makes ugly ships into beautiful ships all glittering and clean. It can briefly turn even a sow's ear like the *Charon* into a silken whatever-it-is, concealing her rust-dank surfaces below a pure white blanket of swans-down. Which is OK if you are mindful of the dangers hidden beneath such treacherous cosmetic; made sure you don't reach out an unthinking hand to steady yourself only to discover, too late, that snow doesn't do a damn thing to counter the underlying threats from corrosion. All it will mean is that the section of parted safety rail you still clutch in a bewildered fist as you plummet to meet Davey Jones, will continue to look a lot more user-friendly than it did when it had simply been raining.

But then there's the downside of snow. We entered the downside phase very quickly. Because snow, if it keeps on snowing as it did during that afternoon following the raids, can become an enemy every bit as threatening as those who've just dumped a hundred-plus tons of high explosive on you. On a personal level it blinds you. You peer into it through eyes already narrowed to ineffectual slits and it even fills the slits and builds up on your lashes and, when you raise a hand to brush *that* away, it drives up your sleeve and down your seaboots an' inside your ears and under your collar an' . . .

Bridge screen wipers can help you see where your going and what may lie just ahead – like another, even bigger ship – although they, those wipers, can themselves be overwhelmed by a concentration of snowflakes, each less than the weight of a weevil but, when mechanically squashed together with a hundred thousand thousand of its brethren, can become as compacted and unyielding as . . . as . . . well, as that same bloody ship which, by then, might just be lying stopped less than a heaving line's throw forward of your bow.

Trapp, never one to be phased by the worst extremes of nature, had first experimented with a strategy to overcome that disadvantage – him never having afforded the *Charon* the luxury of wipers in the first place. Instead, he'd had Gorbals Wullie lashed more or less securely over the starboard bridge front so's that, without hardly having to stretch, he, Wullie, could reach the nearest front wheelhouse window with a broom while Trapp lounged comfortably behind its shelter nursing a giant mug of steaming cocoa and offering loudly expressed criticism of crew who wis aye complainin' aboot their conditions o' bluidy service.

That trial run only lasted minutes before they had to cut a frozen substitute squeegee free and carry him back inside to thaw out. Or roll him back inside to be more accurate; Wullie having mutated into a giant, twinkling chrysalis by then. I had to keep telling them to be careful or they'd snap his arms off, though Trapp said it didn't matter 'cause 'e wus bloody useless anyway.

It was around that time, just when Wullie was getting on everyone's nerves 'cause he wouldn't stop screaming and threshing and crackling about due to the agonies of returning circulation, that the downside of snow became even more apparent.

Because that was when a bitter easterly wind got up, and the wave heights increased until the convoy, instead of sailing with relative, albeit nerve-rackingly blind serenity through an opaque winter wonderland, began to meet steepening head seas. Our consorts took it in their stride; pitching into them and casting great sheets of white water aside. Not so the *Charon*. Stuffed with concrete, our sloped, ice-breaker bow didn't so much carve through the waves as blast them to atoms which whirled high into the air to cascade aft as far as the wheelhouse itself, much as I'd watched her doing when I'd first set eyes on her from that Scottish cliff top.

Within minutes the temperature had fallen dramatically. Unseasonably dramatically. By then the mercury, had we been blessed with a bridge thermometer, would have shown an outside reading in the order of minus 10 °C, and *that* didn't account for the wind chill factor. Sea water freezes at roughly minus 2 °C. The upshot of that combination meant that, instead of spray, which froze the instant it became airborne, the *Charon*'s open bridge wings – unprotected even by her former rotted canvas dodgers which had immediately collapsed in tatters under that first onslaught – were bombarded by scalpel-keen ice crystals sharp enough to flay the hide off a rhinoceros, were it to be so stupid as to sail in a Russian convoy in the first place.

Not that one would be allowed to. Not on the Murmansk run. While a rhinoceros could probably tie sailor's knots better than Trapp's average crewman, it would prove a bugger to fit into a lifeboat.

Anyway . . . all of a sudden, in place of pristine snow affording us a not-unwelcome makeover, those fuzzles of white that had previously dressed our stays and shrouds and rails were becoming compressed into ever-expanding sleeves of solid ice the diameter of a bosun's thigh. Icicles formed everywhere, suspended beneath hatch coamings and winches and davits and overhangs, while her masts grew into tree trunks that would've shamed a giant redwood. Her decks became constantly angling cresta runs, and the superstructure itself began to emulate a drunken pastry chef's wedding cake with icing thick as Gorbals Wullie. The abruptly crowded wheelhouse, into which we'd been hastily forced to seek refuge, became not so much a navigating platform as a windowless igloo inside which Trapp fulminated about the cost of the additional coal required to carry so much extra weight – cost that wasn't even chargeable under the terms of 'is already derisory charter fee from them skinflint Ministry of War Transport pen-pushers.

I'd almost lost it then – yelled, 'Well, whaddya bloody *come* for? You didn't *have* to come, Trapp. You could've easily stayed hidden in bloody *Ireland* . . . !' but I didn't. Even though he'd let slip too many indiscretions to continue to fool even one so gullible as I, it was hardly the moment to pin him down to explaining why he'd embarked on this cartoon-strip charade in the first place.

But at that stage, self-indulgent as ever, I'd become rather more preoccupied with the likelihood that we were about to sink.

Yes, OK: I take the point. I could have pressed my enquiry with firmer resolution and gained at least *some* benefit from my final moments in Trapp's company. After all, sinking wasn't exactly a new experience for me. I'd been sunk before. Regularly. But this was different. In Arctic waters sinking and dying are even more closely related, particularly when your only chance to beat the odds is dependent on the readiness of your vessel's lifeboats. And I'd already been down *that* particularly contentious route my first night aboard.

But, getting back to my journal: we were about to sink because (a) being as visually gifted as . . . well, as Dead-Eye Alf – currently steering a hazy and thus somewhat erratic compass course as helmsman – we could well collide with our next ahead at any moment, and, (b) that dread possibility was only eased by the likelihood that we would capsize before any such event had time to take place.

What's that? Oh, sorry: but *capsize* do I hear you ask now . . . ? Like, do I mean capsize as in turn turtle or, even more specifically, revolve through 180 degrees around our fore and aft axis until we were heading for Russia down-side up . . . ? Well unfortunately, yes I do. Because option (b) arose from yet another of those laws of physics that Trapp constantly chose to ignore on economic grounds.

I'd *tried* to outline my concern to him. I really had. As soon as the spray had begun to freeze I'd pleaded with him to roust the crew out of their blankets and set them to attempting to stave off the build-up of our sub-zero super-cargo with sledges and chisels and, above all, steam hoses, but *that* artery-testing confrontation had proved a complete waste of time. I would've had a better chance of getting Trapp to sign on that bloody rhinoceros than persuade him to countenance such reckless squandering of bunker coal.

Anyway, the point I'm *trying* to make is that, as the *Charon*'s centre of gravity rose higher and higher through her having accumulated several hundred extra tons of top-hamper, so the movement of the ship was becoming even more sluggish than usual. Her ability to recover from each roll was fast diminishing. I could sense her hanging as she lay over, sometimes for what seemed a very long interval – roughly an hour of terrified apprehension condensed into each five-second delay – before slowly, ever so reluctantly, commencing to creak upright again.

It was time to get out of that confined space an' risk being flayed alive. I grabbed the handle of the port side wheelhouse sliding door and hauled. Frozen solid, it didn't budge.

'We're dead,' I said.

'Whass that you're sayin', Mister Miller sir?' Wullie whispered tensely, hesitating in mid-agony.

'It won't budge,' I informed him.

Wullie gave up fruitlessly trying to generate sympathy, shot to his feet, and began to run about waving his arms stiffly, still crackling a bit, and crying, 'We're trapped: we're *trapped*. Trapped like . . . like rats inna trap!'

Despite our increasingly desperate situation, I took considerable umbrage at the inclusive *We*. While Gorbals William may have been eminently qualified to class himself a rodent, I felt courtesy demanded he should credit me, his executive officer, with being of a rather more elevated species.

'Oh, don't be so girlie about it, Mister,' Trapp urged, managing as ever to imply I wasn't trying hard enough. 'Give it a proper pull.'

'*You're* Captain. It's your door that's stuck. *You* give it a proper pull if you're so . . .'

He did. The handle came off in his hand. Simultaneously the ship lay over ten sluggish degrees and, this time, failed to show the slightest enthusiasm for returning to the vertical.

'That's you must've broke it, Mister. Pullin' too hard the first time,' Trapp grumbled.

Anxiously I looked around the angled wheelhouse for an

alternative escape route. By then a veneer of ice was forming even *inside* the space. The perennial Murmansk run quandary: freeze, drown, or – increasingly likely in Trapp's case – have your chief officer strangle you first.

'P'raps we should leg it down the inside stairway, Captin. Find another way out?' Dead-Eye Alf suggested rather ingeniously.

'It's a very old ship. This wheelhouse doesn't *have* an interior stairway,' I explained to the patch gently.

'Ah,' Alf nodded with sudden comprehension. 'I allus wondered why I'd never seed one.'

The *Charon* shuddered a further ten degrees to port and settled temporarily. Tired and top-heavy, one more sag and she'd keep right on going. Wullie tobogganed past me down the ice-treacherous incline and brought up with a crash against the recalcitrant port door.

'Where's yer sea legs, stupid?' Trapp yelled irritably, unmollified by having ensured that he, himself, was securely anchored with one arm around the binnacle. 'If you've damaged them door runners, I'll dock 'em out've yer wages.'

No point in trying to smash a window even if he'd let me, I gloomed. They were made of armoured glass a good inch thick and represented the only components of the *Charon* which hadn't degraded with age. And anyway, even if we *did* make it outside I could forget raising the matter of steam hoses again. He'd much prefer to die than concede I'd been right an' he'd been wrong, so we were doomed to founder anyway . . . apart from which, facing up to reality had never been Trapp's main driving force. His having survived a war in which, without the intervention of a suicidal fish, he should rightfully have died; having jumped his very first coffin ship just before she became one; and dodged the wrath of that Chinee Fu Manchu feller in Macao at the expense of a commercial traveller from Birmingham, only to avoid being topped by the French Foreign Legion through a sheer fluke of luck a short time later – to say nothing of having succeeded in getting our previous Mickey Mouse warship blown up by his own side – an' *still* escaping unscathed . . . Well frankly, those episodes had, in my jaundiced view, a lot to answer for when it came to Trapp's subsequent and unshakeable belief in his capacity for self-survival.

Come to that, Trapp's facility to routinely postpone his final meeting with the Grim Reaper was largely responsible for my continually being at loggerheads with him. His misplaced conviction that he was immortal had long prevented me and him from experiencing the one common emotion we might otherwise have shared. I did fear very well. I was extraordinarily good at it. Trapp wouldn't recognize the sensation if he chanced across it in a dictionary.

Fed up with trying to stand vertical at twenty degrees from the vertical, if you see what I mean, I took my steel helmet off, slumped into a corner, wedged myself in and resigned myself to dying in unattractive company.

'*Now* what are you doin'?' Trapp demanded.

'Wondering what Noel Coward would do.'

'Shit hisself,' Trapp predicted with relish.

'I mean the *movie* Noel Coward. The warship's captain in *In Which We Serve.*'

'I saw that,' Wullie interrupted from the bottom end of the wheelhouse.

'So did I,' Dead-Eye Alf enthused. 'Well, quite a lot of it.'

'Now he wis a *proper* ship's captin, Captin,' Wullie reminisced ill-advisedly. 'A *reel* gentlema— ouch!'

Trapp withdrew a jealous plimsoll and growled dismissively, 'We just picked up a bit of ice. They wus bein' bombed when they sunk. At least we ain't bein' bombed, Miste—'

The explosion of the bomb close alongside caused a shuddering vibration to run right through the *Charon*, accompanied by a series of gunshot-like detonations as frozen snow parted company with corroded steel.

Followed by a rumbling that continued on, and on and on. And on. As if a whole iceberg had begun to deposit itself on our decks.

The first thing I registered when the door blew open of its own accord, was the brilliance of the sunshine outside. Not a cloud in the Arctic sky. The snowstorm had evidently long passed. Heaven only knew how long we'd been stuck in that wheelhouse sailing blind while every other vessel in the convoy stood their extra lookouts down and sent hands to tea.

The lone Condor which had jettisoned its stick of 250-kilo ordnance on us from fifteen thousand feet was already a departing drone in the south east as the *Charon*, relieved of all top hamper, began to right herself. With mastheads swinging through monstrously spiralling arcs she started to bob and wallop from side to side like one of those dipping plastic ducks in a fat man's bath, while flinging huge cobs of dislodged ice a ship's length either way.

'Don't panic and . . .' I attempted to warn urgently, clinging like a leech to Trapp's leg to prevent myself following a similar parabola to the airborne ice.

Of course, Gorbals Wullie did anyway. Panic, I mean. One second he'd been talking up Noel Coward's facility for command; the next he's clawing an' scrabbling to make it through the door into the open air. By the end of the third second, he'd disappeared under the half ton of snow still avalanching from the roof of the wheelhouse.

'. . . try going outside 'til she stops rolling,' I finished wearily.

There followed a very long and somewhat stunned silence. Until.

'Steam hoses, Mister?' a totally vindicated Trapp jeered derisively. 'Didn't I *tell* you we wouldn't need steam hoses?'

'An' I wouldn't have suggested them *either*,' I yelled back defensively, 'if you'd bothered to tell me your list of guardian demons includes some half-witted bomber jockey in the bloody LUFTWAFFE!'

The U-boats closed on the convoy that evening. Well, later that day really; or as good as. Because we'd broached 78 degrees north by then and turned to sail due east, parallel to the seasonal limit of the Polar ice barrier. That placed us only about seven hundred miles from the Pole itself which meant that, as the Arctic sun barely dips below the horizon at that time of year and when it does a ship observed from the south is still silhouetted against the ice blink that never quite fades, even at the darkest time we never really became invisible.

Which was exactly what the wolf packs had been waiting for.

The bigger of the two ammunition carriers died instantaneously. The beautiful new American tanker took a little longer: all of four minutes longer. And there were others.

Within thirty minutes of nautical twilight descending, our

impossibly burdened seadog of a Commodore had been forced to look out over his formerly tight phalanx and order *Close up on next ahead* no less than seven times as ships exploded or listed further and further, or burned, or simply limped wearily out of line.

I never actually saw his last bitter instruction signalled by stuttering Aldis lamp, although I guessed which STUFTs it would have been addressed to – Designators One Four and One Five, previously occupying the chalk boxes behind us.

We'd fallen too far astern to maintain sight of him by then.

The *Charon* being the seventh ship to drop out of convoy on that terrible night.

Twelve

Yes, all right: I concede the point. I *should* have guessed something was afoot long before the U-boats came.

Immediately following our near capsize he'd busied himself with uncharacteristic industry in the chartroom, and that should have served as a warning in itself. Trapp had hardly glanced at a chart since we'd left Scotland: always made it clear the one advantage of sailing in convoy was its cost-effectiveness. According to his philosophy, all you needed to do wus follow the bloke in front and trust to his ability to navigate safely, thus saving the wages of a second certificated officer who would only eat his head off at Trapp's further expense while proving marginally useful, at most, for keeping abreast of trivia.

Trifling detail such as (a) what our position might happen to be at anytime, should we wander off track from the convoy and finish up getting lost. And (b) where Murmansk was. When we did.

Well after midnight the Arctic twilight had finally closed around the *Charon* before, following much frustrated tipping out of drawers and riffling through yellowed, dog-eared chart folios apparently predating Columbus's time as a cabin boy, he'd stuck a flustered red face out've the door and shouted, 'All right, I give up, Mister. Where's that new Polar chart the Navy give us? The one you admitted you 'adn't corrected.'

I refused the bait to engage in fruitless argymint. It was obvious he was still smarting from Wullie's earlier and most cruel Noel Coward slight, and was hunting for someone, anyone, to grouch at. I didn't even attempt to remind him I'd *already* reminded him that our current-use chart, being brand new, was up to date anyway.

'Try looking on *top* of the chart table, where it's supposed to be kept,' I suggested mildly. 'I marked our last dead reckoning position less than an hour ago.'

'You're gettin' far too lippy f'r Crew, you are,' he still pronounced blackly as he disappeared back inside. 'Been talkin' to that bloody cook again, 'aven't you?'

Albeit consumed by curiosity I waited ten minutes before giving in and following my Master afore God. On stepping across the coaming I surprised him hunched over the table, dividers in hand, while poring over the chart with brow-furrowed concentration. A scrappy piece of paper lay next to the parallel rules. The moment he saw me he snatched it away before furtively stuffing it in his pocket, like a schoolboy caught cheating in an exam.

''Ow do I know your last DR position is accurate?' he challenged hastily to head off the interrogatory already framing on my lips.

'You don't,' I retorted. 'But why should you? You've never worked one up yourself since we left Scotland. In fact, my guess is that the last time you actually knew where you were, Trapp, was when you found reason to leg it from Cardiff to that Droolin Bay of yours.'

Well, *that* did it. I could see I'd accidentally hit a nerve soon as his face went puce.

'What do *you* know about my diversion to Ireland, Mister? How did you know what I'd had in mind – putting into Droolin?'

Oh joy of joys: all my earlier strategies to confront him thwarted, and he'd just blundered into laying himself wide open. This time nothing could deflect me from pinning him down to explaining why I – *ex*-Lieutenant Miller RNR, thanks to him – was here, merely a modest if chilly stroll from the North Pole, yet still not knowing why . . . other than nursing a pretty fair hunch it had bugger all to do with any miraculous conversion on Trapp's part to patriotism.

'I didn't,' I beamed. 'But having admitted you *were* planning something – something utterly nefarious, no doubt – you might just as well come clea—'

Reflected through the open door, the flash came white. Magnesium white. Lightning-white. Stroboscopic and dazzling in intensity, it lit up the shambolic interior of the chartroom and burned a lasting image into my retina of Trapp's dividers still pricked into a point on the chart that lay not too far ahead of our current position . . . less than an hour's steaming at convoy speed.

But *why* . . . ? What significance did that particular location, a bleak and featureless place on what was virtually the roof of the world, hold for Trapp? There was nothing out there other than the terrifying, inhospitable rim of the Polar barrier.

My rational attempt to process irrational speculation disintegrated as shock took charge. We were still tumbling out on to the open starboard wing by the time the thunder arrived.

Fifty Three had disappeared completely: one of the ammunition ships from the centre of the convoy.

Only a boiling, incandescent glow below the surface remained to mark where she would have been mere seconds ago, from the core of which spiders' legs of still-detonating ordnance zipped, crackled and screeched; describing long, steam-trailing parabolas arcing for half a mile either side. Atop that Wagnerian celebration of instant death, a rolling column of smoke continued to climb eight . . . nine hundred . . . a *thousand* feet into the sky: smoke such as I'd never witnessed before. A monstrous, spine-chilling maggot of smoke. Jet black smoke entwined with flickering red on its undersides, etched stark against the deep purple of the southern horizon. White hot debris, some large as a windlass or an anchor or an entire deck house were still descending; hurtling from aloft to splash amongst her closer consorts in a stagger of foam-gouting thunderclaps. God help anyone aboard those other vessels caught on deck by that lethal rain.

Ten thousand tons of steel and wood and cordite and seamen – over a hundred men: ordinary blokes like you and I. One moment they're thinking *Must finish that letter to the wife soon as I'm relieved . . .* or *It's bloody cold but thankfully it's stayed quiet so far tonight . . .* or *Is it tomorrow that's a bacon an' eggs day for breakfa—?*

Next instant they aren't thinking anything at all.

Trapp turns without a word, and goes back into the chartroom.

I'm glad he does. No one gets to see me crying.

The American tanker went next.

I'd compelled myself to wrestle with Trapp's bloody one-optic binoculars in a vain attempt to distract me from the horror of our previous casualty, and was actually watching her in relative close-up while thinking enviously on how proud I'd feel to be sailing in her. How elegant she looked: how clean were her lines, and how cruel it would be for such a ship to be destroyed . . . when the strangest thing happened.

She produced a fountain from her after end. Right where her engine room was located. It was the sort of celebratory water wall those stubby little fire tugs display when one of the great Blue Riband Atlantic liners arrives off New York . . . and then a *second* fountain appeared, this time from slightly forward of her midships bridge structure. Then both fountains raced each other into the still purple sky only this time, instead of rising black and sinister as had the smoke from the ammunition carrier, they were clean and white and virginal as sea spray while they hung suspended for a few hesitant moments. Until, almost as quickly, they shrank back down while the tanker continued on course, surrounded by the sister silhouettes which made up our ghostly argosy, as though absolutely nothing had happened, and I was left frowning and wondering if I hadn't imagined it all.

A full minute ticked by. Then, give or take a curse of dawning realization, a further thirty seconds . . . ?

A tiny red glow twinkled mischievously just below her bridge. Then disappeared. Then remanifested itself as if some errant firefly had passed briefly behind a tree in our supposedly protective forest, only now it seemed bigger, even *more* twinkly . . . ?

I heard myself calling automatically, 'Captain! CAP'N to the starb'd wing . . .'

The geyser of flame erupted vertically as the firefly graduated to flame monster. Up the face of her midships island it climbed: up, up, high above her foremast, instantly incinerating anyone and everyone caught outside on her bridge wings – then the monster became a blowtorch and I could hear the gasoline-fuelled roar of it from where I gaped transfixed.

And then Trapp came to the door grumbling 'Bloody First Mates. Allus needin' a nursemai—?' before stopping dead with the red light reflecting from his weather-beaten face affording him a ghastly Satanic appearance, and blurted '*Christ*!', which struck me as being a curious appeal to make from a man who looked like the Devil.

The base of the blowtorch suddenly expanded, racing towards both bow and stern like opposing trails of gunpowder touched by a slow match. In the blink of an eye the whole tanker had ignited along the line of her weather deck as fuel vapour was drawn from her tanks only to be followed by the high octane spirit itself. Most of the seafarers in their cabins below, or on watch in her engine room, would have suffocated immediately; the very oxygen sucked from the air they breathed, to feed the flames. All the hooked-back doors and kick-out panels in the world wouldn't have helped them then. While those very few who were left . . . ?

I didn't want to think of those who were left. She was ablaze from jackstaff to taffrail now, with rivers of fire pouring from her scuppers into the bitter cold sea which, in turn, began to boil with rage as the licking flames, refusing to be extinguished by the element that was their bitterest enemy, spread outwards instead to surround the ship. And then more oxygen, the second element needed to sustain fire, took the side of the flames and fed them further until, refreshed and invigorated, they continued to advance.

I wanted to turn away. God knows I so desperately *wanted* to pull back from that awful scene. But I couldn't. Turned to stone by a paralysis of horrified revulsion, I continued to stare through my one-eyed lens as, incredibly, first one, then two – then several matchstick figures, each a tiny flame in itself, came sightless and blundering from *within* that white hot holocaust to tumble over her rails, and out, and down into . . . !

'God DAMMIT, man!'

Trapp snatched the glasses from my grasp and swung me, startled from my shocked immobility, to face him. His countenance was terrible to gaze upon, yet there was something else there. A sympathy I'd never, ever encountered before.

'They're dying hard, them sailors, Mister: hard as any you an' me 'ave ever been plagued to watch. It isn't good for a man: watching close up like that.'

It was the one kind turn he ever did for me.

We lost four more ships to torpedoes in that first co-ordinated U-boat attack: three merchantmen and a small warship that I think had been a corvette in the few seconds I sighted her before she continued to drive below the surface with all hands still closed up to their action stations: her bows blown off and her screws still racing. Perhaps thirty minutes – although it could equally have been thirty years – passed before the escorts finally succeeded in forcing our torment-ors to dive deep and impose silent routine beneath a sea by then seething from the multiple eruptions of depth charges.

Curiously, while a literal over-kill of fear for my own life combined with shock at witnessing the passing of so many others, had begun to at least anaesthetize, if not completely inure me to the violence of that dreadful period, the reverse seemed to be the case with Trapp.

He'd appeared to grow increasingly more agitated. While I'd determined to be vigilant in maintaining a safe distance from our next ahead; about the only practical measure I could take to aid our survival for as long as she, or we, still existed, he, Trapp, had begun to pace the wing almost aimlessly while, every few minutes, suddenly darting into the wheel-house to frown ferociously at the brass clock affixed to its after bulkhead.

At first I'd assumed it was typical Trapp: focus on some trivial occurrence and totally ignore the approach of Armageddon. That bloody clock, for instance, afforded a classic example. It had resolutely remained stopped at twenty minutes and forty three seconds past eight since I'd joined the *Charon*: had probably been that way since the Russian Revolution, but then, all of a sudden, the bomb that exploded alongside us earlier had traumatized it into ticking again. And to Trapp, having even one piece of equipment aboard that actually worked was a triumph; having two bits of fully functioning kit, counting his new megaphone, was a novelty.

Although I did begin to wonder after a while. About his increasingly erratic behaviour.

Because the next time he disappeared, it was into the *chart-room* which, as I've already mentioned, represented a hitherto unexplored region of the ship for Trapp.

I snatched a quick glance around. Some time had passed since the last attack. I decided to chance following him in since, the way our tardy steering gear responded, there was little or no chance of avoiding an incoming torpedo's track anyway: not even if it came fitted with a flashing blue light.

He didn't attempt to cover up this time. Just glanced up as I entered, and growled sceptically, 'You *sure* you got this last position right, Mister?'

'Positive.'

'What time is it now?'

'Two minutes later than when you last looked at the clock.'

'An' how far d'you reckon we've run since you marked it?'

I glanced at my own watch and did a quick time and distance calculation. 'Ten point three miles.'

'Which places us . . .' he stubbed a grubby forefinger on the chart. 'Here?'

Reaching for the dividers, I laid off a quick measurement to double-check.

'Can I go home now?' I asked. 'You've just passed your navigator's exam.'

There was no answer.

When I raised my head to frown uncertainly around, he'd vanished.

He was nowhere to be seen in the wheelhouse, or out on either wing.

Only Wullie remained to greet me from the wheel with a mystified, and mystifying, 'You *sure* you know where we are, Mister Miller sir? Cause I hate tae tell ye, but ah jist seen Gibraltar aboot five mile dead ahead.'

From the front rank the Commodore's Aldis flickered in anticipation of some three hundred-thousand tons of shipping collectively ramming Gibraltar. *Convoy will turn to starboard two zero degrees. Execute immediate.*

'It's an iceberg *shaped* like Gibraltar,' I explained patiently. 'And you're the second person to question my navigation in the past couple of minutes. Do so again and I shall leave you marooned upon it, without even a bagful of sandwiches, when we pass . . . now, starboard ten the wheel if you will.'

I wasn't surprised we were wheeling to the south again. In a vain attempt to stay outwith the operating range of the Luftwaffe while this damned clear visibility persisted; a strategy supported, presumably, by what was currently proving to be woefully inadequate forecasts from the Admiralty regarding the likely disposition of Dönitz's wolf packs, we'd been driven steadily north until we could go no further. The near proximity of the ice barrier had made itself evident for a good forty-eight hours. A steady rumbling transmitted throughout the ship from under our forefoot as we steamed through ice rind and brash of ever more dense concentration. Here and there, glimpsed through the short night gloom, small floes glistened and twinkled; occasionally glowing sinister red as the seafire from the cremated tanker astern still flared to illuminate the convoy.

'I *still* says it wis an easy mistake to make,' Wullie continued to mutter, very *very* discreetly, to hisself. 'Well, it could've been. If it ever snowed on Gibraltar.'

'Where's the Captain?'

'How would *I* know?' Wullie retorted, persistent in his resentment. 'There's some on this ship would claim ah dinnae even know where *Gibraltar* is.'

'Here, Mister,' Trapp growled; suddenly reappearing at my shoulder.

I started involuntarily. Enough potential menaces were abroad to play on my nerves that night without him joining in. 'Where did *you* disappear to?'

He looked surprised. Somewhat ham-actorish, over-the-top surprised his response struck me as being. Almost as if he'd been *rehearsing* looking surprised. 'Why, the *engine room*, o' course. Surely you heard the Chief call up on the voice pipe as well?'

The brass stopper in the engine room voice pipe had a whistle piercing enough to drown out a diving Stuka. I eyed him sceptically. 'No. So considering you were with me in the chartroom for ages prior to your doing a runner, I'd like to know when he *did* call?'

The bobbing cap, the shifty eyes and the bluster conspired to deliver Trapp's standard evasion package. 'Nit-pick, nit-pick: it's like sailin' with a bloody seawife . . . anyway, more to the point, Mister – jus' what d'you think *you're* doing?'

'Your job. Ensuring the responsible navigation of this vessel.'

'I'm talking about making a course alteration without my permission.'

'Convoy order: execute immediate. Apart from which I would have altered anyway, to avoid the nuisance caused by hitting that iceberg ahead. It's what we deck officers do.'

'Well, we *deck* officers ain't doing either. Not this time,' he announced with what I considered misplaced relish. 'Seems we got a problem.'

More in hope than conviction, I fought the unease that suddenly assailed me. 'Please tell me you're only referring to a very minor problem, Trapp. Like in how we transfer Wullie on to that iceberg, for instance?'

'I mean a major problem. Like in engine,' he retorted flatly. 'Chief says he's got to shut it down f'r repair, or . . .' He hesitated then, seemingly loath to be drawn into explaining further.

'Or *what*?' I snarled, cutting out the middle emotion and going straight to panic.

'Or it's buggered,' Trapp specified, reaching for the telegraph's worn brass handle. 'Which means so are we, Mister.'

The discordant jangle of bells must have caused every man aboard to explode from his blanket huddle like ferrets from a sack the instant Trapp swung the handle, first astern then halfway back up to leave it at rest on the topmost segment marked *Stop Engine*.

Which, translated into U-boat German, suggests roughly: *Dann angegangen, wenn irgendein von Ihnen Kohl-cabbage-munching scaredy Katzen denkt, sind Sie genug groß! Jetzt allem, das Sie erhielten zu tun, wird ein GESTOPPTES Ziel geschlagen.*

'. . . c'm ON then! Assuming any o' you cabbage-munching scaredy cats think you're big enough. Now all you needs to do is hit a *stopped* target!'

But then, Trapp had never been much of a diplomat. No more than he was one to soften the blow in times of looming despair.

Instantly the steam-syncopated vibration that had so far accompanied us from Iceland, the one shred of on-going comfort I'd been able to cling to during the voyage so far, died away, whereupon we continued to coast through a hushed silence broken only by the steadily diminishing rumble of ice parting before our bow.

'Pass the word: everyone quiet as mice. Them U-boats'll be able to hear a pin drop in these latitudes,' Trapp ordered with irritating matter-of-factness, before adding slyly, 'Oh, an' you'd better enter it in the Log, Mister. What with you bein' a perfectionist an' everythin'.'

'Enter what?' I demanded. Already I'd detected at least four periscope lenses out there, camouflaged as ice floes. 'That we're good as dead already?'

He chuckled amusedly. Like I've said before: Trapp *never* chuckled. ''Course not, silly. I means that we just become a straggler.'

I delayed my descent into hysteria long enough to frown. No yelling? No histrionics? As Master, wasn't there something wanting in his overall response to our condition? One couldn't help wondering: particularly when all he'd done after that was wander off and drape himself comfortably over his usual spot at the rail and start to hum a catchy little ditty.

Meanwhile: *Poor devils,* they'd be saying at that moment on the Commodore's bridge when they saw us veer out of column. *Sitting duck. Won't stand a chance now they've dropped out, even if she can effect repairs and proceed independently to Murman—*

. . . But hang *on* a minute! Hadn't we found ourselves in this precise situation, give or take a wolf pack or two, on a previous occasion . . . ? Because our engine had allegedly broken down once before, remember? Shortly after Trapp inexplicably disappeared from the bridge that last time – once again in the middle of the night – while on our first leg to Seidisfjord.

Funny, that. How I'd never really felt convinced by the technicalities of over and under thingummies as explained by Trapp the last time. No more than I'd been able to fathom how he'd managed to remain so unconcerned during *that* incident too. But they must have been true. I mean, what could he possibly have stood to gain by subterfuge? All he'd managed to achieve was to establish in the Navy's thinking that we were just the sort of unreliable STUFT one might *expect* to become a straggle—?

Precisely the official mindset that some observer more cynical than I might have suspected Trapp of having engineered from day one.

. . . *So we'll just have to leave her to fend for herself. Little point in detaching an escort to stand by her even if we could spare one*, they'd be saying. *And after all, she* does *have a previous track record of sheer incompetence, combined with a history of engine failure.*

A conclusion Trapp had now succeeded in reinforcing.

Thirteen

I'm sorry, but I simply have to ask once again. Have *you* ever drifted, alone and vulnerable, at the edge of the Polar ice barrier nor'east by something-or-other of Bear Island, part way between Franz Josef Land and sudden death?

Have you ever done an unsettling thing like that with your ship's engine stopped and the Judas-benevolent wavelets slap, slap, slapping against your already dangerously submerged war loading marks, and no one daring to drop a spanner, clatter a plate: make the slightest noise that might act as a magnet for the searching hydrophones of the wolf pack you just know is out there?

Even more disturbingly: have you done it at the worst possible time of year? In the middle of a seasonally-brief autumn night when, each minute by nerve-corroding minute, a star-laden sky made you clearly visible through a Zeiss attack lens from miles away . . . ? Had reduced your floating refuge to being a black cut-out target marker silhouetted against that never-quite-dark ice blink of the Arctic horizon.

Have you ever done all that, and done it with your throat so dry with apprehension that not even the frozen crystals inhaled with each laboured breath can alleviate the discomfort – and simply waited for the first torpedo to strike?

You *have*, you say . . . ?

Then by all means feel proud of the valour you displayed, anyone among you who now reads this, my own account of having experienced such a knuckle-gnawing, courage-sapping event. Do, by all means, feel free to nod in grim recall of how you, too, must have felt.

But wait: I haven't quite finished yet. Because next you must multiply, by a factor of at least ten, the psychological trauma you endured during that time of dread anticipation – and *then* some!

Otherwise you won't have allowed for the consequences of having a megalomaniac control freak like Trapp as your captain. Not unless there'd been two of 'em in our war – not counting that chap directing it from Berlin. Otherwise you must further add confusion, growing suspicion, slowly dawning disbelief, and, ultimately, outraged resentment to the mix.

Include all those emotions, and you're just about qualified to imagine *my* depth of suffering.

I'd watched hope steam remorselessly into the distance until the serried ranks of silhouettes faded hull down below the cobalt horizon. A shuddering sniff or two later and even the last illusion of security afforded by the convoy's rearmost escort, had become only a precious memory.

Still in a daze, I made my first entry in the Log as chief officer of an officially designated straggler. Not even Number Thirteen now, we weren't. Just a discarded legend in an Admiralty *Out* tray marked Billy No-name.

Engine revolutions *nil*, I'd written. Present speed: *nil*. Distance run in past hour: *nil*. Wind force: *nil*. Sea state: *flat as a floundering sailor's cardiogram*. Prospects: *nil . . .*

According to the Almanac, dawn would arrive in twenty-two minutes. Only the indefatigable Dead-Eye Alf felt his way below for breakfast.

I reckoned he had twenty-three minutes left in which to finish it.

Those minutes dragged by with excruciating slowness. Every few seconds I found myself staring fixedly at the engine room voice pipe: willing it to whistle as a precursor to the Chief calling to say all systems go; we could get under way again. Only grudgingly did I eventually walk to lean beside Trapp, resolved to be seen maintaining some vestige of sangfroid by the crew – most of whom had, by then, congregated abaft the bridge within elbowing distance of our remaining lifeboats while, devoid of forward motion, we continued to roll gently to the creak of the old ship's bones.

Probably with a good half-dozen U-boats already forming a ring around us, I speculated morosely; simply waiting for full, trigger-friendly daylight to arrive while their commanders meticulously double-checked the data entered on their attack plot.

But it would have been crucial for them to get it just right. Miss the *Charon*, they were likely to torpedo one of their own guys on the opposite side of the circle.

'So what do we do next?' I asked. 'Assuming Oily Rag gets the engine going and we do have a *next* to plan for?'

'P'raps you should be askin' Noel Coward, Mister,' Trapp retorted waspishly; never one to let an indiscretion drop, no more than he was capable of maintaining a tolerable humour for long.

'It was him, not me, made that remark,' I protested disloyally.

'Judas!' Wullie hissed, halfway through trying to figure how to tie his lifejacket the right way up.

It promised to turn out to be a beautiful day. Meteorologically speaking. The sun came up, bathing the ship in a chill-crisp brilliance, and I braced myself for the first explosion. Trapp, on the other hand, merely stirred, stretched, yawned, then rubbed his hands briskly together. Unpredictable as ever, the wasp had turned back into a butterfly, flitting from mood swing to mood swing.

'Right, Mister. The sun 'as got its hat on, meaning we got things to do an' fish to fry,' he announced somewhat obscurely. 'Please be so good as to go an' get your sextant an' them astronomic tables the Navy give us. I wants to confirm our *exact* position, or near as it's possible to in these high latitudes.'

I frowned. I'd been doing a lot of frowning since we'd stopped. This time it wasn't so much his unsettling courtesy as his current obsession with pinpointing our precise whereabouts that concerned me. Throughout life he'd blundered from one ocean to another with only the scantiest concession to any recognized navigational technique. Not that he needed such formal education, it seemed. Trapp had always possessed the directional facility of a homing pigeon. A sniff o' the wind, a glance at the sky, a quick scan of that archive of charts so antiquated that most've them boasted hand-etched designs of spouting whales and dugout canoes an' copperplate legends like *'Ere be Sea Monsters . . .* yet next thing he'd be calling a course accurate enough to make a landfall any battleship captain would be proud to boast.

I shrugged. Anything to pass the minutes until *untersee-boot knocken-knocken.*

On reaching the bottom of the bridge ladder en route to my cabin to collect the sextant, I chanced by two figures engaged in leisurely contemplation of life as they saw it aboard Trapp's Queen o' the Seas. Meaning they were muttering darkly while hanging over the rail. I couldn't help but overhear the title *Captin* being bandied about quite often, invariably preceded by a less respectful adjective. One wore a filthy chef's apron and the sort of disgruntled expression Fletcher Christian must've evinced just before the mutiny on the *Bounty*; his companion revealing an angry swelling above his left eye caused, I suspected, by recent contact with a clenched object like, say, a fist. Nothing new there, then. Like I say, this *was* the *Charon*.

'Mornin', gentleme—?' I acknowledged automatically on my way past.

Half a dozen steps further, and realization dawned.

With Trapp not having expected me back so soon, my pell-mell return caught him red-handed: denied him enough warning to snatch the parallel rules he'd been using, from the chart. Immediately I registered that they neatly bisected the cross marking my last estimated position of where we'd broken down and thus become official members of the Russian Convoy Stragglers' Club: the position he now wanted me to double-check with a sun sight.

OK, so that realization in itself didn't give cause for suspicion. No more than did the fact that the instrument was still placed to plot a track almost exactly north to south – after all, it was self-evident that our first act, once we got under way again, *had* to be to head south. It didn't need Marco Polo to figure we had no option. Apart from Franz Josef Land – at 80 degrees of latitude a barren and forbidding archipelago consisting of icebound islands that only walrus, arctic foxes an' polar bloody bears inhabit out of choice – the area offered even the most intrepid . . . even the most suicidal mariner, nothing other than several thousand square miles of sea ice, snow, and freeze-dried misery.

. . . Except it didn't quite work out that way. Because, you see, I'd *also* managed to register, in the split second before

I started screaming at him, that Trapp had already pencilled *in* his proposed route to escape the pickle we were in . . . heading virtually due NORTH!

Going THAT way, the *Charon* should hit the ice barrier after roughly five miles steaming.

Yes, I know: I can see you scratching your head at this point. What's Miller *on* about, you must be asking yourself. All that north and south stuff, and why such abrupt abandonment of faith in his captain's integrity? Trapp might well have provided a *perfectly* reasonable explanation as to why he proposed to kill his crew, given time to think one up. And anyway, you'll be grumbling: why make a big deal out of it? You didn't have any means of propulsion, Miller, so you weren't heading anywhere other than vertically – one way or another – once a U-boat found you. While all said and done, shouting at him has never got you anywhere before. So why didn't you just get on with it and ask . . . nay – *demand* he account for his intended action?

All right, maybe I should have done. Maybe I would have got to the truth quicker by adopting a more reasoned approach. Except that *wasn't* what had made me hopping mad in the first bloody place! I'd got to the vein-bulging, incandescent stage long before I'd clocked his plan of action: even before I'd raced all the way back up the bridge ladder without hardly touching a rung, to confront him.

'*Engine* trouble?' I bawled from the edge of hysteria. 'ENGINE trouble is it . . . ? You said . . . no – you *assured* me, Trapp! – we gotta stop 'cos of an over-an'-under thingum-myjig problem. Jus' float around obvious as a black duck inna white basin, waiting the outcome of a race between the Kriegsmarine Underwater Branch an' that . . . that useless *motor* car washer of yours! Slaving down the engine room he was, you said. Urgently trying to *fix* things so's we c'n move again, you said . . .'

'Er . . . is there some sort of point you're tryin' to make, Mister?' he fenced uncomfortably. I could see his mind working flat out to contrive some other crisis that might serve to take the heat from this current one, but I'd finally caught him out. And terror being a great motivator, I felt pressed to complete before some voice not too far away ordered, *Torpedos einer, zwei, drei . . . FEUER*!

'. . . then how COME, Trapp,' I screamed, every nerve strung tight as banjo catgut, 'how come I jus' passed your bloody Chief ENGINEER out there?'

'Get away,' he said, utterly astonished. 'So where wus that, then?'

'Up on the fuckin' BOAT deck. Loungin' around in the sunshine like he's killing time 'til YOU tell him the engine's fixed!'

Gorbals Wullie's left ear had retained the imprint of a keyhole for hours after I'd slammed the chartroom door shut on it before launching myself, arms outstretched to grab Trapp by the throat.

. . . But I stay my writing hand at this point. Out of defer-ence to the more sensitive follower of this journal, I propose to touch only briefly on the detail of our subsequent discourse. There are some events which any responsible narrator must concede, however grudgingly, are simply too harrowing: too awful to record. Suffice to say heated words were spoken. That I'd given vent to saying cruel things . . . *terrible* things to Trapp while shaking him; and that only by threatening to clamp off his oxygen completely did I finally manage to persuade him to admit the truth.

To explain *why* he'd scuttled off in precisely the opposite direction to Russia despite having been entrusted by – *and* paid good money by – a hard-pressed nation to do the Right Thing for once in his misbegotten life, an' bloody *go* where he'd promised to go!

To subsequently explain *why* he'd changed his mind, tooted a warship, and done the Right Thing anyway.

And above all: especially from *my* point of view . . . to explain why he'd *then* gone out of his way to persuade the convoy, our only means of protection, to abandon us halfway through that voyage to hell, just so's *he* could deliberately wreck us – with no one other than the odd hunter-killer sub-marine watching – within roughly a couple of weeks' sleigh ride from Santa Claus's bloody GROTTO!

Fourteen

According to my satisfyingly strangulating Master afore God, Droolin's Atlantic-battered *Fenian Boy Inn* had turned out to be just the sort of seagoing gentleman's hostelry Trapp felt most at home in.

A thatched hovel dim-lit by rush lights and only marginally more spacious than those other poor dwellings comprising the harbour's housing stock, it boasted an earthen floor and a few crude sticks of furniture long fractured by repeated contact with the skulls of travellers injudicious enough to betray an English accent. Beneath its rough-sawn ceiling beams, a layered fug of contraband tobacco neatly complemented the aroma of locally distilled Irish *poteen*: that illegal fuel favoured by patrons averse to paying excise duty on non-paralysing spirits.

In one dim corner five Galway pigs and four worthies with three teeth atween 'em played dominoes; the worthies playing the dominoes, that was; not the pigs. And not counting any teeth the pigs possessed . . . anyway, add to that rural ambience a makeshift dartboard with a bull's-eye comprising a yellowed photogravure of the corpse of a British Black and Tan officer murdered sometime before the Easter Uprising: stir in a suspicion of incomers so tangible you could cut it with a potato peeler, and you had the perfect venue in which Trapp felt comfortable doing business.

The moment he and Wullie entered the clatter of dominoes froze suspended, whereupon a deathly hush descended upon the establishment. Gradually, as one's eyes adjusted to that early experiment in sophisticated cocktail bar lighting, further groups of drinking men could be detected observing warily from the shadows.

'This is nice. Very nice,' Trapp said before addressing mine host with the cauliflower ears. 'A pint o' Guinness an' a grog chaser f'r me, bartender, if you would be so kind. An' a small lemonade, nothin' too expensive, for my friend.'

Then, unruffled as you like, he'd turned to face his glowering audience.

'Now, which o' you fine fellers knows a man . . . 'oo *might* know a man . . . 'oo *might* be interested in acquiring a bit o' war surplus?'

Wullie's lemonade hadn't even stopped fizzing before Trapp got his answer.

The soft voice came from astern just as its owner placed the muzzle of a large revolver under Trapp's starboard ear.

'Sure and wad ye not rather die and go to Heaven straight away, Englishman,' it enquired solicitously. 'To save yourself the cost of the little feller's drink altogether?'

But British spies abounded in the neutral territory of Eire in 1942. For citizens of a certain political persuasion, shooting one came high on their list of things to do as soon, and as often as possible: ideally in the convivial atmosphere of a pub.

Reaching to pinch the barrel of the ex-British Army issue Webley and Scott between forefinger and thumb, Trapp swivelled it fastidiously to point at Wullie before growling, 'I'm an internashnulist, mister. Cap'n of that ship in the bay. An' he's Scotch, so 'e don't count.'

'Then oi'm truly sorry, sor,' the voice said.

'That's all right. 'E can't *help* being a Jock,' Trapp assured the Invisible Man.

'Oi mean sorry for yourself, sor. Having the terrible misfortune to be captain of that ship out there.'

Trapp let it go, being intent on other matters, and swivelled cautiously to appraise his welcomer. 'So, assumin' you ain't no public relations greeter from the tourist board, who might you be?'

'Father O'Donnelly, parish priest of this, our toiny community,' his new acquaintance advised, hospitably averting the weapon. And it must have been true because, as he stepped forward into the rushlight, a clerical collar did indeed glint softly around his neck.

'Then pardon my Frog, but it's a bloody awkward-shaped Bible you carries, Vicar,' Trapp grunted, eyeing the Webley as it disappeared beneath the Father's cassock.

'The Boible oi carry for me Sunday job, Captain, and talk with a Dublin University-educated voice. Mondays to Saturdays oi carry the gun, and converse in this excruciating Oirish accent because that's what a man in my position is expected to do,' the curious cleric of Droolin retorted. 'Not that oi don't spread the Good Lord's Gospel every day of the week, mind? Tis a grand theological tool for persuading sinners to move closer to God, is the gun.'

'It must be awfy hard for ye, Fayther,' Wullie broke in sympathetically. 'No' bein' able tae speak proper English.'

'Oi can shoot him for you now, if you like,' the cleric offered generously.

'Too late: 'e's brain dead already,' Trapp growled. 'So, this being Wednesday an' you talkin' pure Paddy, that makes your position . . . ?'

'Quartermaster-Major Shamus O'Donnelly it is today, sor. Droolin Volunteers, Third Battalion, Oirish Republican Army. Now, what was that you were saying about war surplus?'

. . . And so it was that Edward Trapp had come to the very brink of abandoning one of his own most strictly held principles – that of never selling the cargo entrusted to him.

Although I do feel bound to spring to his defence here. I'm prepared to concede I don't blame Trapp for acting as he did on that occasion. The way our mutually detested Admiral had blackmailed him simply because he'd forgotten to resign from the Navy. Had, without compunction, resorted to the threat of using King's Regulations as an excuse to have him shot if he refused to volunteer his ship for war the first time, flying right in the face of the Captain's most devoutly held principle of all, then had subsequently pulled exactly the same stunt on him soon as he'd acquired his replacement Queen o' the Se—?

Beg pardon, again . . . what's that you interrupt my flow with this time – that it's been niggling you since page forty-odd, you say? My having shied from relating how Trapp ever so conveniently manages to reappear in this journal complete with steamboat, despite my having clearly stated earlier that he'd sunk his. Indeed, that you consider it little more than a cheap literary device on my part – reintroducing him already established as the proud proprietor of another СИДЯОИ, without a word of explanation as to how he'd come by her.

Oh, all right – I'll *tell* you, then. If only to prove this isn't a work of pure fiction, and that I *can* claim some integrity as its author. I mean, we *were* nearly at the North Pole f'r cryin' out loud, but I'd thought I was being helpful. Had merely rewound my tale back to Ireland for the sake of clarity and understanding: not to invite a bloody argument with anyone an' everyone reading it.

Well, jus' for the record: there had been these three White Russian fellers, exiles in North Africa, who'd owned a ship berthed not too far from where Trapp and Gorbals Wullie had contrived to escape ashore from our first *Charon*. She was an old ship – I mean, *tell* me about it – a *very* old ship indeed, being even older and more frail than Trapp's last hulk. A ship so old that those Russians had searched unsuccessfully for weeks beforehand to find some renegade captain stupid enough to take her out an' sink her in the time-honoured tradition of coffin ship insurance scams. All of 'em, even the ones blind drunk, reckoned she wouldn't reach water deep enough to submerge her masts, never mind destroy the evidence, before she went down without even a stick of gelignite to help her on her way.

Until Trapp and Wullie washed ashore. And after that, it had been like picking fruit in The Cherry Orchard for Trapp. The Russians insured the valueless СИДЯОИ and her non-existent cargo for three million Libyan *dinars*, paying the understandably substantial premium in cash – wink-wink – to a highly recommended, albeit rather small person with a curiously broad Scottish accent who he'd hastily introduced as 'is agent at the *Banco de Beirut*, Glasgow Sauchiehall Street Branch, then the Russians had given Trapp the gelignite and the СИДЯОИ's official papers, and happily sat back in the local *souk* downing vodka chasers while waiting for the cheque to arrive.

Meanwhile Trapp sailed off into the war-torn Mediterranean sunset yet again; threw the gelignite overboard on the grounds she wus far too fine a ship ter waste, and the three million along with it on account of discovering the notes had been counterfeit anyway, and promptly recommenced his contraband running career until . . . yes, *now* you've got it! . . . until *another* British warship put *another* shell through his funnel an' Lieutenant Commander Trapp RN finished up on the carpet in front of the *same* bloody Admiral as last time.

So now, if you could be so good as to resist the temptation to seek out further flaws in Trapp's – no, in *my* story – I can return with you to that hostelry in the Emerald Isle.

On the surface it seemed a fair deal Trapp had struck with the IRA. He would begin to discharge his cargo at dawn, while the schizophrenic O'Donnelly's Fenian bhoys went and robbed their nearest branch of some English banking house to pay for it.

Trapp didn't know it then, of course – and be advised, I *have* been forced to assume some of this next bit through drawing from Trapp's previous history of business dealings – but it seems reasonable to imagine such a Devil's pact could never have concluded in a straightforward, totally honourable manner. That Quartermaster-Major O'Donnelly's alter ego, *Father* O'Donnelly, might well, on the other hand, have found himself embroiled in a conflict of interest.

He'd've realized that, as soon as next Sunday morning dawned, the cleric in him would become much disturbed at having handed over such a terrible big sum of money to a sinner so plainly beyond redemption as Trapp: money that could be better spent in relieving the desperate poverty which abounded in his parish. After a bit of an argument between them in two different dialects, they – both O'Donnelly's – could well have agreed that topping Trapp before he sailed off with the loot might well offer a solution acceptable to the Church, the Republican High Command and, in the longer term, afford the Irish Customs and Excise Service a Divine bonus as well, considering a bullet in the head might just prevent the ould scallywag from returning to the Emerald Isle after the war.

By coincidence Trapp, too, had suffered a crisis of conscience when it actually came to the bit. In his case he'd been finding it increasingly difficult to reconcile his cunning plan to fund the *Charon*'s extraction from the war with yet another of his firmly held principles: that of never committing any act which would prejudice the Allied cause. And certainly not one which would afford sworn enemies of the Crown like O'Donnelly the kind of logistical support that could lead to the deaths of British soldiers.

The Captain's solution was equally pragmatic. He'd checked

to ensure the telephone box outside the harbourmaster's ramshackled office was still working before he went along to the *Fenian Boy* with Wullie. Just before casting off the *Charon*'s last mooring line he proposed to call *Garda* headquarters and suggest to them that, should one or two of their officers – more prudently, a whole armed response unit – chance to pass by Droolin later that same morning, they may well notice a consignment of snow warfare-camouflaged kit lying around on the dockside large enough to severely embarrass the Eire Government should it cross the Northern Ireland border.

Both plans looked equally promising.

Until around midnight on that day of amiable skulduggery.

When everything changed.

By that hour the *poteen* had flowed unrestricted, the dominoes had chattered like the teeth of frozen dead men, the pigs had *oinked* and the hens had *clucked*; the accordions had been elbow-pumped to bursting and the penny whistles blown into shillings; the jigs had become wilder and wilder, with lumpen boots pounding the earthen floor into the semblance of linoleum . . . and everyone, Republican or principled atheist, wus having a good time so they were, in anticipation of the morrow.

Until, just as the clock struck twelve, Trapp overheard the one word in that merry throng that was guaranteed to capture his undivided attention.

'Gold,' that word was.

Gold!

The ould feller had been wild-eyed and toothless, with hair so unkempt and matted it stuck from his head like the twigs of a mulberry bush. His fingernails were black-ingrained and broken: his clothes pathetic weeds. Edward Trapp had noticed him only briefly part-way through the evening as he'd sat, hunched and alone, in the darkest corner of all. He gave the impression of having once been a seafaring man, though possibly the fact he bore a tattoo of a fouled anchor on the back of one grimy hand and a mermaid on the other had helped point to that conclusion. But that aside, Trapp had ignored the apparition. He'd seen dozens in his time; just another maritime derelict reduced to the indignity of cadging booze in whatever grog shop he'd washed up alongside. And he'd collected quite enough losers of that sort already, thank yer very much. The ones he called 'is crew.

Wullie, of course, had been fascinated by the chap. He'd always aspired to be like that when he matured. A career village idiot. Free drinks; never havin' tae wash; nae forced haircuts: spend all day inna pub that couldnae sink . . . ? But then, when it came to picking role models, Gorbals Wullie never had been too selective. And anyway, as Trapp kept telling him: he'd have to study too hard to qualify f'r such a job.

But then it happened.

Trapp's dream came true.

''Oo wants ter buy me SECRET – me secret of the GOLD?'' the previously brooding creature cackled unexpectedly from the shadows. ''Oo among you landlubbers 'as courage enough to take on the quest for Murphy's *Gold*?'

Trapp choked over his Guinness. 'What's 'e say . . . ? *What's* 'e sayin'?'

''*Ooooo* wants to buy an old seadog's secret?' the creature obligingly repeated. 'Me secret o' the *gold*?'

'A glass of yer special liniment, bartender. And an extra chair if you please,' Trapp called, rising hospitably.

Well, of course they'd *tried* to tell him, had the locals. The ould feller was plainly mad as O'Grady's rabbit and a terrible loiar to boot. Six months he'd lodged in that corner livin' off pork scratchings and scraps while trying his best to blarney some eejit into buying that tatty ould map of hi—

'Map? *What* map?' the Eejit spluttered. But Trapp always had been cursed with a chronic affliction of the inner ear canals leading to his brain. Soon as gold was mentioned within a heaving line's throw of either one of them, both became deaf to common sense and to reason.

'*This* map, Captin,' the wild-eyed creature offered helpfully; producing a dank and mildewed oilskin envelope from beneath his coat tails after pausing briefly for dramatic effect. 'This map as can point 'ooever musters the fortitude to return along a course already sailed by twenty-two dead men, to where the *treasure* still lies.'

'Twenty-two *deid* men?' Wullie whispered nervously, eyes like organ stops. 'Sailing inna boat, were they?'

'Well, them as goes sailin' generally *does* do it in a boat, shipmate,' his new acquaintance endorsed reasonably. 'Whiles ter be strictly accurate, there wus twenty-three o' us in her. But seein' as how I ain't parted me own cable yet, I 'olds by my original tally. And naturally they wusn't none of 'em dead when we started off.'

'Frum where? Started off from *where*?' Trapp urged, completely entranced by then.

'Frum the wreck, sir,' the old sailor whispered, then shook his matted head in sad recall.

'Wreck? *What* wre—'

'There's only the one of him. So why dae ye keep askin' everything twice, Captin?' Wullie frowned before Trapp kneed him under the table.

'The wreck o' the S.S. *Salamander*, sir: out o' Liverpool. Passed the Formby Light an' never seed again. Driven ashore by an icy tempest an' stranded in the 'igh latitudes these eight years since.'

'Just exac'ly how high are these latitudes you talk about, mister?'

'*Aaaaar*, that's f'r me to sell an' you to buy, Captin,' the man said, placing a knowing finger alongside his somewhat unsanitary nose: a response which proved that, while he may have been a bit over the top as a nautical character actor, he wasn't stupid. 'But if you wants a hint ter show good faith, then you'll still be steamin' north when you passes through 79 degrees.'

'That's awfy hot if he's talkin' centygrade,' Wullie pointed out apprehensively.

''E means 79 degrees *latitude*, ratface,' Trapp snarled, fed up with being interrupted. 'Bloody near up to the North Po—? But *hang* on a minnit, mister – ain't that even up past the ice barrier?'

'Well past, Captin,' the man agreed cheerfully, draining his grog. 'Twenty-two dead men past, and only yours truly 'aving survived to tell the tale.'

'So 'ow . . . ?'

'There be a warm water current at a certain place in the Barents Sea, sir. Not warm enough so's you'd notice dippin' yer toe in it, but warm enough ter form a lead o' thinner brash an' pancake north. It's up through there the *Salamander* wus blowed 'elpless right to the island, rudder torn clean off its pintles, and where me twenty-two shipmates perished on our attempt to escape back south.'

'I got twenty-two blokes I'd be 'appy to see perish: one in partic'lar,' Trapp growled, eyeing Wullie pointedly. 'But I ain't daft enough to end up in a dive like this as number twenty-three.'

'We come down in an open boat, Captin, wi' barely a blanket atween us. But, if me rheumy old eyes didn't deceive me when I see'd you anchoring, you'll prove a very different kettle o' fish. You 'ave a fine ice-breaker in which ter seek yer fortune in the frozen waste.'

There came a long silence as Trapp digested that counter argymint while his informant ostentatiously inspected his empty glass before hopefully prompting, 'Where the *treasure* still awaits aboard the *Salamander*, sir? Stacked in 'er number two hold it is. Boxes an' boxes of it. Boxes o' Murphy's Gold.'

Well, it was at that point that even *Trapp*, a martyr to his own naiveté, nearly told the apparition to sling 'is hook. Boxes and boxes indeed. Ever since he'd been a tadpole pirate in Macao he'd been privy to throatily whispered tales of golden wrecks. Every low-life grog shop from Shanghai ter Valpariso abounded with 'em. And they all 'ad one thing in common: a romantic etymology designed to whet the appetite of any wannabe fortune-seeker naive enough to pay for the map that allus seemed to come with 'em . . . *Solomon's* Gold: *Pharaoh's* Gold: *Lasseter's* Gold: *Black Tench's* Gold . . . a bar or two 'ere, a buried sea chest of it there, a brass-bound case locked in a sunken liner's strongroom, even one ingot worth a king's ransom . . . but this wus over the top, straining even Trapp's credulity. I mean: *boxes* of it? Jus' stacked casual as you please in a ship's hold?

Mind you, admittedly he'd never heard tell o' *Murphy's* Gold afore. And hardly surprising. Didn't exac'ly smack of allure and intrigue in treasure hunting circles, did the name Murphy. No more than did the mention of frozen wastes and boatloads o' corpses appear designed to suck in even the most avaricious investor with a promise of easy money.

So, on the other hand; might that not afford a certain credibility to . . . ?

''Ow many boxes?' he asked suspiciously.

'Off the cuff, sir?' It was the sailorman's turn to mull, 'I'd say near enough eight.'

'*Eight*?' Trapp jeered, albeit conscious of an unexpected sense of disappointment. 'Eight boxes hardly takes much stackin', mister.'

'. . . thousand, sir,' the apparition clarified to avoid confusion. 'Eight *thousand* boxes o' gold.'

Well, Trapp's face must have been an absolute *picture* at that point, the Internashnul bullion market having made a particular study of his. All relevant data lay ready-programmed into the computer powering the financial lobe of his brain; it being the dominant, if not the only lobe he possessed.

So he'd allus been wistfully aware that yer standard gold bar held by the world central banks, known to aficionados of refined metals as the *London Good Delivery Bar*, weighs anything between 350 an' 430 troy ounces, or around 27.4 avoirdupois pounds on average. An' being that heavy, they generally comes one to a box f'r easy handling; suggesting there 'ad to be a minimum of eight *thousand* individually cased bars aboard the S.S. *Salamander* altogether. OK, so even overlooking the nitty-gritty difference between troy an' avoirdupois measurement – and being conservative in one's expectations, assume each bar weighed no more'n 25 proper British pounds – then multiplying by 8,000 cases gives you 200,000 pounds total weight. Then start dividin' by 112 pounds to get 'undredweights . . . then . . . then factor in *twenty* 'undredweights ter the ton . . . ?

'But if they wis all *deid*,' Wullie still frowned, having rather lagged behind in the discussion. 'Did that mean youse had tae do the rest of the rowin' yoursel'?'

'Near enough ninety *ton*,' Trapp whispered ecstatically before slipping into a brief coma. 'Ninety TONS o' gold!'

. . . And that disclosure, albeit obtained under duress and still going only part-way to explaining why I was throttling my captain a spit from the North Pole while waiting helplessly to be torpedoed, must suffice for the moment to allow our return to that gloriously sunny morning in the Barents Sea.

Fifteen

Yes, I do understand your scepticism. And your growing sense of disillusionment at having been carried so far through this journal only to discover it's in danger of becoming far-fetched. But please be assured I, myself, had experienced much the same reaction when Trapp first mentioned that estimate of ninety tons to me . . . in between sucking great breaths of oxygen through his windpipe soon as I'd eased my grip on it.

'You didn't fall for *that*?' I'd said disbelievingly. 'That's probably more gold than they keep in the Bank of England. Talk about bloody overkill.'

''Course I didn't,' he spluttered, kneading his Adam's apple experimentally. 'Not until 'e'd told me the full story, Mister.'

'Oh yeah?' I jeered. 'Did he include the bit where little green men came down in a flying saucer an' saved him alone from his lifeboat?'

'No,' he said, seemingly refusing to be drawn into another barney; a reluctance uncharacteristic enough in itself to worry me. 'But he did provide proof that the gold was loaded aboard the *Salamander* in the first place.'

I gazed hard at him. The crucified cap sat steady as a rock on his head. Not a bob.

'*Proof*?'

'Proof, Mister.'

'I think,' I frowned uneasily, forgetting all about U-boats, 'you'd better come clean, Trapp . . .'

It seemed that, for three days, the Steamship *Salamander* had been driven steadily north under the press of that Arctic summer storm; rudderless and with even her boiler fires finally extinguished. At least that was according to Trapp anyway, who, in turn, had recounted it according to his whiskery new most-bestest friend ever from the *Fenian Boy Inn.*

But were I to transcribe every tortuous meandering of that grog-slurred conversation in detail; were I to include every throaty 'aaaaar' and every 'shipmate' and every knowing wink of an increasingly bleary eye; then I would be laboriously scrawling 'til a month cum Tuesday and you'd have fallen asleep by page 1,387. Suffice once again then, for me to recall the bones of it as best I can.

In 1935 her peace-time course to Archangel would have taken her further south of that followed by our Convoy PQ whatever-it-was. Near enough due east past Norway's North Cape she'd have steamed, effectively heading for Novaya Zemlya until she reached her point of departure and altered sou'westward to make for the Kola Inlet.

But once she'd lost her rudder and thus her ability to steer any course at all, then the only route she could follow was whichever way the shrieking tempest chose to drive her. And for the already mortally-stricken *Salamander* and her fearful crew, that was up towards the Pole.

On that first terrible day her number one hatch was stove in by mountainous seas. By the second, numbers two and five went also, and had begun to fill so fast the pumps could barely keep pace with the water. Then, on the morning of the third day of screaming gales and white-outs and fog thick as a polar bear's fur coat, even the bare comfort of the pumps abandoned them when the water level finally rose above her fireboxes and she lost all ability to maintain a head of steam.

By noon she'd become sluggish, but not so her captain. A master mariner fashioned from shipyard steel, he had meticulously recorded her drift by dead reckonings based on a lifetime's experience in murky waters. He'd known what terrible misfortune lay ahead but he'd kept it from the others – until that terrifying moment when the fog lifted and they could see for themselves the gouting columns of breaking seas less than a mile abeam, and hear the thunderous rumbling and cracking of grinding floes that marked the limit of the Arctic ice shelf. Twas like being cast helpless on a Biscay lee shore, but colder.

Closer and closer they drifted. Half a sea mile, a quarter . . . two cables . . . one, with the freezing spray now flying above the height of her masts. Some among them cursed their misfortune, others took to prayer . . . the captain took a final note of her position, entered it bravely in the Log, finished off the last tot in the rum bottle he'd always kept 'idden behind the chartroom fiddley in anticipation of such a time, then composed hisself to dying 'ard but quick. An' very, very happy.

Still running fast before the crests there came a jolt and a bump and a screeching of plates under pressure as the ice first swallowed, then began to close about her. She listed further and great sheets of it began to build up along her port side, some actually sliding inboard over the bulwarks to grate monstrously across her deck causing the cabin boy to cry aloud for his mother and the mate, another fatalistic seadog and a crusty one at that who had no love of children, to tell 'im to shut up an' stop getting' on 'is nerves while he wus makin' 'is number wiv 'is Maker.

. . . Until suddenly, unbelievably, instead of capsizing the *Salamander* near enough *righted* herself, and instead of being ground and crushed into oblivion by the outermost fangs of the ice shelf, they found themselves floating, calm and serene, in a gently billowing wilderness of constantly moving brash and rotten ice just piled up into hummocks and down into bummocks . . .

. . . And *that*, according to Trapp, according to a man in a pub, was how the Steamship *Salamander* out of Liverpool had come to finish up stranded on some island up near the North Pole eight years before. Because the wind and the anomalous current had carried her further and further north over the succeeding weeks until, finally, they had ground to a gentle halt in a bay surrounded by towering snow cliffs and icebound rock faces and . . . ?

'Hang on a minute, Trapp,' I'd broken in at that moment. 'If that all happened in 1935, then how come it took eight years and twenty-two dead men for this scarecrow pal of yours to finish up sole survivor in some scruffy west coast Irish pub flogging a treasure map? Or are you saying he'd sat in that corner f'r roughly seven of 'em waiting for someone as naive as you to turn up?'

''*Course* not, Mister,' he said huffily. 'That would be silly.'
'So?'

'So they'd stayed with the ship over two Arctic winters in the hope of rescue. A bit like Ernest Shackleton's crew 'ad to sit it out on Elephant Island after the *Endurance* got herself icebound down the Antarctic in 1916, only a bloody sight longer – but then the *Salamanders* wusn't in the same hurry, bein' better provided for. She wus general cargo, remember: plenty of quality export British grub in her. But eventually they got bored; took a vote, and most've 'em reckoned it was time to make tracks home. Fixed up the only boat she had left after the storm, an' set sail. Only it didn't quite work out as planned. The weight of a trampship's one thing: a lifeboat's a different kettle o' fish – they finished up havin' to pull it *across* the ice more'n sail through it like they thought. An' on top of all that, with a magnetic compass only good to tell you where your boots are, that close to the pole, they got lost.

'Wandered round in circles, droppin' like flies with the cold. Passed the same bloody *island* three times, they did. Seemed 'er Old Man weren't no Shackleton when it come to findin' his way without a tot o' grog behind the fiddley and a proper ship under 'im.'

He paused to draw breath, then his eyes went pensive. 'Anyroad, there they wus. Just a shrinking band o' survivors with ice ter the back of 'em, ice ter port, ice ter starboard an' *ice* still ahead o' . . .'

'Trapp,' I interrupted anxiously, recognizing the symptom. He was about to launch into Part the Third of that already interminable, salty recounting. 'I really don't care *how* they died. At this moment, I don't care whether they even existed in the first place. What I *am* concerned with is the odds-on likelihood that *we* are about to, if we hang around here any longer. So can you now please tell the Chief to restart the bloody engine that didn't break down in the first place, and try to catch up with the CONVOY?'

'Oh, I'll tell the Chief to restart the engine all right, Mister,' he said.

'Thank you. Then I apologize for trying to strangle you,' I accepted magnanimously. At least he wasn't being awkward any longer.

'. . . but we ain't going chasin' after no convoy.'

                    *   *   *

At first I hadn't registered the punchline.

'Whaddyou *mean* – AIN'T?' I'd yelled when I finally did. 'We can't just turn round and go back to Scotland unescorted. Statistically we have less chance of surviving as a straggler than we do of that . . . that Gorbals Wullie person stuck to the keyhole out there volunteering to take a bath.'

'I knows that. You must think I'm reely stupid,' Trapp jeered, proving he was a mind-reader. 'Lissen, Mister, let's get things straight. Why d'you think I volunteered my ship for this convoy lark in the first place?'

'At a rough guess, because the Admiral proposed to shoot you if you didn't.'

'I mean *after* that. I still didn't have to come, remember? Not once I'd shaken the Navy off an' negotiated a nice little IRA-funded pension plan f'r me an' my lads.'

'The day I understand how your mind works, Trapp, I'll *know* I'm crazy as you are.'

'Only to change me mind an' sail out've Droolin before dawn without collecting from O'Donnelly?'

'Like I said, the day I understa—' I broke off to stare at him incredulously. 'No. No, you *can't* be serious, Trapp. You didn't *really* fall for that yarn the old soak spun you about ninety tons of gold, did you?'

'Like I told you: I didn't 'til he produced the proof,' he retorted. 'Which only left me with one problem. I knew well as you that the *Charon* couldn't make it this far on her own. Not up against the Luftwaffe an' them wolf packs.'

A nasty suspicion began to raise its ugly head. Remember how I'd formed the impression that he'd never really considered himself a part of any great patriotic endeavour? That view being further reinforced by his unguarded references to 'them' and 'us' . . . ? Plus all that fuss he'd made about double checking our precise position in relation to the ice barrier last night . . . topped off by the *Charon*'s unquestionably contrived – and if I was right – seemingly carefully timed 'breakdown'?

I found myself firmly shaking my head. No way. Not even Edward Trapp could be *that* devious. I mean, *no* one could be THAT dev—?

I still asked him anyway.

'You're not trying to tell me you planned to use the Royal

Navy as a matter of convenience. An escort to bring you this far, then simply allow you to drop out when it suited?'

'I just did, Mister.'

Ask a silly question.

'So what do you . . . do WE, dammit! – do now?'

'Straightforward enough, Mister. We just nips up to where the *Salamander* lies . . .'

Nips up, he said? A grand master of understatement, Trapp. God only knew how many leagues of ice lay between us and this mythical wreck, with us in an ice-breaker that offered a fifty-fifty prospect of caving in first if we tried to force her through a bowl of particularly thick gravy . . . while even if we did achieve the impossible and return in one piece, we *still* had to face the same certainty of dying alone soon as we made it back to the open sea to face the U-boats.

'No we don't,' he argued with terrifying logic. 'There'll be another outbound convoy along in a couple of weeks. We just lies low, hides behind a berg 'til they comes abeam, then join on. Make our apologies f'r the unavoidable delay; gratefully accept their protection; finish the last leg to Archangel; unload our cargo to keep the Admiral frum shootin' us, then sail back with the empty returners.'

'While you earn a double-whammy income. Get paid your charter fee in addition to having exploited the Allied fleet by conning them into funding an all expenses paid search for treasure,' I concluded faintly.

'I 'adn't thought of that, Mister,' he lied without a trace of shame. 'So accordin' to your own lights, you'd better watch out. You reely *are* beginnin' to figure like me.'

'No, I'm not, Trapp!' I snarled defensively. 'Because I'll never be stupid enough to believe everything I'm told by an old soak in a pub.'

'No more than I am,' Trapp retorted triumphantly. He'd obviously been waiting a long time for that moment.

'Not unless 'e backs it up with evidence, Mister. Like producing this first page from the *Salamander*'s original cargo manifest.'

The document he extracted from the oilskin envelope was water-stained and yellow, folded several times and scrumpled up tight in addition. It had torn edges and one corner was missing altogether but I'd handled enough Bills of Lading, effectively consignment notes, to concede it may well have been genuine. Even the faded official Customs and port authority stamps it bore appeared authentic.

SHIPPED in good Order and well conditioned by the good Steam Ship Salamander, it stated in spidery copperplate. *Here Berthed in This, the Port of Liverpool on This the 10th day of August in the Year of Our Lord 1935 and now bound for the Port of Archangel. The undernoted Goods being marked and numbered in the Margin, and are to be delivered in like good Order and well conditioned at the aforesaid Port of . . .*

'Read on, Mister,' Trapp urged.

'. . . notwithstanding the Act of God, the King's Enemies, Fire, Machinery, Boiler, Steam, and all and every other Dangers and Accidents of the Seas, Rivers an' . . .'

'Down the bottom,' he grumbled tensely. 'Read the bits at the *bottom!*'

He was right. In calling them bits, that was. A good quarter of the yellowing page faded into illegibility having been water-marked and ink-run, although most of the general cargo listings were still discernible.

. . . Shipper: *Preston Knittinghouse Limited.* Quantity and Description: *1,763 boxes Elegant Brand gentlemen's woollen socks, sizes various.* Consignee: *Mr Sergei Tkachenko, Novosibirsk Importers Incorp—*

'Further down,' he hissed.

. . . Shipper: *Kent Farm Implements.* Quantity and Description: *3,200 bales Muscle Brand galvanized shovels.* Consignee: *c/o Senior Commissar (Current), Nizhny-Novgorod Agricultural Co-operative . . .*

'Further!'

'Shipper: *Sheffield Ironworks.* Quantity and Description: *1,028 cases Superior Brand canteens cutlery, electro-plated silv—*

'I already said down near enough the bloody BOTTOM!' Trapp yelled.

I stole a quick, uneasy glance through the hole in the chart-room corner chopped out by the Junkers. No torpedo tracks so far that I could see. And still not a periscope in sight.

Yet.

While, until Trapp decided the time had come to tell the Chief to start the bloody engine again, there was sod all I could do about it anyway, even if there wus . . . *was*!

It was becoming harder to make out the writing. 'Reels Lancashire cotton: colours various?'

'No!'

'Egg cups, Royal Doulton?'

'NO!'

'Three thousand cases, bottles, onions, pickled . . . ?'

Obviously the *Salamander* had been a typical Red Duster tramp of the era – *if*, that was, she'd ever existed outside the imagination of a wild-eyed old grifter. General cargo carried in open stows, they used to call it. A rusting, puffing argosy of delights and dreams rolling and corkscrewing and panting and criss-crossing the seven seas bearing opportunity for Chinaman and Javanese, Egyptian, Easter Islander, Thai or Esquimau to experience, if only for a fleeting moment, the British way of life.

'Custard powder . . . leather boots . . . Worcestershire sauce . . .'

'Bloody NO!'

'. . . rolls Axminster carpet. Walking sticks, silver toppe—?'

I broke off abruptly. Trapp was watching me closely.

'*NOW* you got it, Mister,' he nodded.

Gold, the Bill of Lading said.

Murphy's Gold.

It was there, all right. At the bottom. Except that deciphering each line in full had by then begun to present some difficulty as the manifest's bottom right corner – its crucial bloody corner! – had been torn off part-way across, while any remaining script penned by that long-ago shipping agent's clerk was further smudged and corrupted by water.

Nevertheless the start of each line in the left-hand margin showed up clear.

Shipper: *House of Murphy, Bond Street, London . . .*

By Royal Appointment, Purveyors of Refined Me—

Quantity and Description: *8,021 boxes Gold B—*

'Bloody *hell*,' I muttered.

'Read ON!'

'. . . consignee: Mister *Jo—*!'

I broke of to stare at him. Not because the rest was missing, this time. No. No, simply because of what remained. The part I *could* distinguish plain as the triumph in Trapp's eyes.

'*Consignee* – Mister Josif Vissarionovich STALIN,' he filled in for me, largely on account of the fact that I was still struggling to regain the power of speech.

'General Secretary of the Union of Soviet Socialist Republics, Mister. Care o' The *Kremlin*. Mosco—'

Sixteen

'I'm still not convinced,' I grumbled later. We still had forty minutes to run before we hit, and I do mean 'hit', the ice edge itself. Which probably meant, in my jaded view, that we'd roughly forty-one minutes of seagoing left before we began walking the rest of the way to the *Salamander*.

He sighed. 'What's wrong now?'

'That manifest. It doesn't actually *say* gold bars.'

'Bullion. We Internashnul Purveyors allus use the term bullion in the Refined Metals market. An' it don't say it in full because it's a bit torn.'

'It don't – *doesn't* – actually say Refined Metals either. Just Refined Me.'

'But it *does* say Jo Stalin, the Kremlin, clear as a pikestaff, and *that* ain't been ripped off. *And* it's addressed to him personally. What more proof do yer need it's got to be a priceless consignment, Mister? Uncle Joe's a busy man already, what with fightin' Hitler and organizing them purges of his, and choosin' who next to send ter the Gulags.'

True, I conceded. It was the one piece of evidence he'd bought for fifteen Irish quid and a bag of pork scratchings, that did appear incontrovertible. As, for once, did Trapp's logic. If you were expected to dictate the USSR at the same time as pursuing a war, it would indeed take something as important as a consignment note for ninety tons of gold to reach even the in-tray on your desk.

'An' another thing you can't argue with is Murphy's trading address – *Bond* Street, London, Mister,' Trapp added persuasively. 'Everyone knows London's Bond Street is the centre o' the world gold market.'

I took a deep breath and promptly started to cough. It was getting colder and colder the closer we approached the ice. Now, with every laboured inhalation the air really did freeze to crystals before it reached the back of your throat. I wandered into the chartroom to try to warm up.

The scrap of paper came from the old salt's oilskin envelope too. It was the one Trapp reckoned gave the coordinates leading to the wreck of the *Salamander*: presumably a hastily scribbled extract from her Log. There wasn't much to go on: just a succession of lats and longs plotting her drift north, with a final underlined entry that, on any self-respecting treasure trail, might at least have been marked *'Ere be GOLD* but as the old sailor had said, the doomed vessel's old man, denied sight of the sun for days on end, had been working by dead reckoning and rum alone.

The only hard fact came from my own observations. I was confident that, in another forty minutes, our position would tally precisely with the *Salamander* skipper's estimate of where she'd allegedly been swallowed by the ice. If a warmer water lead did exist, then in theory the *Charon* should find it. If it didn't – if the ice shelf was solid and thus hard as diamond when we tested it with our cement-filled bow while employing Trapp's usual degree of finesse – then . . . ?

I blanched and hurriedly turned to studying yet again our projected line of passage. I didn't want to think about the ice proving hard as diamond. I still considered myself fortunate to have been observing from a safe distance while Trapp made his approach to the convoy assembly anchorage that last time. When he'd tried to sink Scotland?

The chart showed several small islands lying outwith the main cluster that formed the desolate archipelago of Franz Joseph Land. Few bore names and none of them lay along the line of the theoretical lead I'd plotted. That in itself was worrying. It implied that if Trapp's dream island did exist, then it was so remote that not even the hardy Norwegian and Greenland sealers had come across it. Well, come across it and returned to tell the tale, anyway.

I rubbed my unshaven chin speculatively. I really must spare a moment for a quick scrape 'cause it could well be the last I ever enjoyed. The supposed experience of the *Salamander*'s lost crew didn't exactly fill me full of confidence. The way they'd wandered around in circles, dropping off the perch one by one whilst, presumably, enduring unimaginable privations

caused by running out of British seamen's staples like pickled
onions, custard powder . . . even Worcester *sauce*, Gawd 'elp
'em, to help the odd seal liver goulash or polar bear stew
down . . .

I thought about that a moment then shuddered although,
recalling the appreciation Gorbals Wullie accorded to the ship's
cat, no doubt *he'd* consider such a varied menu as on a par
with being marooned in a gourmet paradise, with or without
the Worcestershire.

I wandered back out to the open wing where Trapp leaned,
unphased by the prospect of what now lay less than a half-
hour ahead. A movement aloft caught my attention.

Trapp beat me to it. 'I posted a lookout up in the crow's
nest, Mister. So's you couldn't accuse me of not takin' precau-
tions to avoid any half-submerged floes.'

. . . To say nothing of any last-minute torpedoes from totally
submerged U-boats.

'Who?'

'Dead-Eye Alf.'

I rest my case. Raising his game to arranging that level of
emergency response, we were good as dead.

Ten minutes to go, with the raised line of the ice edge now
clearly visible just over a mile ahead yet the volume of tell-
tale smoke pouring from the *Charon*'s spindleshank funnel
still undiminished, her crankshafts still cranking, her pistons
still clamouring fit to bust.

The matter of finding the *Salamander*'s final resting place
still niggled at me. The fact that it appeared to be missing
from the chart.

'What's the name of this supposed treasure island of yours,
Trapp?'

'Tiger Island.'

'*Tiger* Island?' I repeated sceptically. 'There's no such
place.'

'Yus there is. Called after the tigers wot used to roam there.'

'Don't be silly,' I jeered. 'Who came up with that nonsense?'

'Amundsen did. Mad keen on 'is big game hunting when
he wasn't out discoverin' the South Pole, was Amundsen. Used
to shoot there.'

'But there *aren't* any tigers in the Arctic, Trapp.'

'Not nowadays there ain't, Mister,' Trapp retorted trium-phantly. 'Not *nowadays*. Not since Amundsen shot 'em all.'

'I think we should slow down now,' I suggested, gripping the rail straight-armed while steadying my legs apart.

'Trust me, Mister,' Trapp invited somewhat over-optimistically. 'She'll need a bit o' momentum behind 'er to break through even rotten ice.'

'Whit do I dae?' Wullie squeaked apprehensively from where he stood braced at the wheel; eyes like saucers.

'Keep yer mouth shut, steady as she goes – an' don't dare run away this time,' Trapp advised.

Two hundred yards to go. It wasn't so much the frozen shore one could clearly detect now, its glittering edge rising the height of a man's knee above sea level to block our path, that frightened me – sheets and sheets of ice-jumble seemingly stretching ahead of us into infinity – as what lay below it. That eerie, pallid green of submerged horrors only hinted at, fading down into the depths until lost from sight. And this was calm weather: barely a swell you'd even notice. I could only imagine the terror those sailors of the *Salamander* must have experienced while she was driven inexorably closer by the storm, with great rollers breaking and the whole line of the ice a threshing, spume-hazed night-mare . . .

Mind you, she'd been drifting slow. We were approaching like a great rusty behemoth with the radiated temperature drop-ping like a stone, the ash still whirling from the funnel, and the continual grinding and crunching of small floes and nilus ice being trampled aside to tumble and split and rear angrily, hard against our hu—?

'There's Bear Island,' Trapp announced thoughtfully out of the blue.

'Where?'

'No, I don't mean I c'n ackshully *see* it, Mister. I means there *is* a Bear Island,' he qualified helpfully. 'We passed it earlier in the voyage.'

I stared at him in disbelief.

'You're not *still* going on about names?'

'Tiger Island – Bear Island: what's the difference?'

'The difference is, there *are* bears on Bear Island, Trapp . . .'
This was bloody ridiculous.

'. . . in fact it was named Bear Island in 1596 by its Dutch discoverer, Willem Barents. The first thing his landing party met on the beach was a polar bear which, incidentally, they killed and ate. Meaning *our* Wullie, his namesake, had at least one more thing in common with him. An' don't bother arguing the point. I looked it up in the Arctic Pilot.'

'There you goes: undermining my authority yet again. Always havin' to be right,' he grumbled.

ONE hundred yards to run . . . !

FIFTY YARDS!

. . . Whereupon another thought struck him. An absolute coup de grâce of an afterthought.

'Then wot about . . . wot *about* Shackleton's island, eh, Mister? Down the Antarctic? Or are you goin' to tell me Shackleton met an *elephant* on *his* beac—?'

We hit the suburban limit of the North Polar ice shelf travelling at approximately eleven knots.

There came the most deafening *crash* . . . then she just kept going on and on and ON with a screeling and grinding and rumbling and thundering of tortured steel plates worse than a giant dragging 'is fingernails across a screechy mirror.

On and *on* we continued to carry. On and on, and up and *up* an' . . . ?

But wait a minute – we really *were* going *UP*! The *Charon*'s overhanging bow rising remorselessly before us to point to the azure blue sky well *above* the bloody horizon while Gorbals *Wullie* who, honed by his last experience off Scotland, had prepared with rat-like cunning to brace away from the wheel to prevent being thrown forward over it by the anticipated abrupt deceleration, promptly overcompensated *back*wards instead to finish up in a disenchanted muttering heap at the after end of the wheelhouse.

Dead-Eye Alf, for his part, had been fired from his crow's nest fifty feet above the deck like a stone from a sling when the foremasthead had first canted aft, then whipped forward again. Now he pendulumed, suspended only by a snapped halyard tangled around his ankle, reporting triumphantly, 'There be *ice* ahead, Captin! I thinks I sees ICE ahead.'

The rumbling stopped. And so did the angled *Charon*.

We'd arrived at our scheduled point of land – well, icefall, according to Trapp's scrap of paper.

That *bloody* ould liar in Droolin!

It appeared we'd driven to roughly a quarter of the ship's length clear up on to the ice. Not a movement, hardly a sound disturbed the Polar silence other than the gentle putter of smoke still pouring from the funnel to lay a carpet of ash across an otherwise pristine white landscape, accompanied only by the now-somewhat pointless *thresh, thresh, thresh* of our still revolving propeller. I swear I saw what I took to be an Arctic fox watching with mystified interest from a snow hummock. Then even the fox decided it must've been seeing things, and loped off.

I stared hard at Trapp, and he looked back at me. Very uncomfortably. Without a word I relaxed my vice-like grip on the rail then crabbed past him along the canted deck until I could reach the telegraph and ring down *Stop Engine*. No point in wasting steam. We'd need all we could save to keep warm. And for pressure-cooking Arctic foxes. We had at least two winters ahead of us according to tradition.

The propeller stopped turning and the smoke decreased in volume. It was very peaceful in the sub-zero sun.

Trapp was the one who gave in eventually; tentatively breaking the silence.

'Well, Mister: lookin' on the bright side, at least we, ah . . . least we don't seem to be makin' any water.'

'That, Trapp,' I retorted heavily, 'is because we're hardly *in* the bloody wat—?'

Then came an ear-splitting CRACK! and the entire ship shuddered. Then another followed . . . then a third.

'She's broken her back,' I cursed.

'*Wait*, Mister, afore you panics the crew,' Trapp cautioned tightly.

I glanced along the boat deck. The shoving and the jostling. Panic the *crew*, he said? It was like overseeing an Alcoholics Anonymous convention when someone's raised the bar shutters by mistake.

. . . Another thunderous CRACK . . . ! *Jesus!*

Then the *Charon*'s bow began to descend, slowly at first then faster and faster as several thousand tons of deadweight forced down and clear through the ice, with great rotting pancakes of it rearing and growling and standing on end above the height of the foc'slehead.

And then we were floating serene with a jaunty, told-you-so bob to the old ice-breaker.

He didn't actually say anything. He knew he didn't dare *say* anything. But the smug expression alone on Trapp's face made me want to strangle him properly this time as he side-stepped cautiously past me to ringle-tingle *Full Ahead Engine* on the telegraph.

'Our next course if you please, Mister Miller,' he requested, polite and posh as the captain of the *Titanic*. '... for *Tiger Island?*'

Seventeen

I won't weary you with the finer detail of our passage through the ice field. Not even if I could bear to recall it. Mercifully only flashbacks come to mind now, since the Colonel helped me forget.

But first, you should understand: I'd never, ever wanted to go to the Arctic, not even before I'd met Trapp. Not since my friend Ellis had told me of the odds against surviving in that wretched place, when we were apprentices together. Dead now, poor Ellis. Mate of the old *Olympian* he'd been last I heard, when she was torpedoed in the North Atlantic over a year ago on one of the HX convoys . . . but I digress again. The point is, I knew enough to know I didn't want to learn more the hard way. And certainly not Trapp's way.

I knew, for instance, that while fresh water ice requires only half the amount of heat to thaw out than does snow itself, you still had to hunt for clear blue second- and third-year ice because only then will the salt have leached from it, especially if it has thawed then refrozen. But that, however thirsty you become, you should never eat snow itself because that will dehydrate and, ultimately, kill you.

I'd been surprised to hear that rabbits were remarkably prolific up there, but that you must never eat rabbit for more than a few days no matter how desperate you are because, after that they won't satisfy your hunger; they will give you excruciating diarrhoea instead and you will die within a matter of weeks.

I'd gathered you can make a fishhook by sharpening a sliver of metal, or even wood, at both ends before suspending it in the middle, and that you could bait it, if all else failed, with a scrap of coloured cloth smeared with grease. But unless you happen to have a fire handy on which you can cook, you don't dare eat it raw anyway. The parasites in ice-water fish can rot human gut like acid.

While even if you *do* have a handy fire on which to griddle your hard-won fish, you *still* have to be very careful. A fire might well attract a polar bear which will kill you quicker than your short-term fish 'n rabbit dinner will – except you mustn't run away from that polar bear about to eat you for *his* because, if you do, then exertion will make you pant very easily in the Arctic, and a man panting is a man drawing in great gouts of super-frozen air – an' *then* you'll die in agony from internal frost bite anyway.

So, as I've said: I didn't want to go to the Arctic and, having been, I don't want to reprise any more of that dreadful experience than I have to.

. . . Although some memories do stick in my mind nevertheless. For instance I *do* still remember the constant tension. The minute by minute expectation of our bows surrendering to the inevitable, or our rudder finally ripping off as Trapp worked the *Charon*: backing and filling, always full ahead or full astern, hard a port, hard a starb'd, never cautiously, always recklessly; steadily carving a herringbone channel north through what even I was forced to concede – when I dared open my eyes to watch – did appear to be that lead of softer, rotten ice promised by his wild-eyed interlocutor.

I particularly remember the strain of navigating at the top of the world where navigation itself becomes an inexact, if not impossible science. Where the magnetic compass proves ever more valueless the closer your proximity to the Pole. Where celestial observation is made impossible by poor visibility for a large proportion of the time and, even when clear skies do favour you, as they did in our case, the margin for error is still great because the meridians converge while the longitudinal curvature renders the parallels impracticable. I did recall from my apprentice days, the art of the Dutchman's log, where a float is dropped in the water from the bow and, by calculating time measured in conjunction with the ship's known length, a rough estimate of speed and distance covered can be arrived at . . . until your bloody captain goes full astern to try and sink you once more, an' the whole tedious process has to start again.

Trapp had proposed a variation of that, although I felt I had to veto it on health and safety grounds. It would have entailed us lowering Wullie down to wait on the ice with a carefully measured quarter-mile ball of yarn. When it was all payed out, we could note how long it took, then Wullie could floe-hop back to us while rewinding the yarn to begin the process again. Assuming 'e he didn't take too long to defrost. And didn't get eaten by a polar bear in the interim, which was where the health and safety aspect came in – for the polar bear, that was. Polar bears are noted for having very delicate digestive systems.

Trapp had even planned to call it the Scotchman's log.

But above all, I remember thinking that even *then*, despite all that strain, I was still wasting my time. I mean, think about it. I was sweating cobs to guide us along a series of waypoints worked out by a possibly fictional captain who'd got lost so completely he'd passed his own original point of departure three bloody *times* before 'e give up the ghost as a navigator, an' died!

So imagine my surprise – nay, to be strictly truthful; my utter disbelief when, after several days of such misery, the impossible occurred.

When the first hint of Tiger Island's actual existence rose, clear and forbidding, out of the frost smoke blanketing the horizon ahead.

Forbidding from a distance, did I say? It looked bloody ter-rifying in close proximity. Even Edward Trapp fell strangely quiet as we neared that threatening, absurdly over-the-top Gothic horror arising sheer from an otherwise frozen, deathly silent ocean. Think of the mountain on which stood the Evil Queen's castle from the Brothers Grimm's *Snow White*, and you've conjured a vision of Tiger Island. We even had the seven dwarfs, albeit they were still aboard. Including MacDopey.

For most of that morning we laboured and smashed full ahead, full astern, along the sou'eastern perimeter of the island's black, ice-dank cliffs towards a promontory jutting like a black-boned finger into the white void; even Trapp again constrained by a novel sense of prudence as we scanned miles of floes and ice boulders piled higgledy-piggledy, end-on-end a hundred tons apiece against its base, to sight some trace – some hint – of the wreck of the *Salamander*.

I remember lowering Trapp's damned monocular-binoculars in mounting frustration tinged with – OK I admit it now – a previously unthinkable sense of disappointment.

'Nothing, Trapp. Not a snowball's chance in . . .' I hesitated, reflecting on the irony of that particular expression. 'Not the slightest chance of her surviving the pressure. She'll have been ground into iron filings years back, even if she did exist.'

'It's thinkin' on *gold* filings that pisses me off, Mister,' Trapp snarled.

'I sees an island, Captin,' Dead-Eye Alf interrupted out of the blue.

'Get 'im off the bridge, Mister,' Trapp bawled, finally snapping and losing all faith in his gem' o' a lookout. 'I won't *'ave* 'im on me bridge!'

'. . . there's smoke comin' frum it,' Alf supplemented as an afterthought.

I lifted the glasses again, scrunched my eye up, and muttered 'Bloody hell, he's right.'

'Don't *you* start, Mister. I already KNOWS there's an island there. We bin steamin' *round* it fur . . .'

'I mean about the smoke,' I said faintly.

We'd both failed to detect it.

Alf's Elastoplast-suspended spectacle glittered happily in the sun. Just as the brightest facet of any precious gem would.

You will, of course, appreciate the import of that impossible phenomenon – the smoke I mean: not Alf's intermittently superhuman vision. That either someone, or some *Thing* possessing a box of matches, was already there on Tiger Island. And given my previous unsettling reflections on that stuff of children's nightmares conjured by the Brothers Grimm, I reckoned it was anyone's guess as to which of the two it might prove to be.

The smoke still continued to spiral lazily into the mercifully windless sky two hours later as we finally rounded the headland, whereupon the north eastern flank of the island was revealed: seemingly every bit as impregnable in its malevolent, brooding majesty. By then Trapp had managed to persuade me we were merely observing a natural phenomenon, undoubtedly volcanic in origin. Me happy to believe it because I didn't dare visualize an alternative: Trapp because he couldn't bring himself to even contemplate the prospect of someone else having got to the gold first.

'Still nothin', Mister,' he muttered gloomily. I'd never seen him so down. 'No entry, no break in the cliffs. Just ice an' fang-toothed rock.'

It was my turn to snap. *He* was the one supposed to keep morale up. 'Well, whaddya *expect*, Trapp: sun-sweltered beaches an' fuckin' *palm* trees? It's the fuckin' ARCTIC f'r Chris—'

'You're jus' tired, Mister Miller. Per'aps the Captin could take us back to that entrance an' let you 'ave a bit of a lie down,' the astonishing Alf suggested solicitously.

'WHAT fuckin' entrance?'

'The one we jus' sailed past,' the also-very-dense Alf said. 'About twenty minnits ago?'

Even on closer approach it was difficult to identify, the way one headland overlapped and virtually merged into the other when observed from seaward. Nor was it to prove so much an entrance as an ice-fouled dog leg: a rock-lined chicane through which we eventually pushed and shoved with growing anxiety: our trepidation not merely generated by what hidden dangers might lie below the keel but also because, high *above* the *Charon* and spilling out from either wall, teetered great overhangs of age-compacted snow seemingly ready to fall should even the weight of a snow bunting alight on them. Rather, I found myself reflecting bizarrely, as the fluff-puff crust of an overcooked soufflé will expand to overspill the edge of its dish. Except those particular soufflés weighed thousands of tons and, indeed, had extended until they were nearly touching. So much so, in fact, that for several tense minutes we found ourselves sliding through a virtual ice tunnel within which the light dimmed to a sickly, malevolent green and where the beat of even the stoutest heart could be heard louder than the pulse of the slowly turning engine.

And then the sun returned, washing first across the foc'sle then aft along the foredeck until, a moment later, its welcome cheer reached the bridge itself. Trapp turned her short round to starb'd with a skilfully orchestrated jangling of telegraph bells and a great spurting of ash from the funnel, to clear the last ice buttress by the width of a hand.

Whereupon each and every one of us gazed in silent awe on the panorama which opened before us.

We found we'd entered an inland lagoon a good mile wide. It twinkled placid in the sun, with little convoys of brash ice bobbing and swirling and running away from us in excitement, propelled by the thrust from our screw as we threshed and juddered astern, then stopped.

On either side of that unexpected topographical anomaly, a continuation of brooding frost-rhymed cliff faces encircled the *Charon* but ahead, perhaps half a mile ahead, appeared to lie nothing more menacing than a gently shelving beach littered with nothing more threatening than clusters of ice boulders.

. . . And *that* discovery marked the point when my jaw did literally drop. This time I really was gazing on the impossible. For on what had promised otherwise to prove an ideal landing place for anyone sending a boat ashore, someone – or maybe that Some*thing* I've already referred to – had built a . . . ?

'Mister,' Trapp hissed urgently. '*Mister*!'

'Dammit!' I exploded aggrievedly. Just as I'm workin' on conjuring a good Grimm bugaboo in the dripping flesh, so to speak, *he* goes an' interrupts.

When he next called, it was in a reverential whisper. '*Look*, Mister.'

Reluctantly I dragged my eyes from the beach to follow his pointing finger.

. . . Only to find myself staring, still open-mouthed, at the wreck of the Steamship *Salamander*.

She lay within a fissure where beach merged with rock face: wedding cake white as the *Charon* herself had appeared several days earlier, with every surviving wire and rail spun in strands of gossamer ice; careened to port with her tramp-typical funnel leaning drunkenly, her foremast sheered off clean below the crosstrees, and her mainmast overlaying that frozen inland sea. Even from a distance one could understand why her crew hadn't simply rigged a jury rudder and at least attempted to break their way back through the ice field. I could make out the great gash in way of her numbers four and five holds through which, over the intervening years, countless tons of ice had since clambered. A fatal incision inflicted, presumably, as she was carried helplessly through that macerator of an entrance, or otherwise she would have foundered before arriving at the island.

'Can you make out if 'er number two's still sound?' Trapp agitated. 'Thass where the gold wus stowed, Mister. *Murphy's* Gold.'

'Bugger Murphy's anything. First things first, Trapp,' I muttered, switching my gaze uneasily back inland . . . no, not uneasily – damned *apprehensively* back to that beach, with the short hairs at the back of my neck already beginning to creep. 'Concentrate on the beach, Trapp. Tell me what you see.'

He went all huffy at being diverted but, maybe reading my expression, spared a moment for a quick glance.

'Nuthin'. Just piles o' ice cast up on the shoreline, an' a . . . ?'

'A volcano, you reckon? Like you'd decided an hour ago that's the only thing it could be?' I asked.

'No,' he muttered, shuffling awkwardly.

'Pardon? I didn't quite hear that.'

'NO it's *not* a volcano!' he shouted. 'It's a bloody BONFIRE.'

. . . All of which confirmed the origin and source of the unsettling smoke, but failed to explain what manner of creature had ignited it, or why, as not a sign of movement could be seen.

Trapp took the first boat ashore, I followed in the second. In keeping with the *Charon*'s established tradition of boat handling incompetence, it was like helming a race between *two* dysfunctional water-beetles, with the added handicap of having to break through wafer ice at the same time.

Wullie the Movie Buff didn't help boost my morale much, either. 'Dae ye remember that King Kong film, Mister Miller sir? Made in 1933 it wis. Jist before yon *Salamander* disappeared. That one where the sailors row ashore tae that creepy island wi' all they prehistoric monsters, then finds theirsel's chased by a giant griller? Bruce Cabot wis in that. An' Fay Wray wis the lady screamin' in the palm o' the big monkey's hand . . .'

'Shurrup an' row,' I grated. 'Although personally, for the

record, I think Noel Coward would have played the explorer's role much more convincingly.'

Trapp met us on the beach. 'Just had a look at the bonfire. I was wonderin' what you could find to burn in the Arctic. It's all ship's gear cannibalized frum the *Salamander*. Couple o' doors, mess tables, a few broke-up packin' cases . . .'

He broke off, narrowing his eyes. ''Ang on – what's that?'

'What's *what*?' I yelped, whirling like a top. His suspicious stare had been focused on a spot *behind* me.

'Over there. Behind that ice boulder. Somethin' moved.'

'Could be King Kong,' Wullie observed sagaciously. 'Mind youse, it wid have tae be an awfy *wee* King Kong.'

'I saw that one too, shipmate,' Dead-Eye supplemented, predictable as ever. 'Where them sailors rows ashore to that creepy islan—'

. . . Then *I* saw it! No, *not* that ridiculous Hollywood griller . . . *gorilla*! I mean my own personal, straight-from-the-quills of the Brothers Grimm monster. Well, part of it at first. Lord it was hairy. Fur all matted and sticking up above the ice, spiky as a greaser's mop. Then an eye appeared round the side of the boulder, and fixed us with a malevolent stare. A horrible, glittering, mad eye . . .

'Come out, yer wastin' my time,' Trapp bellowed, desperate to get over to the wreck and unimaginative with it. 'Come out, come out 'ooever you are.'

There hung a pregnant silence. Until . . .

'Come OUT, is it?' the monster retorted in a high-pitched, quavering voice. 'When it comes to comin' anywheres, YOU lot 'as been a bloody long time coming in the fust place.'

'I lights a fire: an internashnully recognized distress signal,' the seemingly grumpy monster continued unabated. Almost as if It hadn't had opportunity to converse with a single soul for many years. 'An' wot does you do, Captin? Sails right on past, you do.'

Ohhhh shit, *another* one can't speak proper, I reflected dispiritedly while surreptitiously sidling to place Wullie between It and me. All this crude seaman dialogue's going to be a bugger to transcribe once I get down to writing that journal of mine after this war's over. *If* I should be so lucky, which hardly appears likely under the circumstances.

Ever so cautiously the monster shuffled from behind its refuge and became, instead, your straightforward, common-or-garden Polar apparition. Wild-eyed, raggedy . . . you know the sort of Thing. The kind of ancient mariner anyone might come across in an Irish pub although, paradoxically, I *did* notice that, sticking from beneath tattered trousers, he displayed a pair of Preston Knittinghouse Elegant Brand gentlemen's woollen socks that nicely complemented brand new, shiny leather boots. And in addition, that he clutched a most stylish silver-topped walking stick that could well have come straight from the box.

Trapp looked him up and down, then frowned. 'You don't happen to 'ave a brother in Spud Land, do yer?'

'Not unless me mother, Missis Gunn, may she Rest in Peace Bless 'er, done somethin' me dad di'n't know about.'

'Gunn?' I hazarded incredulously. 'You wouldn't, by any chance, be . . . *Ben* Gunn?'

'BERT Gunn, matey,' the irritable Apparition snapped. '*Bert* Gunn. This ain't a fuckin' remake o' Treasure Island, you knows.'

'Well, would yer believe it. I see'd *that* too,' Dead-Eye announced, shaking his head in wonderment.

'You'll get on well with me cook; a turn of invective like that,' Trapp approved cheerfully. 'So why ain't you dead, then?'

''Oo's dead?'

'Yer shipmates. All but one of 'em.'

'I allus knew it.' He shook his head, more vindicated than grief-stricken. 'I told 'em they wus leavin' too premature, but they wus never the same after the Worcester sauce run out. Which one made it 'ome?'

'Hairy feller. Tattood anchor starb'd paw: mermaid on the other?'

'Silver, that'd be. Mad as a brush, Silver wus.'

It was Wullie's turn to reprise movie magic. 'Not . . . no' Long *John* Silver?'

'FRED Silver, matey. That Robert Louis Stevenson's gotter lot ter answer for,' our crusty new companion snorted aggrievedly. 'An' anyways, by my recollection 'e wus more short than long, wus Fred. Especially in the 'ead.'

But obviously you must be getting impatient to find out about the gold. Just as Trapp had been, to say the least. Especially after Gunn airily confirmed its existence.

'Murphy's Gold?' he'd nodded with remarkable phlegm. But then, after eight years, most of 'em spent in sub-zero solitary, the custodianship of ninety tons of bullion had probably lost its novelty. 'Ho yus, it still be there, Captin. Safe stowed down number two atween the pickled 'errings an' the liquorish all-sorts.'

Oh, dear: you should have *seen* Trapp's expression . . . anyway, moving on – we'd slipped and scrambled up a cobbled-together side ladder leading to the *Salamander*'s listing forr'ad decks: the ladder so rickety it was a wonder Gunn survived as long as he had. I mean, what *else* other than securing things properly, had he found to pass the time during the endless Arctic summer days? Mind you, at least he'll feel at home when we take him back aboard the *Charon*, I thought; albeit our crew are even lazier, and the *Salamander*'s still in better condition.

'I been livin' in the old man's cabin, o' course. Since he didn't 'ave use for it no more,' he volunteered conversation-ally as we ploughed and panted through uncleared snow to reach number two hatch. In fact he'd never stopped bloody talking since we'd come upon him. 'Plenty o' grub in the cargo, though I'd runned out o' Darjeeling tea by 1939. Otherwise nice; very comfy altogether. The Chief Engineer 'ad a lot o' books ter pass the time with. Pity I never learned ter rea—'

'Please make 'im shut up, Mister,' Trapp snarled eventu-ally, driven to distraction despite being only moments away from achieving his life's ambition as he hauled impatiently at the hatch canvas draped over one corner of the coaming from which the boards had already been removed.

It was eerie down there in the tweendeck: dim and dank and frost-encrusted, with mini snowdrifts settled in corners whence it had blown. It became immediately evident that parts of her cargo had been breached. Gaps in the stow revealed splintered packing cases and wrenched open cardboard boxes jumbled together with broken spars of dunnage and grass-matting separ-ators; all scattered carelessly across the rusted deck.

'Me pantry,' our host said proudly. 'I jus' never seems ter find the time to tidy up.'

'Like I said, you *will* get on well with our cook,' Trapp growled sardonically. ''E's as house-proud as you are . . . now where's the Murphy's consignment?'

'Be'ind yer, on yer port hand,' Gunn pointed. 'Boxes an' boxes of it, see?'

Trapp whirled, blinked, then looked disconcerted. 'Where?'

'That can't be it,' I frowned, eyeing ranks of cases stretching clear across the hold until lost in the darkness. 'They're too big, Trapp. Each box could hold twenty bars, never mind one apiece like you reckoned. And that's plainly inconceivable as it would imply that each case weighs over a ton. *And* they're only cardboard boxes at that.'

His mouth dropped open while his eyes rounded to twice their normal diameter. But as ever, Trapp being Trapp, greed triumphed over logic as sure as gold is for fools. 'That'd be eight thousand times *twenty* bars . . . ? Comes to, ah, one 'undred an' *sixty* thou—'

'Just say eighteen hundred tons and be done with it,' I said. 'Now you can add the United States Federal reserve to the Bank of England's, and you'll still be richest.'

'Maybe it's the wrong parcel o' cargo,' he blurted.

'No, it's no',' Wullie called from the gloom. 'It says on this label: *Mister Josif Stalin, care of The Kremlin, Moscow.*'

'O' course, I've et a fair bit of it,' Bert Gunn supplemented, to further confuse the issue. 'Very tasty it wus.'

'ET it . . . ? 'Ow *much* 'ave you et?' Trapp screamed, practically beside himself and thus somewhat overlooking the fundamental flaw implicit in Gunn's claim.

'Ohhhh, about two thousand one 'undred cases. Jus' last week I'd reckoned there wus still enough left ter keep me goin' another thirty years.'

'I think, Trapp,' I interrupted gently as I could, 'the time has come for us to open the box.'

According to Trapp's educated guess, the text lost by virtue of the manifest page's corner having gone missing wus *bound* – unless yer *reely* stupid, Mister – to have read:

> Shipper: *House of Murphy, Bond Street, London.*
> *By Royal Appointment, Purveyors of Refined Me . . . tals.*
> Quantity and Description: *8,021 boxes Gold B . . . ullion.*

The printed label on the first tin I withdrew after Trapp had broken every fingernail while desperately ripping apart the nearest cardboard box, begged to be at slight variance with his interpretation.

IT said:

> *House of Murphy, Bond Street, London**derry**,*
> **Northern Ireland**
> *By Royal Appointment*
> *Purveyors of Refined **Meals** and **Treats** for Gentlefolk*
> MURPHY'S GOLD B**RAND**
> **BAKED BEANS**
> *Finest quality Fagioli Beans in Rich Tomato Sauce*

Trapp had been absolutely spot on with one aspect of his argument, mind you.

'Very fond o' his Murphy's Gold, Joe Stalin is,' Bert Gunn said, innocently unaware of the storm about to break over his *Salamander*. 'This wus the third batch this ship had loaded for Archangel, addressed to 'im personally.'

Well, an incandescent Trapp kicked the *shit* out've Murphy's bloody Beans for a good ten minutes after that. So violently that Wullie shot up the hatch ladder and on to the deck like a rat up a drainpipe, so scared of being next was he. But that was one of the things that made me feel sympathetic towards Gorbals Wullie, albeit infrequently. After years of sailing with Trapp, his self-esteem had fallen so low he was even content to accept he came second place to a row of beans.

Me? I didn't mind. I was just glad we could now extricate ourselves from Disneyland and try to thumb an escorted passage onward to Murmansk with the next passing PQ convoy. Assuming the old *Charon* contrived to hold her bones together for long enough to punch her way back to the Barents in the first place, that was.

. . . While you, my steadfast companion throughout that terrible voyage? I can only apologize if this, my faithfully recorded journal of Trapp's search for a treasure beyond any sensible man's dream appears to have concluded with something of an anticlimax. There isn't even some wise maxim one might have hoped to draw from its pages. It turned out that Trapp hadn't even got what you might consider his just desserts: being conned by a rogue even more adept at skulduggery than he. Because it seemed, according to a slightly surprised Bert Gunn, unused to observing such unconstrained displays of pique, that there'd been no question of the undoubtedly plausible Short Fred Silver having lied to Trapp in the *Fenian Boy*. Turned out simple old Fred really *had* believed they wus carryin' bullion f'r Joe Stalin in number two. Apparently the rest of her crew had thought it a great joke: kidding 'im they had boxes an' boxes o' gold aboard a rusty old tramp . . . and it 'adn't been hard convincing 'im. Like Bert said, 'e'd been mad as a brush frum the start.

. . . Which, of course, he must have been, poor fellow. I mean, who *else* in their right mind could possibly have fallen for an old sailor's yarn like *that*?

But WAIT . . . ! Do I sense you're about to close these pages and shuffle, disillusioned, off to bed?

Because, begging your pardon, but I haven't quite finished my tale. There's more. We haven't actually got back to the Barents Sea yet, remember? And surely you don't imagine Trapp would have managed to achieve such a straightforward, if admittedly formidable endeavour without once succumbing to his own stubbornly held conviction that he was immortal. Just as he was inclined to loftily disregard the possibility that the rest of us weren't.

It all began with a casual remark.

'Never mind,' I'd offered consolingly once he'd calmed down enough to kick only the odd can in despondent ill-humour. 'At least you haven't sunk us this time. So far. And there's probably a thriving black market for pickled onions in Murmansk.'

'It's this bloody war,' he sighed. 'I wouldn't never have gone to Ireland in the fust place if it 'adn't been f'r the bloody war.'

'War?' Gunn frowned blankly. 'Wot war?'

'*The* war.'

'That wus over ages ago. The Kaiser lost.'

'I mean this next one. Hitler's War.'

''Oo's 'Itler?'

It had been a long time, eight years, to be unaware of what's going on around you in the world. Although Gorbals Wullie had managed to achieve that blissful state all his life, no problem.

'The bloke we're fighting. Again. And all his other Germans, of course. And the Italians *and* the Japanese and, in Captain Trapp's case, our own Admiralty. And we used to be fighting the Russians but now we're allies and we send them stuff.'

'More Murphy's beans?' Bert hazarded. 'Joe Stalin loves 'is Murph—'

'If 'e mentions beans again, I'll kill 'im quicker than the torpedoes will,' Trapp said.

'What torpedoes?'

'The torpedoes they kept firing at us on our way up here,' I expanded.

'Ahhhhh,' Gunn nodded sagely. 'That explains it then.'

'Explains what?'

'Them U-boats I keeps seein'.'

I looked at Trapp and Trapp looked at me.

'WHAT U-boats you keeps seein'?' we roared in unison.

'Them U-boats as comes in 'ere reg'lar as clockwork. Enjoy a bit o' relaxation frum the daily slog. Do a bit o' fishin': poke around the old *Salamander*. Run up an' down on the beach. Personally I keeps me 'ead tucked in when they comes – won't 'ave no truck with German fellers . . . an' there's *no* need ter shout.'

He drew back the frayed cuff of his sleeve. I noted he was wearing a most elegant *Jaeger-le-Coultre* gold watch with platinum wrist band and date-month facility. Useful when no one posts you a calendar every Christmas. But like I've said: tramps under the Red Duster carried the argosies of the world; especially in their strongrooms.

'In fac' the next one's due in day after tomorrow,' Gunn added. 'Bout ten o clock.'

Eighteen

She was one of Dönitz's new VII-C *Atlantic* class boats. Long and lean, black and rapacious-looking as a killer whale to every Allied merchant seaman. She mounted a 105-millimetre cannon forr'ad, and twin Oerlikons in anti-aircraft configuration on the stepped, rail-enclosed platform abaft her conning tower. *Der Wintergarten* the Arctic U-boat men called it, and most aptly to my way of thinking. As she nosed round the last bluff I swear the chill in that brooding inland sea plummetted a further ten degrees.

I stole a tense glance along the beach to my right. Trapp crouched stony-faced ten yards from me, then Gorbals Wullie then Dead-Eye, then, making up our flank, Trapp's favourite antagonist, the Cook; still wearing his butchers apron and still muttering in black-browed resentment at having been dragged frum 'is galley ter do a job totally outwith 'is bloody mandate as flat bread baker an' chairperson of the S.S. *Charon* Debating Society.

. . . But muttering very, *very* softly. Even concealed as we were behind those hastily fashioned parapets of snow, each of us felt horribly vulnerable. Apart from Trapp, of course. But him an' his bloody immortality was our problem. Otherwise we wouldn't've been there at all.

Hastily I switched my eyes back to the transit I'd pre-selected. An imaginary fixed line drawn from a wind-eroded rock column perched on the top of the cliffs to seaward, to ourselves. It cut straight across the middle of the lagoon. I was banking on the U-boat turning short round to starboard as Trapp had done, and thus presenting her broadside as she then moved to seek the deeper water in the centre. Twenty fathoms I'd sounded it to after breaking through the slush ice, and still not found bottom.

I tensed. She *was* beginning to swing. Half ahead port, full astern starboard . . . the snub bow now pointing directly at us with the bulge of her saddle tanks glinting red rusted under the patina of ice already forming over water spilled from her casing when she'd surfaced before entry. She'd spent a long time on patrol it seemed. Could well be one from the wolf pack that had savaged our own convoy before we'd, ah . . . parted company with it.

Dangerously distracted for a moment, I thought about the Navy carrier and wondered if she'd made it back to Iceland. I hoped they had. Then I thought about the little Greek *Λουλούδι*, and whether she'd reached the ice barrier before she finally sank. I hoped she hadn't. From what I'd since observed for myself, the two minutes it takes to lapse into unconsciousness before drowning up past 79 degrees North is a far kinder way for a seaman to die.

The subdued mutter of her diesel engines carried clear, as did low voices, an occasional laugh from those crewmen already savouring the luxury of daylight however lacking in warmth. Otherwise there wasn't a sound to break the silence. Rest and recreation, Bert Gunn had reckoned, and he was right. No one manned her guns: only a skeleton watch below and the rest of her complement already spilling from her hatches to suck deep and appreciatively of the bitter cold oxygen. Secure in that secret harbour they could relax, forget their personal terrors which mirrored our own and, for a precious few hours, become carefree men again.

It was understandable. But ill-advised.

Ever so surreptitiously I raised my arm. Three and a half pairs of eyes locked on to it. The U-boat was heading broadside on to me now. Her bow touched, then passed through my imaginary line of transit, followed by the saw-toothed net cutters that marked the base of her forestay. Then her deck gun, still secured precisely fore and aft as would be expected of any warship when not in harm's way . . . *then* the forward round of her conning tower – three bright yellow oilskin sou'westers projecting above its armoured rim to mark her watch look-outs, with a fourth head, this time wearing a white cap, turned to face towards me. I took two seconds to digest the import of the flash that suddenly reflected the sun – *Jesus*: the flash from Zeiss binocular lenses scanning the beach where we waited.

I wrenched my hand down.

'FIIĴIIRE . . . !' I roared. 'Shoot – *shoot* – SHOO—?'

Oh, f'r *cryin'* out loud. Just as I've come to the crucial pa—

What's that? What's that you interrupt my flow with yet *again*?

'FIRE?' did you ask? 'Fire *what* . . . ?' are you yelling in purple-faced frustration at the pages of this journal. '*Another* short cut, is it . . . ? *Another* of the damn fellow's literary devices to save himself the effort of offering even the most convoluted explanation, as any half-competent author would?'

'How come,' do I hear you further snarl, 'How *come* you're down the *Salamander*'s number two on one page, watching Trapp kick beans about, then by the next you've adopted a totally new role – one never previously even *hinted* at in the text, one might add – in which you're making like some kind of naval *gunnery* officer?'

Well, I'm sorry, pal. I'm a merchant bloody seaman, not bloody Tolstoy.

But seeing you've been so fu— so *considerate* as to raise the issue, then I'll rewind an hour or two . . .

I'd made it halfway up the ladder by the time Bert Gunn had finished delivering his bombshell.

'NOW where are you goin', Mister?' Trapp had bawled, still grumpy-faced over losing ninety tons of gold he'd never had.

'Back to the *Charon* to prepare her for sea. We have to get out of here fast.'

'To where? There's miles of ice out there, an' a U-boat comin' the same track we got to go follow back. Even submerged she'll be using her periscopes. We'll stick out like a stoker's thumb poked up through a slice o' bread.'

True, I mulled. For once I couldn't disagree with his logic. Which meant we *had* no way out: nowhere to run to. And because, for some inexplicable reason, the Royal Navy hadn't felt able to trust Trapp, no way to even attempt to defend ourselves.

Which meant we were dead.

'Oh, I wish we had a gun,' I'd gloomed a few minutes later, too dejected to care that I was becoming more like Trapp than

Trapp by the day. 'It's all your fault they didn't give us a gun. If you hadn't been so irresponsible in the old *Charon*, an' the Admiral didn't hate you so much, they'd've given us a DEMS gun like everybody else.'

'If *you'd* bothered to question that Fred Silver's cargo manifest more closely when I asked yer to, Mister,' he'd grumbled back, 'you might've persuaded me beans di'n't mean bullion an' we wouldn't 'ave come in the first place.'

Persuade him? Yeah, right, I thought morosely. And Wullie might turn out to be Einstein cruising incognito, an' pigs might overtake Stukas in a dive.

'Yeah, right,' I snapped. 'An' Wullie might turn out to be . . .'

'*Cargo* manifest,' he interrupted rudely.

'We've been there, done that bit.'

'I means our *Charon*'s manifest, Mister. You're the Mate. You should know what cargo she's carrying for Joe Stalin's benefit.'

I'd done a pierhead jump. Trapp's paperwork was an even greater shambles than his ship. I hadn't had two minutes spare to read anything without him shouting at me since we left Scotland.

'Not more Murphy's Beans?' I retorted sourly.

'The IRA wusn't planning to buy beans, Mister. No more'n the Russkis are planning to throw tins at the Nazis. That's a *war* cargo we got below the hatches.'

I stared at him. There was a look in his eye: a frightening look I hadn't seen since we'd sunk our last enemy ship together. Hard. Cold as the steel of a Toledo sword. Merciless as . . . as a U-boat.

'Including forty British Army 6-pounder anti-tank guns.'

The good news was they were stowed, easily accessible, in number five upper tween deck. Along with two thousand rounds of armour-piercing ammunition designed to kill tanks. Even better, U-boats are thinner-skinned than tanks. Otherwise, Panzers or U-boats: not much difference. They both bucket around a lot when they're moving fast, and are vulnerable when they go slow. Unless they fire first, then it's you that dies.

The bad news was that, according to Gunn's *Jaeger-le-Coultre* we had less than thirty-six hours to transport them from ship

to shore: a formidable seamanship challenge in itself considering each gun weighed 2,520 pounds, roughly a ton, while we
only had two semi-derelict lifeboats to tackle it with . . . then
while I set up the guns, Trapp would have to take the *Charon*
back out under that bloody terrifying arch before anchoring her
out of sight the other side of the headland. *Then*, because he'd
insisted on being in at the kill, return overland to the beach on
his own in sub-zero temperatures through God only knew *what*
depths of drifted snow . . .

I rather enjoyed that bit of the plan. Surviving that, I thought
cheerfully, he'll *need* to be immortal.

'We got ten packing cases o' snow-shoes down number one,
Captin. Makes f'r a nice easy stroll,' Gunn had assured him.
'Very bracing.'

The ubiquitous Red Duster cargo again. But then, the old
salt had had eight bloody years to practise with them. Trapp
had spent his last eight years slouching over a bridge rail. Oh
I *did* enjoy that part of the plan.

The worst news of all was I had the *Charon*'s crew to
contend with. Turning them into even half-competent sailors
would require twelve months shouting, if ever. Turning them
into fighting soldiers, a further year. Turning them into heroes
on *top* of that would need a bloody miracle.

Mind you their only alternative – having their various body
parts spread across the Arctic by a Krupps 105-millimetre
cannon – was to prove a great motivator in that respect.

And anyway, had it been easy, Trapp wouldn't have dreamed
up such a plan in the first place.

With Trapp bawling at everybody, and me checking their
knots, wearily re-tying any girlie bows they'd made, we lashed
the two boats together catamaran-fashion with stout spars
between to provide a platform on which to ferry each gun
laboriously to the beach. We managed to lose three overboard
before they got the hang of rowing together while learning
that two inflated rubber tyres simply couldn't keep a one-ton
weapon afloat.

We managed to get five ashore, with two rounds of ammunition apiece, before running out of time. We wouldn't need
more than two rounds apiece. In fact I suspected we wouldn't
need more than one round apiece. Assuming Trapp's master

plan worked as effectively as all his previous master plans had done, the second shells fired would be coming inward.

We laboured to haul the guns in place before I hastily set up the killing ground: selecting, literally, the dead centre of the lagoon as my aiming point. That's where my imaginary line came in. The U-boat would have to pass through it as she'd no other option. There wasn't enough sea room to anchor short of it. Meticulously I laid each gunsight with its cross hairs precisely aligne—

Pardon . . . ? What's that now? How could I, a common trade sailor, possibly have known how to aim and fire an army anti-tank gun. Aren't I stretching your credulousness too far yet again . . . ?

Well, apart from having acquired extra-curricular gunnery skills from serving in my first destroyer, then honing them razor sharp as Trapp's number one in the old HMS *Charon*, what d'you *think* I'd spent my time in the desert doing? Potting the odd Panzerkampfwagen had proved a bloody sight more fulfilling than lying around in a hospital and anyway, a steel gunshield offered rather better protection than a canvas tent. I was good with big guns, naval or field artillery. Just ask all those poor sods I'd already murdered in the name of war, down the Mediterranean.

So, with your permission, might I presume to continue . . . ?

Meticulously I'd laid each gunsight with the cross hairs precisely aligned along the transit, and the barrel elevation set to zero. At point-blank range like that a monkey could put a round through a teaplate. Unfortunately I didn't have the advantage of commanding monkeys. Apart from Trapp, who just managed to make it back in time looking rather like an angry, panting yeti after parking the ship, I had Gorbals Wullie – who I'd had to drag kicking an' screaming up the beach to volunteer as one of my suicide artillerymen – plus Dead-Eye Alf and the Cook. Certainly the latter possesses all the aggression needed to make a good gunner. Never mind Grumpy Gunn: our pugnacious Cook would've got on well with *Hitler*.

'Who did you leave in charge,' I asked Trapp.

'That Bosun bloke,' he growled, snapping icicles off the peak of his cap. 'Told 'im not to touch anything.'

'Dick Head?'

'No. Jus' dickhead!'

And by ten minutes to ten, we were ready. I'd reduced the requirement for intelligent thought to a minimum. All they had to do was squeeze a trigger grip. And hope Hermann the German at the other end didn't beat them to it.

At one minute past ten, thanks to Teutonic punctuality, I raised my hand.

By two minutes past, I'd screamed, 'FIIIIIRE . . . ! Shoot – *shoot* – SHOOT!'

It was slaughter. One round would have been enough. It must have hit the submarine's ready-use ammunition locker located at the base of her conning tower, being her main armament bin containing up to ten 105-millimetre shells. Enough of them detonated simultaneously to blow the entire structure over the side along with most of her crewmen enjoying the sun. I glimpsed a white cap falling, fluttering and spiralling like a dead leaf through the fireball. Before it landed I caught sight of Trapp's eyes. They were flint hard, as were mine. Rules of war again: them or us. That could've been our caps a few days ago when we were defenceless. Well, my cap anyway. Trapp's was already in a worse condition than the U-boat Kapitan's: even after the explosion.

Three more AP rounds hit her saddle tanks just above the waterline. At least two penetrated clear through her pressure hull to explode inside the boat itself. Great fingers of white-hot flame licked up through her already open hatches and she rolled to port with a few dazed, terrified men still clinging to her casing, then sank quietly beneath the fractured skin of ice. Only one or two heads resurfaced above the oil-fouled water.

'Leave 'em be, Mister,' Trapp said tonelessly. 'We can't get to 'em. An' they only got minutes. If the oil don't kill 'em first.'

I was still frowning uncertainly, thinking I'd only been aware of four rounds having been fired, when I heard the amiable Alf down the end of the line muttering in what, for him, was strong language. 'Dash an' fiddlesticks,' he was grumbling in evident frustration. 'I jus' *can't* get this gun ter fire.'

'That's because you're turning the wrong wheel,' I called consolingly. He'd already managed to elevate the muzzle high enough to double as a howitzer. 'The trigger's on the other side . . . but *don't* squeeze it now.'

'Shouldn't we reload, Mister Miller sir?' Wullie asked

enthusiastically. He'd always been a feisty, brave little tiger. *After* we'd won a battle.

I shuddered at the thought of Gorbals Wullie handling an armour-piercing shell, even if he knew which end of the barrel to stuff it in. Anything with gunpowder in it, he tended to set off accidentally.

'Negative. No need. Leave the gun alone.'

'You sure?' he said, looking slightly perplexed.

'Course I'm sure.'

There followed an expressive silence.

'*Now* what's wrong?' I queried tentatively, aware he was disappointed. Firing guns at people can become addictive.

'Nuthin'.'

Shit, I thought. He's going all precious and awkward on me. 'OUT with it, man!'

'I jist wondered,' Wullie grumbled reluctantly, 'what you wis going tae dae aboot . . .'

He shrugged. Be it on my own head was the clear implication.

'Aboo— about *what*?'

'Yon other submarine,' Wullie muttered sullenly. 'The wan that's jist come in through the tunnel.'

Nineteen

We didn't stand a chance. Four guns empty, our last hope of staying alive elevated high enough to shoot albatrosses, an' manned by a guy who couldn't even clock where its trigger was. It struck me then that Dead-Eye Alf's good eye was only a dead-eye when the object of its attention was a long way away. He was blind as a bat when it came to seeing in close-up. It was why he'd kept walking into things like doors and stuff.

I tried. Me and Trapp an' the Cook, we all *tried* to reload: snatching to yank open the breeches, spent brass shell cases expelling through an acrid pulse of cordite smoke – clawing to grip the ice-cold tube of the next . . . Wullie doing bugger all; adopting a policy of non-cooperation, just kneeling with elbow on *his* gun, chin on hand, eyes pointedly studying the sky; makin' it plain he was in a black huff and had no intention of participating further in Miller's War.

'No way we'll make it, Mister,' Trapp bellowed furiously, affording me my Sunday name for what was probably the last time ever. 'They been alerted. Stood to at action stations, gun crew closed up an' ready.'

And they were. I couldn't even detect the barrel of their cannon, largely because it was pointing straight *at* me! Even as the submarine swung to clear the bluff it continued to train on us. *Bloody* U-boats! You wait scared, heart in your mouth f'r days, then all of a sudden two come along at once.

Roughly four seconds left . . . *three* . . . WHY didn't they *fire*? I punched the shell into the breech and slammed the block, damn near amputating my thumb in the process – not that it mattered: Herr Krupps had devised something far more effective at amputating things. I still lunged hopelessly for the trigger grip.

Two seconds. Christ it was cold. My numbed fingers could hardly close around the trigger.

ONE secon—?

'Well, would yer believe it,' Trapp said.

I froze altogether then. And stared.

The flag running up the conning tower halyard afforded a pleasing splash of colour against the towering, ice-fouled background of the entrance.

Red, white and blue it was. Horizontally striped . . . stars in the upper quadrant?

That battle Ensign of the United States Navy.

Twenty

They never spoke to us, you know. The whole way back to the Barents Sea, they'd refused to speak to us: them simmering at one end of the *Charon* and us feeling embarrassed at the other.

I mean, they hadn't *had* to hold fire with such steely discipline. They could easily have shot first and apologized to the ice craters within which parts of us still frizzled, later. It was very decent of the Lootenant Commander to show such restraint, and smart of him to appraise the situation so quickly. It seemed he'd been stalking the U-boat under the ice, curious to discover why Grand Admiral Dönitz was allowing his captains to sneak off up towards the Pole in between PQ convoys. Even more fortunate for us, he'd been quick to put two and two together soon as he'd heard the explosions and identified the swirling wreckage as having come from a German boat. Meaning it could only have arisen – or rather, submerged – as a result of friendly fire.

Well, friendly from an Allied point of view anyway.

So I could appreciate the American submariners' resentment, and why they'd felt such disenchantment. In fact I sympathized with them unreservedly. But to make a whole international *incident* out of it – to allow any subsequent co-operation between the US and British navies to be placed in jeopardy throughout the rest of the war . . . ?

Yes, all *right* – I haven't overlooked your previous criticisms. I *am* going to explain without being pushed this time.

It had all been Dead-Eye Alf's fault. See?

'DON'T FIRE!' I'd screamed the moment I'd recognized they were on our side. 'Check, *check* . . . CHECK!'

'Fire . . . dinnae fire. Fire – *dinnae* fire. Don't lissen,' Wullie advised a seagull. 'Bluidy officers. Aye indecisive.'

'It's orlright, I found it Mister Miller sir,' Alf called delight-
edly, having been totally absorbed until that point with
fumbling for his field gun's trigger.

'STOP 'IM!' Trapp bawled.

'BOOOOM,' the gun roared.

'That'll show them bastards,' the Cook shouted fiercely an'
with enormous satisfaction, having somewhat lost the point of
why we were there; carried away as he was with the euphoria
of finally being allowed to kill those he disapproved of.

'Shit.'

I muttered.

Happily Dead-Eye, a misnomer if ever there was one, missed
the submarine. Which was good.

Less happily, he didn't miss the cliffs behind it, the barrel
of his 6-pounder being elevated but not elevated high enough
to fire clear.

Which was bad.

Being an armour-piercing round, the shell penetrated clear
through metres of ancient, compacted snow and ice before detonating against the high rocky outcrop forming the starboard hand
of the entrance itself. There was no evident trace of the explosion; just a puff and a muffled, echoing *thud*, and a sudden flurry
of startled snow buntings taking wing while concluding the
Antarctic would've afforded a safer haven to emigrate to. Even
the American captain must've have evinced a wry, if slightly
shaky, smile at the quality of my gunnery direction.

Nothing else happened.

'That wus lucky,' Trapp said. 'Panic over, Mister.'

'No, Trapp,' I appealed. 'Please don't . . .'

A trickle of powdered snow spilled from the edge of the
overhang.

'. . . say any more.'

A further curtain of powder drifted seawards.

'I fink I sees anuther submarine comin' in, Captin,' Alf
announced helpfully.

Trapp ignored him. 'D'you hear it?' he asked, cocking an
ear intently.

My eyes stayed fixed on the drifting snow curtain. There
seemed to be more of it trickling down.

'Hear what?'

'Thunder,' Trapp diagnosed authoritatively. 'The good weather's goin' to break. It's startin' to thunder, Mister.'

The crack that suddenly appeared at the edge of the icebound overhang zigzagged all the way to the top. Then started to get wider.

'No it's not,' I disputed, feeling the ground beginning to tremble beneath my feet even at that distance. 'It's not the weather that's about to break.'

The thunder got louder and louder.

'RUN,' I yelled.

'Run? Run where?' Trapp growled, resentful as ever at having his judgement questioned.

'*Any* fuckin' where,' I screamed, already slipping and scrambling for the cliff rearing behind us on the beach. 'So long as it's high above the SHORE line!'

How come Gorbals Wullie made it before me? Clamped up there against the rock face above my head like a bluebottle stuck to flypaper, an' still climbing. One minute he ignores my order: next he beats me to it. *Bloody* ordinary seamen. Always indecisi—

At the other end of the ice lagoon twenty thousand tons of consolidated snow parted their moorin—?

What's that? '*How* much snow?' you question dubiously, a critic to the endpaper.

Well, *I* don't know exactly, do I? I mean, I wasn't bloody measuring it inna a bucket, was I? Oh, call it a *thousand* tons . . . no, five thou— no, *ten* thousand tons then. Conservatively! Jus' concede *ten* thousand tons of consolidated snow parted their moorings and avalanched into the entrance, with the ice bridge snaking down after them and an ever-swelling roar and a splashing and gouting of foam and spray high enough to start a new layer above that will probably build, winter over Arctic winter, until the next millennium dawns across that desolate, frozen splinter called, improbably, Tiger Island.

Unless Trapp returns in the interim, of course, and does even more damage to it. In the process of making sure there hadn't been a silly mistake in the *Salamander*'s manifest, and the *real* Murphy's Gold wusn't still stowed in some other part of the ship.

I've never believed it myself. It had obviously been a

complete fabrication conjured by the mind of some dissolute old sailor in an Irish pub.

I swear to you now. I *never* believed that story about Amundsen shooting all the tigers.

The tidal wave I'd anticipated only reached to just below our scrambling seaboots. Otherwise, it stands to reason, you would hardly be reading this. It did, however, carry the USN *Whatever-She-Was* clear across the lagoon, twirling helpless as a drunken matelot on a merry-go-round while defying her captain's stoutest efforts to control her, before depositing his submarine gently in the northern rock fissure: there doomed to sail in company with the wreck of the SS *Salamander* for ever.

But even had he managed to defy that monstrous swell, it wouldn't have helped.

The entrance had become permanently sealed by ten . . . *twenty* thousand tons of ice, reaching halfway up each side. Not even the United States Navy could have retrieved her from there. Not even after the war. Not even if they'd put skis on her.

International incident, did I say? International fracture more like. No wonder the British Government placed that blanket decree that all involved should remain silent to prevent the Royal Navy's continuing embarrassment.

And to the nation's continuing cost, I might add. I mean, have you ever wondered why the US Treasury has always been so insistent that the UK pays back every penny of the Lend-Lease money Churchill borrowed to finance our part in the war against Nazi tyranny?

That's all been Trapp's fault.

And Dead-Eye Alf's, of course. But at least the valiant Alf could claim there were mitigating factors involved for his part.

When we returned home as distressed British seamen, Alf was excused further service with the Merchant Navy on medical grounds. Which was strange because he'd never been in the Merchant Navy in the first place: he'd been a pirate. But either way, the authorities found him a shoreside job instead. A quality control inspector, they made him. Of really tiny light bulbs.

The Cook . . . funny that: I never knew his name other than that his first was Bloody, according to Trapp anyway . . . they insisted he stayed ashore for the rest of the war too, on account of his being too aggressive towards Germans, Americans, and shipmasters. Last I heard of the Cook he was head pastry chef of a specialist Asian bakery. They made the most wonderful flat breads; especially their chapattis.

Flags: my spiteful adversary all that time ago in Scotland? Run over by a tramcar in Glasgow the day after we'd sailed. On his way to the naval tailor's to be measured for a smart new staff uniform to replace his accidentally sodden one, he'd been. I have to acknowledge he'd been made of the Right Stuff, Flags. Done his duty to the last. Had his measurements taken exactly as ordered by his Admiral. Only not for a uniform.

Crusty old Bert Gunn . . . ? He'd refused to leave the *Salamander* when we set off across the island to rejoin the *Charon*, trailing a convoy of dejected allies. Claimed that, having been forced to lissen to Gorbals Wullie f'r near enough a whole day, 'e'd had a bellyful o' conversation, an' wus happier to stay marooned in hell. Besides, he did have plenty o' grub to work through. Much better than yer average Red Duster tramp's galley fare, too. *By Royal Appointment*, Murphy's purveyances wus. Fit even f'r Joe Stalin's delectation, no less . . . whilst on top o' that, he could remain confident 'e would *never* run out o' Preston Knittinghouse Elegant Brand gentlemen's woollen socks.

And me . . . ? Well, first I spent a few weeks back on the funny far— in military *hospital* under the ear of the Colonel who, despite my entreaties, still insisted that no way, therapeutically speaking, could this, my Russian convoy account, be justifiably titled *Miller's War* any more than could my last. He'd been very forcible when pointing out that Trapp had, once more, dominated all the best bits – while at the same time, threatening not to discharge me 'til hell froze over, unless I accepted his prescription once and for all.

Subsequently I was posted back to sea. In the oldest minesweeping trawler the Navy could find. Working up the Greenland Gap. Which was where hell froze over *anyway*!

And worse: as a Royal Naval Reserve Lieutenant.

. . . And *that*, before you raise your next obvious protest, returns us full circle back to the Admiral.

He'd grudgingly reinstated my King's Commission, not because he'd been prepared to overlook my part in almost bringing an end to the Special Relationship – rumour had it that a lot of US admirals cut the boss dead at later Allied staff conferences – but because the only way he could guarantee keeping my mouth shut was by gagging me with the Official Secrets Act as a serving officer. Still had a blazing row with Churchill before he agreed to take me back, though. Never did make it to First Sea Lord, as he'd so desperately yearned to become.

Mind you, the salty old curmudgeon did get his revenge, at least in part. By the time he'd persuaded the Ministry of War Transport to offset Trapp's losing eight field guns and, allowing for depreciation, the cost of an American submarine, against the charter fee due to him for the convoy, Trapp only received fifteen pounds. Precisely the amount he'd paid for the map to Murphy's Gold.

Meant that, for all his Machiavellian ambition, he'd still finished up a bag of pork scratchings down.

While Trapp and Gorbals Wullie themselves . . . ? What happened to *them* after Tiger Island, I hear you ask. Come to that, did they even survive the war, albeit such an outcome seems highly remote?

Ah, well, Dear Reader: you who have proved so faithful by persevering to this final page despite having betrayed an unfortunate tendency to keep pointing out my failings as a raconteur . . . I do apologize. But I really must be resolute in bringing this manuscript to a close.

. . . Because *that's* another story.

Or rather: a lot of stories.

Epilogue

I tell a lie. I haven't quite finished yet. It would be utterly remiss of me to overlook the old *Charon* herself. And unfair to you who, as you have obviously read this far, have proved yourself the staunchest of shipmates through so many bitter cold miles on watch with myself.

We did pick up the next outbound PQ convoy just as Trapp had planned. That was a novelty in itself. Not finding the convoy; simply that one of Trapp's plans had actually gone according to . . . ah . . . ? Yeah, OK, so I can't think of a suitable word. But like I've already said, I'm no Tolstoy.

I suppose I could pen a further chapter – nay, an entire journal – on that gallant endeavour by brave men. But I won't. Suffice to say we did make it to Russia, albeit our port of destination turned out, ironically, to be Archangel.

The Stukas had bombed and strafed us unremittingly all the way, yet had never even managed to shake the snow and rust off the *Charo*— well, off the *СИДЯОИ II* as we'd made clear to the Soviet defence gunners by that time, having erected, at Wullie's insistence, a big cut-out arrow above our bow pointing to the name.

The city was ablaze as we nudged towards the berth. Dense smoke drifting across the inlet; sunken ships everywhere, some partly blocking the fairway. Less than half a mile to go to reach voyage end. Then I tensed. Something was amiss. Something felt, well . . . *wrong*.

'See, Mister. Di'n't I allus tell you we would make it?' Trapp had said proudly. And devastatingly.

Water began to swill inboard across the forward well deck.

By the time she'd settled on the bottom with barely a bump, the water reached nearly to the underside of the gallant old ship's topsy-turvy bridge.

'Can ah have that steel helmet of yours now you've finished

with it, Mister Miller sir?' Wullie asked. 'Ah've always wanted tae look like Noel Coward.'

My last recollection as I trailed down the shell-cratered wharf to join the corvette ordered to repatriate me, was of two dishevelled silhouettes, one very small and the other wearing a bobbing, strangely articulated cap, engaged in animated and seemingly persuasive conversation with an armour plated limousine-full of Soviet gentlemen of criminal mien.

They appeared to be tendering a tattered oilskin envelope for inspection. The kind of envelope in which one might keep, say, an old ship's cargo manifest?

I hesitated. Neither spared me a glance, so preoccupied with getting themselves killed next time round, were they.

Swallowing with some difficulty, I'd turned and walked quickly away bearing an enduring memory of those two raggle-taggle figures slouched so close together.

So *very* close together.

Maybe for ever and ever. Maybe until the very end of Time itself.

But *only* if you truly believe in ghosts.